Readers love The Belladonna Arms
by JOHN INMAN

Serenading Stanley

"I have such respect for this author. He uses both humor and drama to deliver a brilliant love story that never panders but is always intelligent and just pure fun."

—Gay Book Reviews

"If you are interested in a sweet love story and quite a bit of humor, I highly recommend this book. Be prepared to laugh out loud a lot. I did."

—On Top Down Under Book Reviews

Work in Progress

"It's official… I'm head over heels with the Belladonna Arms."

—Sinfully Gay Romance Book Reviews

"Once again we are treated to impeccable writing that produces a fast-paced, funny and sexy story line that never veers off course."

—The Novel Approach

Coming Back

"I loved the witty writing style, the fully realized characters, the emotional storyline, the vivid setting. I loved everything about it and I hope this is not the last we will see of the Belladonna Arms and its tenants."

—Prism Book Alliance

"John Inman just keeps getting better and better, and this was such a pleasure to read."

—My Fiction Nook

By JOHN INMAN

Chasing the Swallows
A Hard Winter Rain
Head-on
Hobbled
Jasper's Mountain
Loving Hector
My Busboy
Paulie
Payback
The Poodle Apocalypse
Scrudge & Barley, Inc.
Shy
Snow on the Roof (Dreamspinner Anthology)
Spirit
Sunset Lake
Two Pet Dicks

THE BELLADONNA ARMS
Serenading Stanley
Work in Progress
Coming Back
Ben and Shiloh

Published by DREAMSPINNER PRESS
www.dreamspinnerpress.com

Ben and Shiloh

JOHN INMAN

Published by

DREAMSPINNER PRESS

5032 Capital Circle SW, Suite 2, PMB# 279, Tallahassee, FL 32305-7886 USA
www.dreamspinnerpress.com

Ben and Shiloh
© 2016 John Inman.

Cover Art
© 2016 Aaron Anderson.
aaronbydesign55@gmail.com
Cover content is for illustrative purposes only and any person depicted on the cover is a model.

ISBN: 978-1-63477-145-0
Digital ISBN: 978-1-63477-146-7
Library of Congress Control Number: 2016907022
Published October 2016
v. 1.0

Printed in the United States of America
∞
This paper meets the requirements of
ANSI/NISO Z39.48-1992 (Permanence of Paper).

Chapter 1

THE RATTLETRAP neon sign atop the century-old structure said it all. Over and over, the sign flashed the words Belladonna Arms, carving a stuttering orange tattoo across the San Diego skyline. The letter *B*, tilted and slightly askew from the other letters, flashed off and on at a different rhythm from the rest, as if about to flicker out or abandon its mates altogether and head off for greener pastures somewhere else.

The run-down six-story building beneath the sign was perched high on a hill overlooking the shimmering city streets below. Those streets were ablaze with the unwavering linear glow of streetlights and the constantly moving headlights of a thousand automobiles tooling this way and that, surging, blending, shooting off here and there like fireworks. The twinkling diamond lights splayed out at the building's feet like a crystalline skirt of fire spread gracefully about the knees of a crouching goddess, only the goddess had most assuredly seen better days.

Beyond the grid of city lights encircling the Belladonna Arms, the lights of the San Diego Bay could be seen less than a mile to the south, with ships and sailboats gliding to and fro and the long, graceful arch of the Coronado Bridge connecting the city to the peninsula beyond. And past the peninsula, past the neighboring city of Coronado, there was nothing but the vast empty blackness of the grand Pacific Ocean, with a spattering of stars shining down to cast an occasional spark of light onto the surging swells below.

Over it all, high in the sky, an October moon gleamed fat and round and proud, surveying its earthly realm and the measly lives of the inhabitants below.

Like mine. My life is pretty darn measly.

My name is Shiloh Smart, and no, you're not seeing things. I am indeed wearing a kilt.

I'm twenty-two, stand about five feet seven, weigh in at about 145, have red hair and freckles, and I work as a waiter in a Scottish restaurant downtown—thus the kilt. I'm not Scottish, by the way. My employers just thought I looked the part because of the red hair and freckles. I tend to turn heads when I walk down the street in this stupid kilt, but I doubt if it's because I'm handsome or anything. I think it has more to do with my pale fuzzy knees and the oddity of seeing a guy in Southern California wearing a skirt. I mean, there are a lot of guys running around in skirts, but they are drag queens, so that doesn't count. I'm not a drag queen. I'm just a redheaded guy pretending to be Scottish so I can work in a Scottish restaurant where they make me wear a kilt.

By the way, I'm not suntanned like every other guy in Southern California, because I'm a redhead. Redheads don't tan; they burn. And peel. And freckle. One of God's little pranks, I suppose. What a card.

Anyway, where was I? Oh yeah. Me. I've been working at The Twisted Kilt for about a year now. Tips are good, so I don't do too badly. I save money by not driving. Someday I'll find a job that pays a decent wage. When that day comes along, I'll buy a car. Until then, I'll scuttle around town on the bus. Or walk. No problem.

Anyhoo….

Being gay—oh, did I mention I'm gay? No? Well, I am—umm, now I've lost my train of thought again. Oh yeah, I remember. Being gay is kind of hard for a guy like me. I hate the forced camaraderie of bars, especially gay bars, and I'm not much of a drinker anyway. I prefer reading to movies, silence to talking, eating in to eating out, and being alone to being in love. I've been in love a couple of times, in case you're wondering, and those two times were enough to convince me not to shoot for it again. The beginning of love is such a rush, such a joy. But the ending of love is like a knife to the heart. Every single time.

Being stabbed twice in the heart is plenty. That's why I've decided to avoid the inevitable mutilation of another love affair. Not that I'm planning to be a monk for the rest of my days, mind you. A man has needs. But the whole romance thing is off the table. Definitely. (Unless, of course, the right man comes along, in which case all bets are off. Nothing is carved in stone, right?)

It's also why I'm presently standing outside the Belladonna Arms in a kilt, hoping people won't think I'm a drag queen.

Not that I have anything against drag queens. I don't. In fact, on that Saturday evening, I was stopping by on my way to work to meet with one, or so I'd been told. His name was Arthur, and he was the owner/manager of the Belladonna Arms, which I had seen from a distance for years, perched as it was atop the one and only hill in downtown San Diego. I hate to say it, but up close the place didn't look half as nice as it did from half a mile away.

But that's okay. I'd heard they had a vacancy, and I'd also heard the rent was cheap. Plus it was within walking distance of where I worked. For a guy who is poor and doesn't drive, those are a couple of pretty big pluses.

Recovering from my second mutilation of the heart, as I currently was, I was here in search of an apartment to rent. My latest mutilator had just thrown me out on my ear after taking up with a guy with a tan, and from what I could see at first glance as I was dragging my clothes out the door, not one fucking freckle anywhere.

My only consolation was that I was pretty sure my ex would stick a knife in *his* heart one of these days too. If the new guy had been a little less supercilious as he held the door open for me, I would have warned him. Since he was being a dick about the whole "I'm moving in, you're moving out" thing, I decided I'd let him figure it out for himself.

Just so you know, I really did think Larry loved me. Sigh. But then we always do, don't we?

I pulled a handkerchief from the sporran hanging at my waist and blew my nose. Stupid Larry. After emptying my sinuses and wiping my eyes and stuffing the hanky back into the stupid sporran, which was really nothing more than a glorified purse that I had to wear with the stupid kilt, I took a deep, shuddery breath and studied the building in front of me.

I noticed right away that the management of the Belladonna Arms wasted no time or money on such frivolities as landscape maintenance. I crossed the dead lawn—the brown, desiccated grass crunching under my feet like Rice Krispies—then ducked between two clumps of sun-limp honeysuckle that flanked the entryway. Climbing the broad wooden steps to the porch above, which was littered with leaves from an ancient eucalyptus tree that stood at the side of the building, I was confronted by the sight of the drag queen I was supposed to meet. I mean, it must be him, right? How many drag queens could there be in a place like this? He was reclining on a chaise lounge with a tall glass of lemonade in his hand, and he was the most heart-stopping creation I had ever happened upon.

And creation was exactly the right word. One simply doesn't roll out of bed looking like he did. It takes some work. Perhaps even hours of preparation and planning. Still, all that preparation and planning seemed to have gone awry at every turn. For truth be told, Arthur was the worst bloody drag queen I had ever seen in my life. And the biggest.

He was adorned in gold lamé from the tips of his toes to the crown of his head. His pointy-toed high heels were gold lamé. His billowing gown was gold lamé. The turban wrapped around his bowling-ball-sized head was gold lamé. Looking at him was equivalent to staring into the sun at high noon in the middle of the Mohave Desert with your eyelids stapled to your forehead.

I suddenly regretted not wearing sunglasses.

There was a slit up the side of Arthur's shimmering gown that exposed a rather humongous leg sheathed in black fishnet nylon. The ham-sized hand dangling over the side of the lounge chair, holding the tinkling glass of iced lemonade, was adorned with what looked like every ring ever churned out by the Avon jewelry department. He also wore gold-painted press-on nails, which protruded from the end of each zirconium-bedecked finger like eagle talons.

Arthur's face was a wonder all by itself. He had ruby-red bow-shaped lips, false eyelashes that sprinkled with gold glitter and were so long they resembled two whisk brooms, and two round blobs of rouge that shone from each cheek like a couple of stoplights. His base makeup looked like rice powder, such as geishas once wore, only God help me, even whiter. I couldn't help wondering if his makeup had been applied at that place where they spray-paint cars. Earl Scheib, is it? You see them on TV all the time. I could imagine the ad. *We'll paint any queen for $499.99!*

Jesus. I gave my head a shake to dislodge that thought.

At the moment, Arthur seemed to be resting his eyes. They were peacefully closed, his brightly painted lips were lazily parted, and a teeny smile made his fat cheeks pooch out into even bigger and rounder stoplights. He looked so content and comfortable, I hated to wake him up.

As luck would have it, I didn't have to. At that moment Arthur gave a jerk, sloshing a bit of lemonade onto the porch, opened his eyes with a snort, and gazed directly at me. The eyes between those cowlike lashes scoped me out from top to bottom but then immediately returned to the kilt, as eyes so often do.

His smile widened as he grunted himself fully awake. "That tartan is lovely," he said around a yawn, as if just now yanking himself out of the dream he'd been having. "Is it worsted wool?"

I gazed down at myself—at my pale legs and the fabric surrounding them. "Hell if I know," I said.

Arthur blinked. I thought maybe I felt the downdraft from his flapping eyelashes when he did, but that might have been my imagination. Although a few eucalyptus leaves did slide past my feet and tumble off the porch.

Arthur finally tore his gaze from my kilt and centered it on my face. A sly expression sparked in his eyes. He looked like a sneaky little kid getting ready to swipe a cookie. "Do you wear underwear with that? I've heard Scotsmen don't," he said.

Again I stared down at the stupid kilt. "I'm not a Scotsman. I only wear this for work. And yes, I wear underwear. If my junk dangled free all night, I'd be sporting a constant boner."

Arthur's mouth twisted into a sensuous leer, sweet and deadly all at the same time. "And wouldn't that be a crying shame," he said. Arthur emitted a grunt, which really wasn't very ladylike, and pulled himself to his feet, unfolding his body from the chaise lounge like a Macy's Thanksgiving Day Parade balloon of Jessica Rabbit being pumped full of air and expanding upright into the New York skyline.

On his feet, Arthur was even more impressive than he was on his back.

He towered over me. And when he set his glass of lemonade aside and approached, with one hand stuck out in greeting, it took a wee bit of courage for me not to cower in his gold lamé shadow. Only the smile on his beaming face kept me feeling safe. And welcome.

His meatloaf-sized paw surrounded mine like a shark swallowing a fish sandwich. "I love gingers," he said, squeezing my fist and pumping it up and down, all the while admiring the hair on my head as well as the hair on my legs, all of it red. "I especially love gingers in kilts. I'm Arthur, honey. And who might you be?"

I forced a smile to my face. I was getting used to the man already. Clearly he was a nice person, although his sense of style sucked. And God forgive me for saying so, but he really did resemble a gilded bratwurst, stuffed in that clingy gold dress the way he was. Still, I've had worse-looking landlords. Might as well be friendly.

"My name is Shiloh Smart."

When I smiled, his face lit up. "That's better," he said with a grin. He patted my cheek. "I like you better happy than sad. And you've got such pretty teeth. You should show them more often."

"I wasn't sad," I said, maybe a little too defensively.

Arthur wasn't buying it for a minute. He batted those long lashes and gave me a *tsk* or two. "You can't fool me, honey. I know heartache when I see it. You're here about an apartment, aren't you? You've just broken up with your lover, and you're suddenly on your own, and you need a nice place to live where you can heal your heart and get your life back on track while you find someone else to love who hopefully will also love you back. Tell me I'm wrong."

I stared at him while my face turned cherry red. I know it did because I could feel it. Redheads always know when they're blushing. Mirrors are superfluous for redheads.

I stepped back a few inches, just until Arthur's hand slipped from my cheek. I was afraid if he touched me there another second, I would start crying. I wasn't sure why. I guess I don't handle sympathy very well.

Clearing my throat, I tried for a more businesslike demeanor. All the while I did, Arthur looked like he knew exactly what I was doing but had decided to let me carry on.

"You're right," I said. "I'm looking for an apartment. And yeah, I just broke up with my lover, or rather he broke up with me."

"I'm sorry," Arthur murmured, his bee-stung lips turning down in a frown.

For some reason I was finding it hard to talk. I suddenly had a beach ball in my throat. "He met somebody else, see, and I had to leave sort of on the spur of the moment. I thought he loved me, but he didn't. Pretty funny, huh?"

"It's not funny at all, honey," Arthur commiserated around a pout, eyeing me with such compassion I felt emotionally naked in front of him.

I rattled on, trying to get a grip on my feelings, trying to talk the heartache away, but somehow that only made it worse. And still I couldn't shut up. "And you're wrong about me looking for another l-lover. I don't want another lover. I don't. I don't want another lover ever."

To my horror, I saw that Arthur's gigantic face start to blur as tears welled up in my eyes. Crap.

I opened my mouth to laugh off the sudden avalanche of emotions going through me, but I suddenly couldn't find my voice at all. All I could do was stand there like a sap and try to choke down the lump in my throat while tears rained down my cheeks like a baby's. Jeez. I was so appalled I wished I could sink through the floor and come out the other side in Beijing. I never show emotion in public. Never. Not until today anyway.

Through my fuzzy vision, I was able to discern tears welling up in Arthur's eyes too as he watched me. Before I knew what was happening, he had stepped forward, folded me in his massive gold lamé arms, and dragged me to his bosom, cooing and tutting and patting my back through it all.

"Let it out, honey," he said. "Let it out."

God help me, I couldn't stop myself. I laid my face between his mountainous breasts—which rustled like bags of chickpeas, I noticed— and the next thing I knew I was quietly sobbing.

Arthur made little baby noises as he held me in his arms and rocked me back and forth. I had never been so mortified in my life, but oddly, I was comforted too.

After a minute or two of Arthur letting me cry myself out, I pulled back enough to gaze up into his face. I was humiliated beyond belief, but I had also witnessed a selfless act by a man who didn't know me from Adam.

I tried to smile. No dice. Then I sucked in a trembling breath, hoping I didn't have snot running out of my nose. The only voice I could dredge up was a crackly, hiccupy whisper. "Thank you, Arthur. I guess I needed a hug."

Arthur winked. "We all do now and then." He pulled a lace handkerchief from the end of his sleeve and shook it out. "Blow your nose, honey."

He pressed the handkerchief to my nose and I blew. Like a four-year-old. Arthur's fat thumbs worked like two windshield wipers squeegeeing the tears from my cheeks while he continued to smile down at me as I shook and trembled there in front of him, trying like crazy to regain my composure. When I finished blowing my nose, Arthur stuck the lace handkerchief back up his sleeve, snot and all.

When I thought I was about as calm as I was ever going to get, I forced a grateful smile. "Thank you," I said again, rubbing my eyes with the heel of my hand. "You must think I'm a twit."

Arthur cocked his head and studied me. "I think you're the cutest and saddest young man I've seen in a long time. I also think you'd make a wonderful tenant. Let me show you what's available, okay? You'll find love here, by the way. Everyone does."

"I told you, Arthur. I don't want love," I said, giving myself a shake, running my fingers through my hair, and sniffing back a little more snot, still trying to make myself presentable.

"Yes, you do. Everybody wants love."

"I don't."

"Yes, you do."

"No, I don't."

Arthur honked out a great laugh. "Fine. You don't want love." He leaned in and planted a kiss on my cheek. "But trust me, Shiloh. It's gonna find you anyway. You're too cute for it not to. Especially in that kilt. And with that flaming red hair. Come on. I'll show you around. And mind the cats. The little boogers are everywhere. You don't have any cats, do you?"

"No."

"Babies? Tell me you don't have any babies."

"Uh, no." I was gaining control of myself again, thank heavens. I'd humiliated myself enough.

Arthur puffed out a big sigh of relief. "No cats or babies," he said to the ceiling, throwing his arms wide like a televangelist. "Thank you, God. Thank you."

With that he crooked an arm through mine, hooking me like a salmon, and dragged me toward the door. I blinked back my last tear or two and humbly followed along, chastened to the core.

But for some unfathomable reason, I also felt… hopeful.

That realization thundered through me like a sonic boom. Jeez, who could have seen hope coming so quickly after Larry broke my heart and threw me out in the street? Not me.

It was then, I think, that I began to understand what a wonderful person Arthur was. With almost no effort at all he had made me feel welcome and safe and wanted. I felt my throat begin to clog up with emotion again, and it took all my willpower to swallow it back down. Good grief. Guys in kilts are supposed to be butch. I was impugning an entire nation of tartan-clad hunks.

Still, I had to show my appreciation. I simply had to. I patted Arthur's arm as he led me through the front door of the Belladonna Arms, and when I did, he gazed down at me through those bedazzling, sparkling eyelashes and gave me a smile.

"Thank you," I said, and he offered me a wink to boot.

At that moment our friendship was born.

THE LOBBY of the Belladonna Arms was about what I expected. A battered bank of mailboxes screwed into the far wall, a couple of wingback chairs that had seen better days parked to either side of a coffee table stacked with all the local gay newspapers, flyers from San Diego gay bars, and a propped-up 9 x 12 portrait of Arthur dressed as a cowgirl—a really big cowgirl—standing in front of a bale of hay with a tall handsome older man in a cowboy hat and snap-button western shirt, along with the obligatory jeans and fancy boots. The tall man, one long drink of water for sure, as John Wayne used to say, had an arm draped across Arthur's shoulder, and they were both grinning from ear to ear.

It stopped me in my tracks, and stopping me, it pretty much stopped Arthur too. Anchors do that. I pointed to the picture and asked, "Who's that you're with?"

I couldn't be sure, but I thought I saw a tinge of pink appear beneath Arthur's rice makeup. He was blushing.

"That's my lover," he said, swelling with pride. "That's Tom. Ain't he a dish?"

I couldn't deny it. For an older man, he most certainly was a dish. "He is," I admitted with stunned honesty. "He really is."

Arthur tittered like a schoolgirl who has just been asked for a kiss by the cutest boy in class. "You're wondering what he's doing with me."

That was exactly what I was thinking.

"No, I'm not," I lied.

Arthur nudged me in the ribs. "Liar. Someday I'll tell you all about it. For now, let's go see your new apartment."

That brought me back to earth. "Arthur, I don't even know how much the apartment costs. I might not be able to afford it. I'm just, you know, looking."

"No, you're not," Arthur said. "You're here to take 4D. The unit is perfect for you. The Belladonna Arms is your new home, kid, whether you know it yet or not. You'll be happy here. I know you will. Don't worry about the rent. It's reasonable, I promise. And if it isn't reasonable enough, we'll make it more reasonable. I'm the arbiter for reasonable rents. It's all up to me."

"I couldn't ask you to...."

Arthur narrowed his eyes and, building up a little momentum again, began tugging me toward the stairs at the back of the lobby. "This would be a good time for you to shut up, Shiloh. Let me tell you something. Some free advice. When people try to help you, you should let them. It makes them feel good, it makes you feel good, and you'll hurt their feelings if you don't."

Again I dragged him to a stop. I took his hand. "I'm sorry, Arthur. I'm a schmuck. I didn't mean to hurt your feelings. Forgive me. I do appreciate what you're doing. Honestly, I do."

He grinned at that. "See? Do I know how to work people, or what?"

Seeing the look of surprise on my face, he laughed. "Ignore me. I'm nuts. And nobody manipulates people like a seven-foot drag queen. Come on, let's show you your new apartment."

This time I kept my mouth shut, and together we began climbing upward.

It didn't take me long to realize Arthur wasn't fond of stairs. Truthfully, I couldn't blame him. A three-hundred-pound man in heels? Why would he be? He grumbled and groused and cursed his way up every step, huffing and puffing and sweating like a steam engine. We passed three cats along the way—they were little more than kittens, really—and Arthur grumbled and groused and cursed at them in passing as well.

"What's with all the cats?" I asked.

"Don't ask."

"Is there a laundry room?"

"When it works."

"Are there other gay people in the building?"

"Everybody's gay."

"What, everybody?"

"Well, except for Sylvia, who just had a sex change operation and married Pete, who was her boyfriend before, so technically I guess she isn't gay anymore, and neither is he." Arthur's face lit up, and he elbowed me hard enough to almost knock me down. "Maybe I should kick them out, huh?" Then he threw his head back and laughed.

"Ha-ha," I droned, rubbing my arm and wondering what I was getting myself into.

By the time we reached the fourth-floor landing, I was scared to death Arthur was about to die on me as he stood there on that last step, gasping and clutching his heart. As if that wasn't bad enough, since we had reached our goal, he decided to celebrate by pulling out a cigar as big as a loaf of french bread from somewhere inside his bodice. He fired that sucker up and puffed away until the stairwell was thick with smoke.

Suddenly I was the one gasping for air and clutching my heart.

Arthur seemed surprised by my reaction. As innocent as a babe, he asked, "Something wrong?"

I coughed, hacked, tried not to barf, squinted through smoke-induced tears, and said, "No, no, no. Why do you ask?"

"Just wondering." He sucked in another great gout of smoke and let it dribble from his nostrils until his head was sheathed in fog like the top of Mount Kilimanjaro, only the fog around Mount Kilimanjaro probably smells better. He leaned in and whispered in my ear. "Listen, cupcake, this cigar is our little secret, okay? My pooty-pie thinks I quit."

I hacked up a lung and gasped, "Okay," even while I was thinking his pooty-pie could probably smell it from five miles off anyway.

"Thanks, honey." Arthur beamed and gave me a conspiratorial wink.

He went into landlord mode while continuing to pat his heart and catch his breath and suck on that godawful cigar. "We have a few vacancies scattered around because we had several tenants who decided to move in together."

"Why would they do that?"

Arthur gazed at me with one eye squeezed shut against the smoke. "It's called love, honey. We had a particularly potent crop of love pollen invade the building this year, and—"

"Love pollen?"

He smirked and leaned in to whisper in my ear again. Arthur seemed to do that a lot. "This building positively reeks of love pollen. Trust me, Shiloh, you'll find out all about it. And don't take my word for it either. Ask anybody who lives here. When the Belladonna Arms love pollen drifts down on your unsuspecting head, your days of being single are numbered. Ask Ramon and Barney who live next door. Or Harlie and Milan down on two. Or Charlie and Bruce on three. Or Stanley and Roger on—"

I waved my arms around like an octopus to shut him up. "I told you before, Arthur. I don't want to number my days of being single. I'm not looking for love. And I really don't think love pollen will be drifting down on my head anyway, be it Belladonna Arms love pollen or any other kind. You're making it up. And even if it did exist, I'm pretty sure I'd be immune. Or it would simply give me a rash. I'm not built for love, Arthur, and frankly I'm okay with that. I've tried it twice, and now I'm done with it. As far as I'm concerned, love is highly overrated."

He gave a dainty chortle, which is really the last thing you expect to hear from a three-hundred-pound drag queen in gold lamé chewing on a cigar as big as a dildo.

"Keep telling yourself that," he said, adjusting his tits. "Are these things crooked?"

"Uh, no, they're lovely."

"Oh, good."

I had to ask. I couldn't stop myself. "What are they? Chickpeas?"

"Nope. Quinoa. Not as noisy. Better heft. Just the right squish factor. And look, they're aerodynamic." He bent over and offered me a Jayne Mansfield tit wag.

"Ah," I said, trying not to look appalled.

He clapped his hands together, gave his bodice one last adjustment, scratched his ass in a lackadaisical sort of way, and said, "Tits are the least of my worries. It's these pantyhose that are killing me."

"Sorry," I said, not knowing what else to say.

He slapped me on the back almost hard enough to drive me to my knees. "Don't worry about it, honey. Squished nuts is a small price to pay for beauty. Let's go see your new apartment. It was freshly painted not more than eight years ago. Ain't that grand?"

"Peachy," I said, wondering if he was joking about his nuts. Not to mention the paint.

Chapter 2

I STUDIED the faded walls. I still didn't know if Arthur was joking about his nuts, but at least now I knew he wasn't joking about the paint. The apartment with 4D on the door was a mess. Old fixtures, an ancient refrigerator, threadbare carpets, a claw-footed bathtub bereft of most of its porcelain, a battered shower curtain sporting an array of gaudy pink flamingos. But in spite of all that, 4D had a certain spartan charm. It was also clean. Even the windows were crystal clear and afforded a hell of a view. I could see all the way to the Pacific Ocean if I hung my head out the kitchen window far enough to not quite topple over and kill myself in a four-floor freefall. From the living room, I could see the downtown skyline shimmering on the horizon. It was a spectacular light show.

While I switched on the lights and ran the water and peeked in the oven, Arthur prattled on, happily consuming a jumbo-sized Kit Kat bar he had pulled from some hidden reservoir in his gold lamé gown. The cigar he tossed in the toilet, thank God. I was pretty sure I could hear my lungs singing "The Hallelujah Chorus" in appreciation. When he flushed the cigar away, the ensuing rattle and bang of sewer pipes somewhere over our heads was a bit disconcerting, but I supposed I'd get used to it. It was an old building, after all. I couldn't expect everything to operate without a hitch.

"People are constantly falling in love in this building," Arthur said, continuing his running commentary. "And every time they fall in love with another tenant, they want to move in together, and when they move in together, I lose a paying tenant, so to speak. For a landlord, love is most definitely a mixed blessing." He coughed up a sardonic chuckle and rolled his eyes, "Frankly, if I didn't love love so much, it would be a pain in the butt. Sort of like these pantyhose." He threw his head back and laughed like a loon, then stifled his hilarity by taking another bite from his Kit Kat.

He stood in the bathroom for a while, studying his reflection in the cracked mirror over the sink, checking his makeup, patting his hair, trying to smooth out his double chins, readjusting his tits. But his booming voice found me no matter where I went. Arthur was a foghorn.

"Did you see the curtains? Only 3.99 at Walmart. Do I know how to shop or what? So what do you think, honey? Isn't this apartment to die for? Don't you love it? Don't you just love it?"

Oddly enough, I did. Even the cheap Walmart curtains were sunny and colorful and managed to camouflage the eight-year-old wall paint. I figured as soon as I tossed the flamingo shower curtain, which really did suck, I could live here quite contentedly.

As I stood in the bedroom, testing the firmness of the mattress and wondering why the bed squeaked so much, a hidden doorway in the wall, which I hadn't noticed before and which didn't have a doorknob on my side, suddenly creaked open and scared the bejesus out of me. Two handsome young heads—one Latino and one white, stacked like figures on a totem pole—peered around the jamb and stared at me as I clutched my heart and tried not to keel over from fright.

"Oops," the Latino said through a dimpled smile. "Didn't mean to startle you. We heard noises, and, well, we thought you might be a burglar. I'm Ramon."

The face beneath Ramon's cracked a smile as well. "And I'm Barney. Are you going to be our new neighbor?"

"Well, I—"

Arthur stormed through the bedroom door behind me like a forklift stacked with gold ingots at Fort Knox. God, he was big. And shiny. And loud.

"Ramon! Barney! Meet our new tenant, Shiloh Smart! Ain't he a dream? Not that you'd be interested, you lovebirds, you."

Arthur slipped an arm around my waist and dragged me forward for inspection, still jabbering on. "Don't you love the kilt, boys? We've never had a Scottish laddie living at the Arms before. I can't wait to linger at the bottom of the stairs and watch him walk up so I can see what's hiding underneath that thing." He snuggled his nose into my neck and giggled. "I'm kidding, honey. I'm kidding."

"I'm not really Scottish, you know. I'm Jewish. At least my mother is. My father wasn't much of any—"

But Arthur gave me another hug and squeezed the words right out of me, obviously not interested in my lineage. Barney and Ramon stepped into the room while I was gasping for breath. We shook hands.

While I tried to be friendly, I also eyed the gaping hole in my bedroom wall. "Um, why is this apartment connected to yours?"

"This used to be a suite," Barney explained. "But don't worry, we'll lock the door behind us when we leave. We just wanted to see what was going on. Didn't mean to intrude."

Ramon slipped an arm around Barney's waist. Both men were smiling as they stood there gazing first at me, then at Arthur.

Arthur eyed the two proudly. "These are two of the latest of the love pollen victims I was telling you about. One of the Belladonna Arms's greatest success stories. They're so in love they're practically joined at the hip."

I couldn't help but smile at the happiness on their faces. "Lucky you," I breathed before I could prevent a pang of jealousy from tearing through me.

"I know we're lucky," Barney said, watching me with a somber gleam in his eye. "We both do."

His partner nodded and snuggled closer to the man beside him.

I wasn't sure why I was so touched by their obvious love for each other, or by the openhearted way they were welcoming me to the building. But I knew I couldn't let it go unacknowledged.

I stepped forward and slipped my arms around the two, giving them a brief hug, all the while hoping I wouldn't start blubbering again. Then I quickly stepped back and studied them, made shy by the fact that for the second time since I walked into the Belladonna Arms, I had managed to fall apart at the seams and flaunt my emotions like a teenage girl. It was embarrassing.

"It's great to meet you," I said, trying to ignore all the blood pumping into my ears and the lump of emotion swelling up in my throat. "I hope I'll be a good neighbor."

Arthur clapped his hands in glee and, coming up behind me, swept me off the floor like he was picking up a basket of laundry. He gave me a hug that dragged my kilt up around my ass and almost popped a rib. "Oh, they won't be your neighbors. Ramon and Barney have agreed to take an apartment on six to free up this apartment for someone else."

"Oh," I said, feeling oddly disappointed as I hung there in Arthur's gigantic hands. "Well, that's nice of them, I guess."

Then Arthur seemed to realize what I'd said about being a good neighbor. Still in midair, he flipped me around to face him like I weighed nothing at all. "So you've decided to take the apartment! I knew you would!"

I hung there like a Christmas ornament, arms akimbo, toes hanging straight down like a ballerina on point. "But I still don't know how much the rent is."

He lowered me to the floor, cupped a bejeweled hand to his mouth, and whispered in my ear.

I jerked back and stared at him. "Really? That's all it is?"

Arthur laughed and nodded. Then he laid a fat finger over his ruby-red lips and shushed me to secrecy.

Barney turned to Ramon and said, "We should probably be worried that Shiloh's rent is cheaper than ours, but somehow I can't bring myself to get too worked up about it since our new apartment will have an even better view than this one. Plus I'll still have you to share it with, and poor Shiloh won't have anybody."

"Why, thank you." Ramon smiled, and taking his lover's hand, he led Barney toward the door in my bedroom wall. "But maybe Shiloh will acquire someone later."

Barney grinned. "He might. He just might. That kilt is a mighty aphrodisiac."

Ramon gave his lover a playful slap.

"No, I won't," I called after them. "I'm not looking for anybody. I don't want anybody. I don't. Honest." But they weren't listening. Nobody was listening. Arthur was adjusting his tits again, and Barney and Ramon were ducking back through the hidden door, giggling between themselves.

Just before the door clicked closed behind them for what I presumed would be the final time, both young men poked their heads back through the crack.

"Welcome to the Belladonna Arms," they said in unison, giving me a wink, and with that they were gone.

I smiled as I heard the turn of a key on the other side of my bedroom wall.

Turning to Arthur, I said, "Thank you. I think I'm going to like it here."

Arthur gave me a gentle wink, just as my new neighbors had. "I know you will. And you're welcome, honey. I'm glad you're here."

Before I could get all choked up again, I hustled off to inspect the kitchen cabinet space.

MY MOTHER followed me through her house like a bloodhound on the trail of a wounded rabbit, snooping out information as we went along.

"I don't mind keeping your stuff here, Shiloh. Just stay forever. Unpack. You can have your old room back. And take that shirt off. It's wrinkled. I'll iron it."

I ignored the shirt comment. My mother always wanted to iron something. "Mom, I'm an adult now. I have my own life."

"No, you don't," she said. "You have a train wreck. Why are you always living with men? Why don't you find a nice girl and get married?"

My mother knew I was gay as well as I did. She just refused to accept the fact. It was pretty funny, really. There she stood with her Clairoled hair in rollers, as always dyed red to within an inch of its life, a June Cleaver housedress on, and an apron with a big rooster sewn over the pocket, which I had given her for her birthday. Beneath the rooster was embroidered the words Kiss the Cock. She had worn the apron for almost a year, and she still hadn't gotten the joke.

And yes, in case you're wondering, I do have a mean streak.

"Mom, you shouldn't be wearing that apron."

"But I love this apron. It was a gift from my only begotten son."

"Oh brother," I mumbled, rolling my eyes so far up into my head I had to grab on to a pole lamp to keep from falling over.

"If your father were here—"

My father died when I was twelve. She had accepted his death about as well as she accepted my homosexuality.

"Mom, please, let me just get my boxes out of your way, and I'll leave you to whatever it is you're doing."

"I'm cooking stuffed bell peppers for the basket dinner. Liza Epstein up the street is making them too, but the rabbi said mine are better."

"Old news. You've told me before. Like once a week since I was two." My mother knew I hated stuffed bell peppers. I hated them as much as she hated Liza Epstein. To me they smelled like stinky socks. My mother knew that too.

"I'll wrap up a dozen for you to take with you."

I sighed. I supposed Arthur might like them. Or the pigeons.

My mom's house, oddly enough, would be within eyeshot of the Belladonna Arms if you could manage to climb onto her roof and peer through the branches of the sycamore tree in the front yard. After my interview with Arthur, I had spent the night with my mother for the first time in three years, sleeping on the sofa in the living room because my old room was filled with everything I owned after Larry threw me out. Now it was time to leave, take my stuff with me, and resume my own existence. Thanks to Arthur—who I suspected was a new friend, and if not a friend, at least an ally—I at least felt I had a life to resume. As my prying Jewish mother trailed me back and forth from the pile of boxes in my room to the front porch, where I was depositing them one by one, she managed to keep up a running commentary on the state of my life, most of which I had heard before. Like every time we got together. Or every time she called. Or every time she wrote a letter or sent a Hanukah card. Sometimes she even nagged me in my dreams, but I suspected that was my psychosis, not hers, so I couldn't really blame her for that.

"You should get a better job. You can't get married on a waiter's pay."

"I don't want to get married. And I like my job. Sort of."

"Your father never waited tables in a skirt."

"It's not a skirt. It's a kilt. And my father never worked at all. He sat in the backyard and drank wine until his liver exploded."

"Don't be mean. You look skinny. Are you eating?"

"Yes, I eat daily."

"What are you eating?"

"When I find time, I'll draw up a spreadsheet for you."

"The other night when Loretta Abramowicz and I had dinner where you work, the hemline on your skirt was too high. Loretta said you looked like a floozy. Bring it by one day and I'll rehem it for you."

"No. And it's not a skirt. It's a kilt. And I'm not a floozy."

"I hear a lot of odd people live in that building you're moving into."

"Good. Then I'll fit right in."

"How are you going to get all those boxes to your new place? I can't loan you my car. It's in the shop. It needs a new doohickey."

"I know. You told me six times. I'll get the boxes there the same way I got the boxes here. Cab."

"Your father never wasted money on cabs."

"That's because he was always too drunk to dial the phone."

"Oh, hush." But I thought I saw a grin twist the corner of her mouth. I'm pretty sure if she had been honest with herself, she wouldn't be missing my dad any more than I did.

She started plucking the rollers from her Hadassah red hair. "I suppose if a cab driver's coming, I should make myself presentable."

"The cab driver won't care if you're presentable."

"Think he'd like coffee? I could brew a fresh pot. I've got chicory."

"No!" I sighed again. It was getting to be a habit. Around Ila Smart, everybody sighs. "I'm calling him for a ride, not to pimp out my mother."

"What does that mean? Pimp out your mother? It sounds dirty."

"Oy. Never mind."

"And don't say oy. You never go to synagogue. You haven't earned the right to say oy."

I dumped the last box on the porch and plucked my cell phone from my pocket to call for a cab, specifically requesting either an SUV or a station wagon, and preferably one that could travel at the speed of light. The dispatcher said she would see what she could do. She said it like I'd just asked her for a kidney.

I plopped my ass down on the front porch and waited. My mom plopped down beside me, smoothing her Kiss the Cock apron daintily over her knees. She had her rollers gathered up in her lap, and she was combing her hair out with her fingers.

I leaned over and gave her a peck on the cheek. "Thanks for putting me up last night."

She harrumphed. "I was in labor with you for two days. Your head was so big I had to crawl out of the stirrups and jump up and down to get your ears out. You were so fat the nurse passed out cold and your father said we should have the bar mitzvah the next day. After all that you think letting you sleep on my couch is such an ordeal?"

I sighed. Where was that cab?

WHILE I was moving in, my next-door neighbors, Barney and Ramon, were moving out and settling into their new digs on the sixth floor. Since they had a lot more stuff than I did, I offered my services, and they gratefully accepted the extra help lugging their shit up two flights of stairs.

Both men thought I was the luckiest man on earth to have acquired an apartment in the Belladonna Arms.

"Especially 4D," Ramon said. "That's the apartment I fell in love in."

Barney beamed. "We both did. With each other, of course. I think the love pollen is really thick in there. By my calculations, Shiloh, your life should be changing any day now."

"I don't want my life to change," I said, gratefully dumping a box of pots and pans on their new kitchen floor. As far as I could tell, the layout of their new digs was exactly the same as the layout of their old one, except their view was better and they didn't have a secret passageway leading to the apartment next door.

"You guys want some stuffed bell peppers?"

"Hell no," Ramon said, poking his finger down his throat and pantomiming the act of barfing up a throw pillow. "They smell like stinky socks."

At least I wasn't the only one who felt that way.

I hooked a thumb at the wall. "Who lives over there?"

"Stanley and Roger," Barney said. "Roger's a nurse and Stanley's a student at Beaumont University. He's studying archeology."

"That's nice," I said. "Who's on the other side?"

Ramon's eyes dimmed. I thought he looked embarrassed. He turned away to fiddle with one of the boxes. It was Barney who finally answered my question.

"Ramon used to live there a long time ago, but we don't talk about that anymore. There's a new tenant in 6D now. We haven't met him yet. He seems nice, though. I think he works at the library."

While I wondered what mystery Barney was referring to concerning his new lover and the apartment next door, I decided not to worry about it. In a place like the Belladonna Arms, I would hear the story sooner or later. Barney didn't give me a chance to dwell on it anyway. Thirty seconds later he deftly steered the conversation elsewhere.

"Have you heard who's taking our old apartment?"

"No," I said. "Why? Have you?"

Barney stepped closer and lowered his voice as if the very walls had ears. Even Ramon perked up and leaned in to listen. "It's Arthur's nephew. He's moving here from somewhere in the Midwest. He grew up on a farm there. Wants to try his life in the big city. We can't wait to meet him."

"Does that mean he's gay?"

Barney shrugged. "Don't know."

"Do you think he's a drag queen like his uncle?"

Barney and Ramon both shuddered. "God, we hope not," they said in unison.

Ramon looked immediately contrite. "Don't get us wrong. We love Arthur. We do. But there isn't room for any more trains of taffeta to be sweeping through this building. Everybody's tripping over Arthur's sartorial splendors now."

I suddenly heard noises from one of the cardboard boxes stacked on the kitchen table. Scratching noises. Little mewling noises.

"What the hell is that?" I asked, watching the box rattle and shake and jerk around.

Barney laughed while Ramon hustled off to close the door leading out into the hall.

"That would be our kids," Barney said, unflapping the lid on the box.

The moment he did, a black cat and five little kittens spilled out onto the table like lava shooting out of Mount Vesuvius. From the table they shot off to explore in every direction. The kittens looked about half-grown, while the mother seemed to share some of Arthur's genes. She was huge. She was also cranky. I knew she was cranky because she hissed at me. The kittens looked remarkably like the ones I had seen on the stairs the day before when Arthur showed me the apartment.

With patience and love illuminating their angelic faces, Barney and Ramon watched their litter of felines scatter to the four winds as they snooped out their new digs.

It was Barney who offered the introductions. "Meet Wilhelmina and her five little rug rats: Pancho, Maria, Yolanda, Jesus, and Chuck."

Two of the kittens were white, two were black, and the fifth was half and half. That was Chuck. Chuck had a white face and a black mustache. He looked like Hitler.

"Need a cat?" Ramon asked hopefully. I mean, really hopefully.

"Uh, I'll think about it."

"You sure? They're going for a song?"

"You mean you're trying to sell them?"

"Hell no. Who'd buy a cat? *We'll* pay *you*."

"I need money, but I don't need it that bad. I'm also Jewish," I explained.

Barney understood right away. "Then you probably won't want Chuck. He's already adopted anyway. Yolanda's sweet, though." Barney wiggled his eyebrows, trying to look clever. "She loves lox."

"No. And that lox remark was a desperate play on my religious heritage."

Barney shrugged. "Worth a shot."

"About Arthur's nephew," I ventured. "What's his name?"

"Benjie," Barney said. "Arthur said his name is Benjie."

Chapter 3

I SETTLED into the Belladonna Arms, determined to make a go of it. The location really was perfect for me. I could walk to work in ten minutes. The rent was less than what I had paid to split the rent with my asshole ex, and I hadn't met a single person in the whole apartment building who was anything but friendly. In my last apartment, I didn't meet anybody *period.* The fact that I was on the fourth floor and there was no elevator assured me my mother wouldn't be dropping by unannounced, and as far as assurances go, that was a pretty good one. Nothing can disrupt a day like an unannounced visit from my mother.

I work evenings at the restaurant, so my days are free. I spent the first weekend at the Arms painting my new digs canary yellow after obtaining Arthur's blessing for the color change. He was so thrilled to be getting free labor, he even bought the paint, which I thought was nice. Since I'm a sloppy painter, and since the weekend had turned out to be a scorcher, and because the temperature in my apartment was about a thousand degrees, I was painting in nothing but a pair of old swimming trunks. I didn't want to ruin any more clothes than I had to. In a fit of gleeful revenge, just because I hated the thing so much, I used my flamingo shower curtain as a drop cloth. Do I know how to have fun, or what?

I had little more than one wall finished when I heard a knock on my door. I wiped the paint off my hand, smearing most of it across my nose—told you I was a sloppy painter—and opened the door to find Arthur and two guys standing there with smiles on their faces. Arthur was dressed like Josephine the Plumber on steroids in white overalls and a white hat with a daisy appliquéd here and there, not to mention full makeup and heels. The guys wore simple shorts and tees. Each of them had a brand-new paintbrush in his hand.

"Volunteers!" Arthur announced gaily, waving his paintbrush over his head like Queen Elizabeth limp-wristing the peons. He stepped aside and ushered in the two behind him. "Shiloh, this is Roger, and this is Stanley. They live right above you, and they're just dying to help you redecorate."

I had to give the two credit. If they had been coerced into assisting my efforts to spruce up my new digs, they hid it well. They truly looked eager to begin. I was rather speechless. Not simply by the kindness of the act, but also by the beauty of the one named Roger. My God, he was stunning. Buzz-cut hair, forest-green eyes, a body straight out of a porno shoot, and the sweetest smile I had ever seen on a human face *ever*.

His partner was a little guy, also cute, with black, geeky glasses, a Narnia-faunish build, golden skin, and a way about himself when he stood next to Roger that told me in no uncertain terms they were an item. And more than happy to be so. In fact, they were so obviously in love, I couldn't help wondering why even in the midst of my longest relationship (thirteen months with fuckface Larry) I had never felt remotely as happy as these two looked. Not on my very best day.

"G-golly," I stammered, passing out handshakes. "That's great. Thanks, guys. Grab a rag and a bucket of paint."

Stanley surveyed the one wall I had painted already. "I like the color. Roger, we should paint our place."

"Let's do it, then," Roger said, ruffling Stanley's hair, then as an afterthought leaning in to chew on his lover's neck. "Yummy," I heard him mumble while Stanley yelped with laughter and pushed him away.

"I'll help you," I volunteered, enjoying a rush of camaraderie. "I mean with painting your apartment, not with chewing on your boyfriend's neck."

Roger eyed me slyly while yanking Stanley back into his arms. "Damn right you won't," he said. "This is a one-man neck. And I'm the man. I don't share this neck with anybody." He stuck his tongue in Stanley's ear and said, "Tell him I'm right, honey buns."

Again Stanley whooped with laughter. "You're right! You're right! Stop!"

A second later Stanley was prancing away, still giggling like a loon, and I was standing there with my paintbrush forgotten, envying them all the more.

I guess Arthur was used to his tenants showing affection for one another. After all, the Belladonna Arms was Love Pollen Central, according to him.

"Don't expect me to be buying paint for *everybody*," he carped. He peered into my fridge while Roger and Stanley prepared to get to work. "Ooh, beer. And pastry!" Arthur clapped his hands. The building shook beneath us as he did a happy little tap dance in front of the refrigerator. I heard the clink of bottles as he grabbed beers for everyone and started passing them out while chomping down on one of my jelly donuts.

"So where do we start?" Roger asked, sipping his Bud and gazing around.

"If it isn't moving," I said, "paint it."

With canary-yellow paint in plastic buckets, rags slung over shoulders, beers placed in out of the way spots where they wouldn't be tipped over or painted, and ABBA cranked up on my CD player, everybody fanned out and went to work.

Within minutes, paint and gossip were flying everywhere.

Arthur shrieked when a teeny spot of paint landed on the back of his hand. He wiped it off with a rag, using the same care a brain surgeon uses to prep a skull for the first incision. Afterward he daintily slipped on a pair of pink kitchen gloves, which he extracted from the back pocket of his Josephine the Plumber overalls. "Almost forgot. This manicure cost twenty bucks. If I ruin it, heads will roll."

"So butch," Roger mumbled, giggling to himself and causing Arthur to stick his tongue out at him, which pretty much belied the "butch" comment.

"I saw Pete this morning," Stanley said, anteing up the first chip for the gossip pot. "He was heading down the stairs with Artie strapped to his chest."

"That little booger," Arthur said on a sigh with a grandmotherly gleam in his eye. "Artie's getting cuter every day and growing like a weed. He'll be walking soon. Driving. Dating. They grow up so *fast*!"

"Arthur, he's barely five months old. All he does is slobber and poop."

"Harrumph."

"Sylvia's so happy she practically coughs up little cartoon hearts every time she opens her mouth."

Arthur caught my eye, registered my confusion, and explained. "Your neighbors. Pete and Sylvia. I told you about her. They have a new baby. Artie. Named after me, of course." He patted the side of his hat like Mae West fluffing her finger waves. "Why wouldn't he be? After all, his parents love me, just love me." Arthur skipped a leery eye from one face to the next as if expecting someone to argue. Since everybody apparently enjoyed living where they lived, nobody did. "He's got lungs like a blue whale and the voice box of a howler monkey," Arthur went on. "My God, that kid can scream. You must have heard him wailing through the bedroom wall."

I laughed. "Oh yeah. I thought it was an ambulance roaring up the street."

"That's him."

Roger had squatted down on his knees to slather paint along the baseboard. "Sylvia will probably be over one of these days with the obligatory plate of Welcome Wagon Toll House cookies. She keeps us all furnished with them since it's the only thing she knows how to cook. Poor Pete's getting fat from all the lard and chocolate chips. I figure his teeth should be falling out any day."

"And he's never been happier," Arthur stated as if standing up for Pete at all costs. He patted his own belly and added, "A few extra pounds never hurt anybody. Look at me. Healthy as an ox."

Everyone hastened to agree. Once again, there was no sense pissing off the landlord. Or landlady. Or whatever Arthur considered himself to be.

We hadn't been at it for more than an hour when I gazed around and realized the living room was almost done. Wow. We were good.

Arthur straightened his little hat and adjusted an earring. "Rumor has it that Charlie and Bruce made a trip to the county courthouse this morning."

"Is he under arrest again?" Stanley asked around a groan. At which Roger leaned in to me and explained in a whisper, "Charlie and Bruce are our resident kleptomaniacs. They both work at UPS. They met in klepto rehab and live on 3. You'll know Charlie when you see him. He's skinny as a rail, stands about twelve feet tall, and his hair is even redder than yours. Bruce is a little pudgy guy who dresses like Gene Autry. They're devoted to each other. Watch your stuff when they're around, though. They are less than diligent when it comes to taking their klepto pills. Other than that they're sweet guys."

I scratched my head, realizing too late I was using the hand with the paintbrush in it when I felt paint drip on my hair. It startled me so I dropped my brush on my foot. "They have meds for being a thief?"

Roger shrugged. "I'm a nurse. Trust me. They have meds for everything except being stupid, which is the one thing the FDA should really invest in research on."

Stanley eyed my newly painted foot. "That and meds for people who can't hold a paintbrush."

"Blow me," I grumped with a grin and chuckled when he pretended to cower in fear.

Arthur prissily dabbed a jot of paint along the side of the kitchen door. So far he had painted approximately one square foot of my living room wall. He was the slowest painter I'd ever seen. I did notice he was pretty good at surreptitiously ogling my paint-splattered swimming trunks whenever the opportunity arose. Now, in the midst of his story about Charlie and Bruce, he reached out and plucked at the reddish fuzz surrounding my belly button, saying, "Sorry, you had a blob of paint there."

Yeah, right. I tap-danced out of reach. "Uh, thank you, Arthur."

He edged closer and whispered, "I think I see some paint on your ass too. Let me just—"

I narrowed my eyes and hissed. "Go paint something, Arthur."

He tinkled out a little laugh, not embarrassed in the least. "Oh, all right," he said and went back to prissily dabbing at the wall with his paintbrush, still smirking to himself. He seemed to have forgotten what he was talking about before his hormones interrupted him.

Stanley hadn't. In fact, Stanley seemed to be the only one who hadn't become sidetracked while watching Arthur make inappropriate passes at me. "So what were Charlie and Bruce doing at the county courthouse, Arthur? Jesus, you never finish a story."

Even Arthur seemed happy to get back into gossip mode. "Oh. Sorry, love." He tore his eyes from my ass and sucked in a great gulp of air as if force-feeding a pregnant pause. When he was sure he had everyone's attention, he said, "They registered for a marriage license!" He squealed a happy squeal.

"No!" Roger beamed, smiling even while he managed to look shocked.

Arthur's head bobbed around like one of those bobblehead dolls in the back car window. "They did! And what's more, they've asked me to be their matron of honor!" He squealed again.

To my surprise, but apparently not Roger's, Stanley teared up at the news. "That's so romantic," he murmured, dabbing at his nose with his paintbrush hand, smearing yellow paint across his cheek. "Two thieves in love."

"Yeah," Arthur sniped. "As in 'do you take this felon to be your lawfully wedded husband?'"

I laughed, but quickly swallowed it back down when I saw Stanley's chin pucker. Roger eyed Stanley with obvious admiration. "There he goes. Crying again." To me he added, "Stanley's a bit of a romantic."

Arthur gave a wry chuckle. "It isn't *that* romantic. Two men's wedding rings fell off the UPS truck, and neither he nor Bruce could bear to see them go to waste."

"Fell off the truck, my ass." Roger laughed and growled at the same time. "Those boys will end up in prison one of these days. I'm going to have another talk with Charlie and Master Bruce about their medications. I'll stuff their pills down their throats like a couple of sick cats if I have to. I've done it before."

Stanley giggled. "I remember. It was after we first met. Charlie stole the books I hung on your doorknob."

At this, Roger shuffled his feet and blushed. "Well, actually the book stealing was prearranged. I was trying to get your attention. I did stuff his meds down his throat, however. That part was real."

Stanley grinned. "Sneaky."

Roger threw him a kiss. "Love and war, pet. Love and war."

Stanley sniffed up a glob of sentimental snot and went back to work.

Everybody suddenly ran out of wall to paint. Looking around, we realized the living room was finished, and it looked great.

"Now you need yellow curtains," Roger said.

"Green," Stanley decided.

"Primrose," Arthur commanded, whatever the hell primrose was.

"Brown," I said, and everybody nodded.

"That'll work," they said in unison. "Nice and masculine."

"Masculine?" Arthur piped, checking his makeup in a purse-sized mirror he pulled from his back pocket. "What's that?"

We gathered up our buckets and rags and beers and headed to the bedroom.

"Ooh, the orgy room," Arthur said, eyeing my ass again.

"Hardly," I replied.

"Sorry to hear it," Arthur muttered, and even Roger and Stanley looked sympathetic.

As soon as the conjecture about my lack of a sex life was out of the way, everybody went to work.

Two minutes in, I said, "I helped Barney and Ramon move to 6 the other day. They tell me, Arthur, that your nephew is moving into their old apartment next door. What's he like?"

Arthur didn't bat an eye. "He likes men, just like you do."

"Gay, huh?" asked Stanley.

Arthur was carefully dipping the tippy tip of his brush bristles in his very own bucket of paint, which had hardly gone down at all. Even his brush was still pristine. Give the guy a mascara brush, he could paint the world. Give him a *paintbrush* and he bogs down like a mastodon in a tar pit.

"Oddly enough," he said, "yes. My nephew is gay."

"What do you mean 'oddly enough'? What's wrong with him?"

"Nothing's wrong with him. It's just that he and I are the only two black sheep in the family. Gay relatives where we come from are shunted off to the corncrib, often as not. I escaped when I was just a lad. Now it's my nephew's turn. He decided to follow me west."

"Is he a drag queen like you?" Stanley asked.

Arthur stopped stooping over his paint bucket and rose up to his full height, which in Josephine the Plumber drag and four-inch heels was pretty darn impressive. "*Nobody* is a drag queen like me! I, my dear, am unique!" Then he wilted a bit and added, "Besides, my nephew is probably too big to dress in drag. He would look totally out of proportion."

"You mean he's bigger than you?" Roger asked.

Arthur flapped his eyelashes, and a sprinkling of glitter drifted down and landed in his bucket of paint. Great. Now my bedroom walls would be glittery. "I haven't seen Benjie since he was ten," he said, "but yes. My guess would be he's as big as me. Or bigger. Voluptuous, if you catch my drift. Heft runs in our family, to put it kindly. At ten Benjie was husky. Well, he was a little *beyond* husky. He was enormous. By now he must be… *mountainous*. The little scamp."

"Oh dear. Poor Pete and Sylvia," Stanley said before he could stop himself. The implication was clear. If Arthur's *mountainous* nephew moved in next door, Pete and Sylvia would be directly beneath him and his *mountainous* clomping footsteps. I wouldn't be far away either, but happily, if Arthur was right about his nephew not dressing in drag, at least we wouldn't be tortured by the sound of the guy clattering around in high heels. The Belladonna Arms wasn't exactly soundproof, after all. A good sneeze could carry two floors in any direction. I knew Arthur was on the prowl before he ever left his apartment four floors down by the way the glasses rattled in the cupboard.

Roger threw himself into the conversation to blunt Stanley's comment about poor Pete and Sylvia. "So his name is Benjie, then. Like the dog. How nice. Well, I'm sure we all can't wait to meet the guy. He sounds wonderful. And any relative of yours, Arthur, is a friend of ours. You know that."

Stanley and I quickly and desperately agreed.

But Arthur wasn't listening. He was eyeing my ass again. Arthur is persistent, if nothing else.

I sighed and went back to painting, wondering what my new neighbor would *really* be like.

BUSINESS AT The Twisted Kilt had been booming all night. Tourists, locals, everybody loved The Twisted Kilt. It was almost midnight, and I was just coming down off my shift.

Since closing time was nigh upon us, I was the last waiter standing. The rest had slipped through the kitchen door and clocked out before heading home. I, on the other hand, had ducked into a back booth to partake of my complimentary meal, which all the employees were offered. Tonight I had a plate heaped with scotch pie, bridies, and rumbledethumps. They were all out of clapshots, my favorite. I had been working at the Kilt for over a year, and I still hadn't dredged up the courage to try the haggis or the black pudding or the fucking headcheese. I guess I'm a culinary coward. Wearing a kilt was humiliating enough.

Barfing all over the diners after consuming some poor sheep's offal wouldn't have been cool either.

I watched the joint from my corner booth. It was kind of boring with all the kilted waiters gone. Usually testosterone ran pretty high at The Twisted Kilt, what with the sexy waiters in their kilts, the sexy gay customers eyeballing the sexy waiters, and the straight married women giggling behind their napkins at the luscious array of hairy male knees parading around in front of them. More than once I had seen a particularly determined diner blithely toss his or her fork to the floor just for the privilege of seeing the kilted waiter bend over and pick it up. To be honest, during my first few weeks working there, I had been just as eager as everybody else to see the occasional Scottish butt make an appearance underneath its tartan hemline, but after twelve months of having the same trick played on me, the novelty had worn off.

I was down to my rumbledethumps and the dregs of my Innis & Gunn (we were allowed one complimentary beer with our meal) when the street door opened and a young man walked in. The man was probably no older than I. And he was huge. Not *fat* huge, but *muscled* huge. His shoulders were so broad, he blocked out the night-lit street behind him. He must have stood six five. He was so tall he had to duck through the door, and he did it with a grace and a forbearance that told me he was used to ducking through doors, as I'm sure he was. Otherwise he would have been knocking himself out every time he entered a building. The man was pale-skinned with white-blond hair worn short, and even from across the restaurant I could see that his eyes were a shimmering blue.

At my first glimpse of those azure orbs, my jaw went slack, and I forgot to finish chewing whatever the hell I had in my mouth. It might have been an inner tube for all I knew. I had never been so mesmerized in my life.

I finally swallowed so I wouldn't choke to death on my rumbledethumps (that would look terrible in an obituary), and my heart quickened when those hypnotic blue eyes did a quick scan of the restaurant and immediately came to rest on me.

My eyebrows shot up involuntarily when he stepped toward me. Weaving in and out of the tables, he came striding across the restaurant, gracefully slipping past diners, his smile continually broadening as he drew ever nearer. The closer he got, the more mesmerized I became.

His legs were long, his jeans-clad hips were lean, and the white T-shirt he wore did absolutely nothing to hide the scrumptious body beneath. His biceps rolled and danced as he moved. Well-worn cowboy boots graced his feet, a simple silver watch was strapped to his fuzzy blond wrist, and the bulge pooching up the fly of his faded denims made me gather up the last bite of rumbledethumps from my plate and nervously stuff it in my mouth just to have something to do other than ogle.

This time when I swallowed, the entire forkful of food went down the wrong pipe. I knew right away I was in trouble. I clutched my throat, trying to look like nothing was wrong, but it's hard to appear nonchalant when you're choking to death. My fork clattered to the table as I clawed for air, gasping like a guppy. I could feel my eyeballs bulge from oxygen deprivation. I watched in horror as my beer bottle toppled over and rolled off the edge of the table. As if choking to death wasn't embarrassing enough, now I was tossing beer bottles around and making a mess.

Before the beer bottle could hit the floor, however, the Adonis with the muscles flew across the last few yards of space separating us and snatched the bottle out of midair. He placed it back on the table in front of me with one fluid motion that, even in my panicked state, I thought was graceful as hell.

He planted his hands on the table and leaned in to study my beet-red face.

"You okay?" he asked.

I pointed to my throat, and gasped, "Cho… cho… cho…."

As luck would have it, he spoke gibberish. "Choking, huh?" he asked, and before I knew what was happening, he had dragged me out of the booth, circled me in those massive arms, lifted me off the floor with my kilt up around my chin, and given me a squeeze.

"*Ptui*," I said, and a glob of rumbledethumps flew out and hit a woman sitting at the next table in her neck. I must say she looked mightily surprised when it did.

Like a bellows, I sucked in air through my newly unclogged pipes, and Lord, it felt good.

My blond savior then flipped me around to face him so he could gaze into my eyes with a quizzical expression that I thought was kind of blasé, considering everything we had just gone through together.

"Can you breathe?" he asked, giving me a shake. "Need mouth-to-mouth?"

"I wish," I sputtered. Then I realized what I'd said, and my blush came back. The surprised expression he gave me in return embarrassed me all the way down to my toes, so I wiggled out of his arms, pulled my kilt down over my balls, and gulped, "Y-yes. I mean, yes. I can breathe."

It was then I realized every eye in the place was on us. As soon as the blood sluiced out of my face and I was finally breathing normally again, a round of applause rose up. A couple of people came over and, ignoring me completely, patted my rescuer on the back, congratulating him on his quick action. They were both gay men, I noticed. Boy, gay dudes never miss a chance to pet a hunky hero. And even though I had just squeaked through death's door and come out on the right side relatively unscathed, I still felt a pang of jealousy that they had gotten to him before I did.

I embarrass easily. I always have. But somehow, at that moment, I wasn't embarrassed at all.

What I was, was grateful.

I stepped forward, still shaking from the experience, and wrapped my arms as far around the hunk as I could get them, resting my head for a moment on that incredible chest. To my surprise, he slid his arms around me and hugged me back. The top of my noggin fit perfectly beneath his chin, tucking in there like it really belonged.

He smelled of clean skin. Nothing else. No colognes, no soaps. Just skin. The scent of the man was so beguiling, I had to close my eyes for a second while my face was still buried in his chest. One of his huge, rolling biceps pressed against the side of my head, so warm and soft and hard all at the same time that it sent a shiver through me that was much closer to sexual than it should have been under the circumstances.

A huge hand patted me gently on the back as I muttered, "Thank you," into his shirt.

He didn't answer, so I pulled back enough to gaze up into his face, although I sure as hell didn't want to leave the comfort of that massive chest or those heavenly arms. When I did, I saw he wasn't pale anymore. Now he was blushing, and his cheeks had gone rosy like mine no doubt were. I must say he looked pleased, though. Before he spoke, he cast his gaze around the restaurant, and I could see that all the attention was making him uncomfortable. Still, when his eyes came back to me, there was a smile in them, although the smile never touched his mouth. At the moment, he seemed more concerned for my well-being than he was about his own embarrassment, which I thought was gentlemanly.

"I'm glad you're okay," he said in a soft, sexy, resonant voice that hummed its way into my ears and made my libido vibrate like a tuning fork. "I guess I startled you."

I swayed with a rush of something. I wasn't quite sure what it was. Adrenaline? Fear? Excitement? "You might have startled me a little," I admitted. Understatement of the year. The fact that he was *still* startling me didn't need to be said either.

He gripped my shoulders, just forcefully enough to keep me standing, and said, "Are you sure you're okay?"

I swallowed hard, and this time all the proper tubing came into play and everything went where it was supposed to go, air down one tube, spit down the other. "I think so. Who—who are you?"

"I'm Arthur's nephew," he said.

That was a shocker. "You're Benjie?" The words *I thought you were fat!* rattled through my head, but thank God I had the quick-witted wherewithal to keep them from running through my voice box.

His eyes narrowed, but there was still humor in them, although it was obvious I had hit some sort of nerve or other. Probably the childhood-nickname nerve, if I was any judge.

"No," he said, rather more forcefully than was really necessary, yet still maintaining a playful edge to his voice, which I thought was sexy as hell. "Actually, I'm Ben. I haven't been Benjie since third grade. I didn't *like* being Benjie even then. Anyhoo, that's neither here nor there. Uncle Arthur sent me over to tell you hi and to ask you if I could maybe get something to eat. He also asked me to bring him back an order of clapshots, whatever the hell that is."

"It's neeps and tatties."

"What the hell are neeps and tatties?"

I grinned. I guess I wasn't the only one who thought Scottish people talked funny. "It's turnips and potatoes. Squish them all together, throw in some other shit, and you've got clapshots. And we're all out."

"Darn."

"Um, did Arthur also tell you to save my life?"

This time when his eyes smiled, the smile also reached his mouth. His lips spread wide in a grin, showing dainty white teeth and two dimples I hadn't known were there before now. He ran a broad hand across his short hair and blushed a little more, but he seemed pleased nonetheless. His eyes softened as he gazed down at me standing there before him, a head shorter but as rapt as I had ever been in my life. I saw kindness. I saw sweetness. And I saw my own reflection staring back at me in the depths of those gorgeous blue eyes. My reflection was smiling. How the hell could it not have been?

"No," he said, finally tearing his eyes from mine. "I ad-libbed the life-saving bit. But I'll still give you mouth-to-mouth if you need it."

"Uh, maybe later."

"You promise?"

I was so surprised by the question, I almost fainted. Jesus, nothing like meeting the hunkiest guy in the world, then choking on your dinner and almost passing out before he jumps in to save your life, and then two minutes after he saves your life, he starts flirting, and then you almost pass out *again*.

I must be making all sorts of wonderful first impressions, I thought. *God knows he is.*

A bolt of common sense struck me. I have no idea where it came from. Bolts of common sense usually miss me completely and nail somebody else.

"Let's get you something to eat," I said, suddenly realizing why he was here and what was expected of me. I pointed toward the booth where I'd been sitting. "Have a seat."

"Will you join me?"

"Sure. Just as soon as I fetch you some dinner."

I was surprised to see a sign of shyness creep over him. Two seconds earlier he was flirting, and now he was blushing again. "I hope it's no trouble," he said.

I couldn't believe he said that. "You just saved my life! *Nothing* would be too much trouble."

"Yeah, but still—"

Shooting for butch, I rose up on tiptoe and growled in his face. "Sit," I commanded. "Don't make me get physical."

The heat that entered his expression when I said those words, not to mention the little twist of a smile that followed along with it, made my dick nudge itself awake beneath my kilt. Christ, getting a boner was the only way this scenario could get any worse.

"I think I'd like to see you getting physical," he said in the sexiest voice ever, causing me to try not to faint again. He said it staring down at my tiny frame rather like a mighty oak gazing on a sapling that's getting a little big for its britches and trying to hog the water supply.

"Sit!" I commanded once more, and this time I didn't wait for a response. I was grateful for the sporran, as all Scotsmen undoubtedly are from time to time, since the weight of it kept my dick from standing and lifting my kilt up around my ears. (Okay, I'll admit it. There was a certain amount of whimsical literary license in that statement, considering the fact my dick isn't *nearly* long enough to lift my kilt up around my ears.)

Anyway, with *that* ridiculous thought out of the way, I hustled my horny ass off to the kitchen to fetch Ben his dinner, all the while flapping a menu in front of my face to cool myself off.

WHILE THE rest of the restaurant closed down, my boss gave me a holy dispensation to feed the man who had saved my life and in saving said life, had prevented a bunch of paramedics and coroner's assistants from traipsing through The Twisted Kilt and disrupting everybody else's dinner. I think the boss was also thankful for the floor show. Most of the remaining customers appeared to have enjoyed it immensely. At my expense, of course. But still, I was alive. That's what counted.

I was also intrigued. Not by the fact I had just escaped death. But by the man who had plucked me out of its slavering jaws.

I gathered up whatever leftovers they had in the kitchen and served it to Ben with an Innis & Gunn on the side, which I paid for myself. My boss's largesse only goes so far.

Ben eyed the unfamiliar food with a cockeyed expression, but he must have been a trusting soul. He lit into it without a moment of hesitation. I had never seen anyone eat so fast. He must have been starving. The haggis alone would have given *me* a reason to at least poke through it with a fork first to try to figure out what I was eating.

When Ben's feeding frenzy began to wind down, and while the two old Mexican ladies who comprised the cleaning crew began vacuuming the restaurant around us after the last customers left, I claimed two more beers from behind the bar and eased myself back into the booth.

"Welcome to San Diego," I said, handing him his Innis.

He smiled a thank-you and held his bottle out for a toast. I tapped it with mine and we drank.

While he fiddled with what little food was left on his plate, he said, "I've never really seen a man in a kilt before."

"I'd never worn one before I started working here."

"You're not Scottish?"

I laughed. "I'm Jewish."

His face softened. He looked down at his hands, and I spotted his shyness rising up once again. It was funny how a man with his physical presence could display such sweet timidity.

"I'm glad you're okay," he said quietly. "I hope I didn't hurt you when I—did what I did. You scared me. I just grabbed you up like a bag of chicken feed and started squeezing."

"You were scared? You looked so calm. At least what I could see through my gasping, gagging panic."

He gave a wry chuckle, and his ears went pink. "I was scared to death. I think I was more scared than you were."

"If you think that, you'd be wrong. It was probably the most frightening thing that's ever happened to me. I'll never forget that you were the one who saved my life. I mean it. I never will."

"And I didn't hurt you?"

I rubbed my chest and decided to be honest. "Come tomorrow morning I think I might have a bruise or two. But I'm not complaining, Benjamin. I could very easily have died. It's only because of you that I didn't."

"Call me Ben," he said. His pale blue eyes were so centered on my face that I couldn't have looked away if I wanted to. Which I didn't. Something about the gentle way he stared out at the world—not just at me, but at everything—reminded me of the wide-eyed innocence of a child. I could actually see the childlike goodness in him simply by gazing into his eyes.

It was kind of heart-stopping.

The beauty and the size of the package all that goodness came in was heart-stopping too. Ben was perhaps the biggest and most incredibly put together man I had ever met. I had known few men in my life whom I would call beautiful, inside or out, but Ben was certainly one of them on both counts.

God help me, I couldn't help thinking how fortunate Ben was that his Uncle Arthur had likely received all the weird genes in the family. I mean, Arthur was a sweetheart, but he certainly wasn't normal, and I was pretty sure he'd be the first to admit it.

I sipped my beer and tried not to let my imagination get too carried away. Ben was my landlord's nephew. He was my new neighbor. He was handy to have around when one was choking to death. And he was pleasing as hell to look at. But that was really all I knew about him. Until I found out if he was a serial killer or someone who eats his boogers, I'd really have to withhold judgment.

Even if he did save my life.

"So Arthur's your uncle," I ventured.

He grinned. "I hadn't seen him since I was a kid. He met me at the airport tonight in a ball gown."

"Well, that's our Arthur."

"We're the only two gays in our family. Where I come from, gay relatives usually end up stomped to death out behind the barn and fed to the hogs. I thought I'd better escape while I could."

"Wise choice."

"But seeing Uncle Arthur now, I'm not so sure I did the right thing."

"What do you mean, Ben?"

He watched one of the cleaning women fight with her vacuum cleaner for a minute before he turned back to me. His eyes were wide and worried, and his mouth was a little pouty. Jesus, I wanted to kiss that pout away. Maybe it was time to ask for that mouth-to-mouth.

"I thought I should come out to California to be with the only other relative I have who's like me."

"And?" I asked.

Ben's ears glowed red again. They must have some wonderful blood circulation, I thought. They went red every time he turned around. "I—I thought being gay made Arthur and me alike." Ben leaned in and whispered frantically, "But I'm not nearly as gay as he is. Nowhere close! He's like *Olympic* gay. I'm clearly an amateur next to him."

I patted Ben's hand. I'd been wanting to do it for the last few minutes anyway, and I finally saw my chance. As I patted that beautiful hand, I noticed it was about twice the size of mine. And oh, how warm it was! The fuzzy feel of the blond hairs sprinkling the back of it sent shivers of delight straight to my crotch. God, I'm a slut.

I snapped myself back to reality. "Listen, Ben. It's true. *Nobody's* as gay as your Uncle Arthur. He's one of a kind. Okay, so he likes to wear women's clothes. *You* don't like to wear women's clothes, do you?"

He looked horrified. "No!"

Thank God, I thought. "But there's something you need to know about your uncle. He's the sweetest man I've ever known. In a pinch he'd give you the camisole off his back. And he's thrilled to have you here. He told everybody in the building you were coming. He loves you very much, even if he *hasn't* seen you since you were ten. Don't look down on your uncle for being who he is. And don't be ashamed of him either. He isn't you. That's all you need to know. Pretty soon you'll love him as much as everybody else does. After a while, you won't even notice the drag outfits and the excess makeup and the size-twelve high heels and the bags of frozen peas he wears for tits when the weather's warm."

"Really?"

I rolled my eyes and bit back a chuckle. "No, Ben. That was a fucking lie. How could you *not* notice that shit? But I will say this. After a while what stands out most is Arthur's good heart and his generous spirit and his humor. Trust me. That's the real meat of the man. All the other stuff you see is what he does for himself because he enjoys it. The culottes, the gowns, the bed jackets, the stiletto heels, the wigs, the eyelashes, the rubber Gloria Swanson mole he drags out on special occasions and glues to the side of his face. It's all icing on the cake. It's what he does for everybody else that makes him special. That makes him loved. When you meet Tom, his other half, you'll understand your uncle a little better. When he's with Tom, that is Arthur at his very, very best."

"You like him," Ben said softly, dragging this lovely sweet smile out for another encore.

"I like him very much. And Arthur is like you in a way. He saved my life too. He took me in when I needed a place to stay after my lover broke up with me."

"Why did your lover do that?"

The question was so surprising, I lost my train of thought. I merely stared back at Ben while my brain did calisthenics inside my head, trying to get its wits about it again. It took a minute, but I finally managed to accept the question for what it was. An attempt to get to know me better.

"He left me, Ben, because he found somebody else he liked better." I shrugged. "It happens."

Ben cocked his head to the side and frowned as he studied my face. "He must be a fool."

For the second time in half a dozen seconds, I was astounded by the words that came out of Ben's mouth.

"Th-thank you," I finally said, wondering if I was going to pull a Stanley and start tearing up. "Actually I called him worse things than a fool after he dumped me."

"Good," Ben said. "I'll bet he misses you. I would."

Okay. Three's the charm. This guy just kept astonishing me with his sweetness. "Would you?" I asked because I simply couldn't seem not to.

But he didn't answer. Instead, he avoided my eyes and fished for his wallet.

I reached over and laid my hand on his arm to stop him. While I was at it, I also managed to enjoy the feel of my fingers rustling through the mass of blond hair that decorated his forearm. "Your dinner is on the house, Ben. For saving my life."

"You sure?"

"Yes, Ben. I'm sure."

He slowly stuffed his wallet back in his pocket, all the while gazing down at my hand on his arm. When he raised his eyes to my face, his smile was back. "I hope we'll be friends," he said quietly.

And just as quietly, I answered back, "I think we already are."

A while later, we bowed our way past the two old Mexican ladies, who giggled when we slipped by them as they were wiping down the tables and chairs. "Buenas noches, niños!" they tittered as we ducked through the door onto the street.

Outside, the night was balmy and clear. A million stars speckled the sky above the streetlights. The hour was so late, the downtown traffic had at long last died down.

"I could be lying in a morgue right now," I said, as we jogged illegally across the street, dodging a city bus.

"You mean from jaywalking?" Ben asked, eyeing the bus with some alarm.

"No. I mean from choking to death."

"Oh, that. Well, you didn't."

Safely off the street, I tugged at Ben's sleeve and pulled him to a stop. He stood there next to a parking meter, polite and expectant, as if wondering what I was about to say. But somehow I couldn't find words at all. I walked into his arms once more, and he accepted my hug as if it made all the sense in the world.

His massive arms gathered me up, making me feel safe and welcome. When I felt his lips in my hair, I closed my eyes and breathed in that luscious clean scent of his. I could hear his heart pounding against my ear, his breath rushing through his body. I heard his stomach growl, probably from the haggis he had for dinner.

"You're really cute in that kilt," he whispered into my hair.

"Uh, thanks, Ben."

I felt his smile on my scalp. "Let's get you home," he said softly. "You've had a rough night."

Taking my hand, he walked me silently along the late-night city streets until we reached the Belladonna Arms. In the fourth-floor hallway, he stepped through his door as I stepped through mine. Our eyes met one last time before we disappeared from each other's sight. He wore a gentle smile as he gave me a little wave, then vanished behind his door.

We hadn't spoken another word since I had hugged him on the street and he'd reciprocated by holding me close.

I could still smell the scent of his skin on my clothes. I could still feel his hands on my back.

I could still hear him tell me how cute I looked in a kilt.

Chapter 4

IN A nutshell, my first impression of Arthur's nephew, Ben, was that I liked him, to say the least. How can you not like someone who saves your life with the Heimlich maneuver and is so gorgeous and hunky your libido kicks into hyperdrive every time you look at him or even *think* of him?

Unfortunately, my second impression of Ben was that he was sort of strange, although the imprint he made on my libido didn't change much in the transition.

That disconcerting second impression began with scuttling noises on the other side of my bedroom wall. The scuttling noises quickly progressed to hammering, thumping, and banging, and the hammering, thumping, and banging went on for hours. What the hell was he doing? Building an ark? Of course, I knew by now those noises weren't simply coming through my bedroom wall. They were coming through the secret door connecting my apartment to Ben's.

I became even more annoyed about it later in the day when something other than noise came through that door.

I had been standing naked at my bathroom mirror, studying the bruise on my stomach I had received from Ben's wristwatch when he saved my life. I wasn't complaining, mind you. A bruise on the belly is way better than a one-way ticket to the crematorium.

Standing there in front of the mirror, my mind went back to the feel of Ben's arms encircling me. Not when I was all bug-eyed and gagging as he was doing the Heimlich thing, but later, when I was thanking him. There was something about the towering size of Ben, the heat and depth of his chest and the gentle way he had held me against him as he accepted my gratitude, that made me tremble as I thought of it. Even my cock responded to the memory. I watched it now as it lengthened and filled and finally stood erect, bobbing around like a party crasher forcing his way into the room to see if there's any cake left.

I tore my eyes away from my dick and gazed at my reflection in the mirror while my fingertips, as if with a mind of their own, played lightly along my shaft, cupped my balls, and caused my hips to buck at the sensation. Shiloh Jr. hadn't had any attention in a while. I could tell he was eager to rumble, even if the rumble was destined to be a one-man show.

I looked down and saw a crystal shimmer of liquid seep from the tip of my cock. That hadn't taken long. I gathered it up on my thumb and slipped it into my mouth, imagining all the while that the salty, delicious precome came from Ben, not me. Again my body trembled as I closed my eyes and savored the taste on my tongue.

My fingers tightened around my cock, and I began to stroke myself, almost lazily at first, as if testing the waters, trying to decide how eager I was for this to happen. It didn't take me long to realize I was pretty damned eager.

It was just as my balls were tightening and I was really getting into my little jerk-off fest that I heard the noises behind my bedroom wall.

I jumped like I had the time my mother caught me whacking off on the commode when I was fourteen, embarrassing her even more than it embarrassed me, or so she said, although I didn't believe it for a minute.

Naturally the merest glimmer of a memory with my mother in it while I was beating off was enough to kill a hard-on deader than a Christmas goose.

I sadly watched as my dick drooped and its fat little corona, so happy and pink and full of life a second ago, suddenly shrank like a leaky balloon.

"Damn!" I said, whirling toward the offending noises.

Still naked, I stalked into the bedroom and stood there with my hands on my hips as I stared at the secret door. With no knob on my side, only on the other, I was surprised to see the door give a tremble, not unlike the way I had been trembling a moment before.

Someone was testing it. Testing the door. And that someone had to be Ben. It also seemed clear he was trying to be quiet about it, which made me suspicious. Had Arthur told him about the door, or had he assumed Ben simply wouldn't notice a door hidden behind the shelves in his bedroom closet? Barney and Ramon said they would lock it. Did that mean there was a key in the door? And did Ben know about the key? On my side, of course, there was nothing. Not only no knob, but no keyhole, no key, nothing. Only me. And my softening dick.

To my horror, I heard a click, and the door swung open a fraction of an inch. Then a fraction more.

Stunned, I stood there in all my naked glory and waited for Ben to poke his head, uninvited, into my private living space. I didn't have long to wait.

The door continued to swing outward—a couple of inches, then a couple more—and suddenly there it was: Ben's blond head poking through the crack. He surveyed the room in front of him—my bedroom!—and slowly his eyes swiveled around to encompass… me! Starkass naked and glaring at him.

He gave a start to see me standing there with my hands on my hips watching him, but even in his shock, I saw him take a moment to let his eyes forage over my body long enough to get a pretty good idea of the terrain I had to offer.

I have to admit, my anger sort of petered out at that point. Having those incredible azure eyes on my naked body was a pretty erotic experience. I might have even felt my dick cough up another drop of precome, although I was afraid to look for fear I would give myself away.

"Oh," Ben said. "It's you."

I stormed toward him, dick swinging, and pulled the door all the way open, jerking it from his grasp. He stood there in a pair of faded blue jeans and nothing else. His torso, uncovered, was just as I had imagined it would be. Deeply muscled, broad shouldered, pale-skinned, and with a dusting of blond chest hair stretching from one bronze nipple to the other. Another tangle of blond hair erupted just beneath his itsy bitsy belly button and disappeared into the top of his jeans where, I couldn't help noticing, the two top buttons were casually undone. Not one little hint of underwear showed beneath. Only a further tangle of blond pubic hair and quite possibly the faintest glimpse of the base of a fairly substantial cock secluded among the shadows.

Or maybe that was wishful thinking.

Ben's feet were bare, his hair was tumbled from sleep, and his eyes were heavy. Or at least they were before they popped open wide at the sight of me staring darts at him as he trespassed into my room.

I tried to ignore the rush of desire that stuttered through me at the sight of those undone buttons at the top of his jeans. It took every ounce of willpower I possessed to drag my eyes away from the treasures hiding there and focus my attention on his face, which, God help me, looked even handsomer this morning than it had last night.

When our eyes connected, I was almost amused to see him wage a battle within himself to maintain the connection. For all his good intentions, his eyes slid away from my face almost immediately and his gaze roamed over my naked body again before settling on my crotch. When he glanced back at my face, I saw the tiniest smile twist his lips.

"You're dripping," he said softly.

"I—I just got out of the shower. I'm wet."

His smile broadened. "You're not wet anywhere else."

I fumbled around for a second, seeking something to say, and then I got mad.

"What the hell do you think you're doing, *Benjie*? This is my private space! You can't just barge in here any time you want!"

At that, the lust fell from his face. His ears turned red and roses bloomed in his cheeks. Unless I was sorely mistaken, at the very same moment, I was almost certain the bulge in his jeans grew. I knew I was right when a mortified look came onto his face and he placed his hands in front of his fly to hide it.

Then it was my turn to be mortified, for at that precise moment, I felt my cock give a lurch and begin lengthening right there in front of God and everybody.

Truly horrified, and so damned turned on I could barely see straight, and still as mad as a hornet, I barked at Ben, "Get out! Get out of my apartment!"

When his mouth opened wide in surprise and I could see he was about to apologize all over the place for doing what he had done, I nipped his apology in the bud, gave him a shove backward, and slammed the secret door in his startled face.

But not before I watched him gaze down at my dick one last time and nervously lick his lips.

And Jesus, wasn't *that* erotic as hell.

Torn between furious and turned on, it took every ounce of strength I possessed to drag the ancient chifforobe that came with the furnished apartment across the bedroom and wedge it against the connecting door. The damn thing must have weighed a ton.

I stood there panting, still naked, and being the wishy-washy guy that I am, I started wondering if I had gone overboard. Maybe Ben had just stumbled on the door by accident and decided to see where it led. Maybe no one had told him about it. After all, it seemed awfully inconsiderate to start raving at the man who less than twelve hours earlier had saved my life.

Plus he was so damn gorgeous. And those half-buttoned blue jeans! Damn!

As if all this wasn't confusing enough, I gazed down and saw that my dick was still dripping. Talk about sending mixed signals. I didn't know whether to go over there and kick him in the nuts, apologize for being mean, or simply stick my head down his pants and have at it. Although I must say, the third option would have been my preference.

Still, privacy is privacy. He had to learn about boundaries and consideration and when not to poke his nose through doors when he hadn't been invited. And how to button his pants.

Well, no. Maybe not that last thing.

BY THE time my breakfast was over, the rest of the world was well into the afternoon. Working nights as I did, mornings did not exist for me; I generally slept right through them. As the day wore on, my anger at Ben mellowed. I simply couldn't believe he had purposely entered my apartment through that hidden door with anything nefarious in mind. There had to be extenuating circumstances. The next time I saw him, I was determined to apologize for jumping down his throat the way I had, although I still wouldn't have minded stuffing something else down his throat.

Or mine.

After gathering up my dirty laundry, I crammed it all in a couple of pillowcases, stuck a bigass box of Tide under my arm, and headed out the door to locate the laundry room, which Arthur had told me was somewhere in the basement. I paused for a moment, eyeing Ben's door, wondering if I should tap on it and apologize for being so mean to him earlier. Then I thought of him poking his head into my apartment without so much as asking first, and I got mad all over again. If anybody needed to apologize, it was Ben, not me.

I turned my back on Ben's front door, and in my usual day-off ensemble of jeans and a T-shirt, I took off, padding barefoot down the stairs.

I was barely on my way when I met a strange young man on the third-floor landing. He stood about twelve feet tall, and his hair was even redder than mine. Putting two and two together, I figured he had to be the kleptomaniac I had heard about the day we painted the apartment. He was traipsing up the stairs, mindlessly picking at a pimple on his chin and not watching where he was going. When he almost walked into me, he lifted his head and grunted a surprised, "Oh."

I juggled my laundry around and stuck out a paw. "You must be Charlie," I said.

He stared at my hand for a minute, then reluctantly stuck his own out to meet it. Happily it wasn't the hand he had been picking the pimple with. "Must be," he said. "Who are you?"

"Shiloh. I just moved in about a week ago."

He answered around a yawn. Apparently he didn't wake up until the afternoon either. "Oh yeah. You're the drag queen on 4."

I blinked in surprise. "Excuse me. I'm not a drag queen."

As if unused to being argued with, his voice took on an insistent tone. "I saw you in a dress."

"You saw me in a kilt."

"Looked like a dress."

I sucked in a great gulp of air and stared at him. "Okay," I said. "Have it your way. I'm the drag queen on 4."

Charlie seemed to think I had inferiority issues. His mouth molded itself into a sympathetic pout that looked remarkably like my mother's when she thought I was being obstinate. Charlie even *tsk*ed like my mother, which was *really* annoying.

Giving me a wink and a chummy pat on the arm, he said, "Never be ashamed of who you are, Shiloh. Everybody's special in their own way." Then he leaned in a little closer, giving me a true bird's-eye view of the seeping pimple on his chin. "Gotta tell you, though, you'd make a much more attractive drag queen if you wore a wig and a little makeup. And stockings. Your legs are too hairy."

I couldn't believe this guy. "Thanks for the beauty tip. Say, aren't you the thief?" I asked, simply because I thought it was time to strike back. I had actually been in a pretty good mood when I left my apartment. Thirty seconds with Charlie the Klepto and I was ready to start swinging.

To my surprise, Charlie didn't cower in shame at my accusation. Instead, he threw his shoulders back and patted himself on the chest. "I'm not just a thief. I'm a kleptomaniac."

"Your mother must be so proud."

A look of doubt crossed his face. "Well, she still wants her blender back." Then he perked up. "My boyfriend's a kleptomaniac too. His name's Bruce."

"How fortuitous for you both."

"I don't know what that word means. So where you headed? Laundry room?"

There I was holding two bags of dirty laundry and a box of Tide. Where else would I be going? Disneyland? "And prescient too," I said. "Bruce is a lucky man."

"For a drag queen, you use a lot of big words. I don't know what that last word means either."

"Then the next time you're in prison maybe you should sign up for a learning annex course so you can keep up." I leaned in and whispered in his ear, "Just so you know, Clearasil is on sale at CVS. You might want to pick up a tub. Get the extra strength. And maybe the economy size. That pimple's a doozy. It looks like Mt. St. Helens just before it blew all those fucking trees over. Toodles."

There's nothing snottier than a Jew who wears a kilt to work and is accused of being a drag queen when he isn't. Or so it would seem.

I felt Charlie's eyes on me as I turned my back on him and blithely skipped off down the stairs, lugging my two bags of laundry and my bigass box of Tide and humming "Hava Nagila" just to be annoying.

One floor down I walked into the midst of a trio of kittens playing on the stairs. They were having so much fun, I thought I'd join them. I plopped my ass down on the top step, and two seconds later they were climbing all over me. Two were black, one was white. I was giggling at their antics as I rubbed their bellies and tweaked their tails when a pretty, petite woman with a baby strapped to her chest came humming up the stairway from the floor below.

Her face lit up at the sight of me. "Hi! You must be my new neighbor! Shiloh, is it?"

I extracted a kitten's claws from first one thigh, then the other, and stood to say hello. Having my hands filled with cats, I merely smiled. "And you must be Sylvia."

Her smile was beautiful. In fact, she was beautiful all over. Her dark hair was cut in a shoulder-length bob, she wore no makeup because she didn't need it, and her body was short and trim and daintily graceful. The baby hanging from her chest was facing outward, and he had a rope of drool leaking out of his mouth that hung all the way down to his foot. He was short too.

"Your child is leaking," I said.

Sylvia laughed. "Artie's always leaking. From some orifice or another."

"Eww," I said.

She reached into the diaper bag hanging from her shoulder and pulled out a ziplock baggie filled with cookies. "Here. A housewarming gift."

The cookies looked great, so I snatched them right up. "Thanks, Sylvia. I was told you'd be delivering cookies one of these days." I reached into the baggie, pinched out a cookie, and went to work on it. It was delicious.

Sitting back on the step with my bag of cookies, I smiled when Sylvia joined me, and also when the kittens came back to climb all over me yet again. Little Artie's eyes popped open wide when he saw the kittens, and he started goo-gooing all over the place, sputtering, spitting, flapping his hands, and kicking his feet. Jeez, the guy was like a whirling dervish. Sylvia was being jerked around like she had an outboard motor nailed to her chest.

Sylvia patted the kid on the head and said, "Easy, big boy." Then to me she said, "These kittens need homes. You should adopt one. Barney and Ramon will love you forever if you do."

"I'm allergic to cats."

"Really?"

"No, I just thought it would make me sound less selfish and self-absorbed."

God help me, something about Sylvia's sweet face and the way she was eyeballing me made me feel like a schmuck, so my mouth took off and left me behind. I hate it when it does that. "I guess I could adopt the little white guy."

"That's Yolanda. She's a girl. The other two are Pancho and Jesus."

"You're shitting me. Are these cats Mexican? I don't speak Spanish."

"Have you had a debilitating brain aneurysm lately?"

"Not that I know of."

"Then shut up," she said. "The longer you talk, the dumber I get."

I studied Sylvia's face, feeling all hurt and offended, and the next thing I knew we were both laughing like idiots. Even Artie was laughing. Then he farted. It sounded like B-flat on a trombone, and Sylvia and I laughed all the harder.

"I saw you going to work one day," she said. "You looked very handsome and sexy in your kilt."

My face got hot. "I hate that thing."

"You shouldn't. It's really quite lovely."

"The klepto just called me a drag queen."

Sylvia threw her head back and laughed. "Charlie?"

"Yeah."

I blushed some more, and Sylvia tapped me on the knee. "I'm sorry. I embarrassed you. And don't worry about what Charlie thinks. He's sweet, but he probably still can't remember the alphabet. All you need to know is you look handsome and sexy in that kilt. Don't let anybody tell you otherwise." She was smiling like even now she thought my embarrassment was endearing.

Hoping to steer the conversation away from me and that fucking kilt, I lifted Yolanda up to my face, and we stared at each other for minute. She didn't seem too appalled by what she was seeing, and I suddenly realized how cute her little white face was. She weighed maybe a pound, tops. Her tiny paw reached out and patted my nose as if she couldn't quite believe it was real.

"So, Yolanda," I said around what I hoped was my most winning smile. "You wanna come live with me?"

Yolanda's purr kicked in.

"I think that's a yes," Sylvia said. "There are two more around somewhere. One is Maria, the other's Chuck. I adopted Chuck."

"Hitler?"

"That's the one."

I had Yolanda in one hand and with the other hand I was fishing out another cookie.

Sylvia watched Yolanda and me for a minute. Her face had gone all soft and mushy seeing the two of us nose to nose. "You two belong together, I think."

I rolled my eyes and set Yolanda down with her siblings. "God help me, I think you're right."

Sylvia and I sat contentedly side by side on the top step while the cats played around us and little Artie goo-gooed. Then little Artie suddenly *stopped* goo-gooing, and he got this really determined look on his face. He looked like he was trying to remember the Fibonacci sequence but wasn't having any luck, sort of like the expression I get when *I* try to remember it. Suddenly a horrendous stench billowed up around us, filling the stairwell. I would have sworn it was swamp gas, but we were hell and gone from the nearest swamp. It might have been my imagination, but I was almost sure I saw paint peel from the walls and flies drop dead out of midair. All three kittens took off running like a Rottweiler was after them. The air around us went foul, as if a dead hippopotamus had been tossed into our midst. And believe me when I say that hippopotamus wasn't recently deceased. It had been dead for *weeks*.

Sylvia blushed while Artie simply looked relieved. I mean *really* relieved.

"Uh-oh," Sylvia groaned. "Hazmat time."

I stared at the baby. "You mean that stench came out of *him*?" I tried to uncross my eyes and speak without sucking in any of the tainted air. "What in God's name are you feeding that kid? Limburger cheese and roadkill?"

Sylvia smirked. "Oh, hush. Go do your laundry. I need to get this one home and cleaned up before they have to evacuate the building."

"I think it's too late."

"I'm going to kick you in the balls if you don't hush."

"Well, that's not very ladylike," I said, and we shared a smile.

"I'm going to run for my life now," I said.

Sylvia nodded. "Yes, I thought you might."

I gathered up my stuff and took off down the stairs, hoping to get as much distance as possible from the reeking creature strapped to Sylvia's chest. I was smiling while I ran, knowing I'd just made a friend. Sylvia, I mean. I wasn't too sure how I felt about the kid.

Downstairs on the bottom floor, still cramming cookies in my mouth, I heard voices. The voices belonged to Arthur and Ben, and they were coming from inside Arthur's apartment. I slipped past his door on tiptoe and quietly oozed my way down the stairs to the basement. The last thing I wanted to do was run into Ben again. I wondered if they were talking about our altercation that morning, and just as quickly, I realized I didn't care if they were. If anyone was in the wrong it was Ben, not me. I had nothing to apologize for.

After first stumbling into a utility closet, a furnace room, and some sort of party room with a bunch of tables set around and, believe it or not, a shiny disco ball hanging from the ceiling, huge and looking sort of like the Death Star, I finally found the laundry room. Without further ado I started cramming my dirty crap into two of the three antique washers. The middle washer looked a little dodgy, so I avoided that one. All three machines were so old I was vaguely surprised that they didn't have washboards and ringers attached.

When my washers started filling, I plopped down on one of a pair of ratty wicker chairs that were placed against the wall, and sat there polishing off the rest of the cookies in reasonable comfort. Knowing two kleptomaniacs were in residence, I thought it prudent to hang around with my laundry so it wouldn't be swiped out from under my nose by either Charlie or Bruce.

The laundry room at the Belladonna Arms didn't appear to have been cleaned since sometime around the Civil War. There were dust balls the size of ferrets rolling around the floor. A horrendous smear of indeterminate orange gunk had dribbled down one wall, coming from God knows where, and the 40-watt light bulb hanging from a grungy string in the middle of the ceiling didn't illuminate much, but what it did illuminate was more than I wanted to see.

Later, I transferred my wet laundry to one of the rusty dryers in the corner. I had to feed it six quarters before it decided to start tumbling, and even then only after I had kicked it in the nuts a couple of times. While my laundry flopped around behind the window in the door and the dryer screamed and shimmied and rattled like a dump truck full of scrap metal, I plopped myself back on the chair, folded my arms across my chest, and fell sound asleep.

I dreamed of Ben. He was standing naked at the edge of a cliff, his perfect body bathed in sunlight. Below, I saw myself, clinging to the rocky cliff and gazing up, lost in the beauty of the man above me. When Ben's eyes slid down to gaze at me, I gasped in surprise, and before I knew what was happening, I was tumbling backward through the air, plummeting toward the rocks below, a silent scream stretching my mouth in horror.

I woke with a start, my heart pounding like a tom-tom. I blinked myself alert, lost for a minute between my dream and the unfamiliar surroundings. Then I realized where I was. The laundry room was silent. The dryer had stopped. I had no idea how long I had been asleep.

A soft scuffling sound drew my attention to the door leading out into the hallway. There, on hands and knees, I saw Ben. He was creeping on all fours along the opposite wall, his nose to the floor, his back to me. It looked as if he was trying to peer beneath the baseboard. He tapped at the wall periodically with a tiny hammer, and between taps he stuck his ear to the wall as if listening for rats. Then he crawled a little farther down the hall and went through the whole process again.

I had no idea what the hell he was doing, and I didn't much care. I held my breath, hoping he wouldn't see me, and apparently he didn't. He crawled on past until he turned a corner about fifteen feet farther on.

As soon as he was out of sight, I quietly scooped my laundry out of the dryer, stuffed it back in the two (now clean) pillowcases, gathered up my box of Tide, and hustled myself up the stairs as quietly as I could.

Halfway up, I stumbled to a stop, recalling the dream. It wasn't the terror of slipping from the cliff, tumbling toward the rocks below, that I remembered. It was Ben I recalled now, still standing above me, his pale naked body so breathtakingly beautiful, bathed as it was in sunlight, the white-blond hair on his chest and legs shimmering in the breeze that swept up the cliff, his young cock snuggled soft and pliant in its nest of blond pubes.

I also remembered how his luscious lips twisted into a smile as he watched me fall.

Chapter 5

WELL, THINGS were moving right along. I'm not sure if they were moving right along in the proper direction or not, but here I was, two weeks into my new life, and I already had a freshly painted apartment that was in walking distance of work. Woohoo. I had a neighbor who was hotter than hell but whom I also suspected was crazy as a bedbug. Hmm. And I owned a cat named Yolanda.

Life is a trip, huh?

Twice in the ensuing days, I stumbled into Ben in the hallway. Both times, we mumbled uncomfortable hellos as both of us blushed, and both times I wanted to thank him again for saving my life, but somehow I couldn't get the words out. Apparently he had the same reticence about apologizing for sticking his head into my apartment without asking permission.

By the third time we ran into each other, I had already come to the conclusion we were both too stubborn to admit we were wrong, and I was determined to set things right. Of course, the *way* we ran into each other that third time was enough to obliterate my pledge right off the bat.

Jesus God, Ben Moss was weird.

It was late at night. I was toddling home after my shift at the restaurant, still wearing my kilt and kneesocks and the whole Scottish drag. All I needed was a stupid bagpipe and a dead goat on my shoulder.

Scuttling up the rickety wooden steps to the Belladonna Arms's front porch, I spotted a gleam of light through the stairs at my feet. Stooping down and peering between the boards to see what the heck it was, I came face-to-face with another set of eyes. Human eyes. Peering back at me.

It startled me so, I bit back a scream, flopped my arms around for a minute while I lost my balance, tumbled backward down the steps with a yelp, and ended up on the sidewalk flat on my back with my kilt up around my ears.

A massive hand came out from between the steps and latched on to my foot. Horrified, I yanked my foot away and scooted backward on my ass until I was out of reach.

"You okay?" a voice said from the shadows underneath the porch. It was a male voice. He had turned his flashlight off, if that's what it was, so I was no longer blinded by the glare.

Still on my back, propped up on my elbows, my legs spread wide, my ass aching from the fall, I frantically studied the eyes staring out at me. Thanks to the streetlight behind me, I could see them clearly. The eyes were blue.

"Ben? Ben Moss?"

"Afraid so. Did I startle you?"

"Jeez, dumbass, what do *you* think? What the hell are you doing under the fucking porch at one o'clock in the morning?"

"Is it that late?"

"Yes!" I barked. "Answer me. What are you doing under the porch? Did you drop something through the boards?"

Ben let that question sink in for a minute. At least that's what I assumed he was doing since he didn't answer right away. Finally he said, "Yeah, that's it. I dropped something through the boards."

"Liar. What the heck were you doing crawling around the basement the other day?"

"How do you know I was crawling around the basement?"

"I was in the laundry room. I saw you. People are starting to talk, you know. The other tenants think you're nuts." This was a lie, of course, but he wouldn't know that. At least I didn't think he would.

"I'm not nuts," he said, sounding rather offended.

"Then why are you always sneaking around? This all has something to do with why you stuck your head into my apartment through that stupid secret door, doesn't it? You weren't just snooping. You were looking for whatever the heck it is you're looking for."

"I'm not looking for *anything*."

"Liar. Does Arthur know you're doing this?"

He sucked in his breath at that. I could hear him in the shadows. His voice took on an edge of desperation. "No, Shiloh. And don't tell him."

I was still sitting with my ass on the sidewalk talking to Ben through the porch steps. *What's wrong with this picture?* I kept asking myself that question, to which I heard no reasonable answers issuing forth except one: *everything's* wrong with this picture!

There was a short silence, during which I assumed Ben was considering the error of his ways. I was soon forced to admit I was wrong about that. He was most definitely considering other things, though.

Ben cleared his throat and stuck a finger through the steps, pointing at my crotch. "So you really *do* wear underwear under that kilt. You have no idea how disappointing that is."

I hastily tucked the kilt around my knees and wondered if I would be physically capable of dragging Ben through that teeny crack in the stairs and gathering up the gumption to beat the living shit out of him. Considering his size, I quickly decided it would be a suicide mission if I did, but that didn't keep me from throwing a snit fit. Snit fits and I go back a long way. I had perfected them over the years with my mother. It seemed perfectly reasonable to drag one out now and hurl it in Ben's direction.

"You have no business saying sexy stuff like that when we're arguing! And I still want to know what you're doing under that fucking porch in the middle of the fucking night with a fucking flashlight."

God help me, I heard a chuckle under the porch. "You're cute when you're mad," he said. "You cuss a lot, but you're still cute. Of course, you'd be cuter without underwear. How's your bruise?"

I touched my belly. "It—it's fine. I've been meaning to thank you again for—hey! Wait a minute! I'm mad here. Stop saying nice stuff when I'm mad. How the hell did you get under there anyway?"

"There's a crawl space that accesses the space under the porch. I found it behind the furnace in the basement."

"Aren't there spiders under there?"

"Yeah. Big ones."

"Then you truly are nuts. Get out of there! We have black widow spiders in California, you know. And rattlesnakes and tarantulas and scorpions and—"

"Golly, you really are cute when you're mad. You want to come up to my apartment for a beer?"

"No, I don't want to come up to your apartment for a beer!" Then my anger petered out. Just like that. It's hard to maintain a good mad when you haven't had sex in over a month and somebody starts talking about your crotch in favorable terms. "What kind of beer is it?"

I heard Ben chuckle again from the shadows. "Go on home and get comfortable. I'll tap on the wall when I get there. It'll take a few minutes for me to worm my way out of here."

"This isn't a date," I said. "And I want some answers."

"Wow, you have a pretty high opinion of yourself, Shiloh. What makes you think I'd want to date *you*?"

That hurt. "Oh," I said. Then I got mad all over again. "Forget it! I don't want a beer."

"Yes, you do."

"No, I don't. And you never did tell me what kind of beer it is."

"It's Heineken."

"Oh. Well, okay. I guess I can stop by for one. But I still want answers!"

"So you keep saying. Go on up. I'll be there in a minute."

Since I had run out of things to argue about, I went. God, he was infuriating.

Still, he was disappointed I was wearing underwear. That was a promising development.

Told you I was a slut.

I dragged myself up the stairs, ducked through my door, greeted Yolanda, who came running to meet me like she'd been abandoned for a month, and after kissing her all over and tickling her belly and pouring her a bowl of warm lactose-free milk (who knew I was such a cat person?), I settled in to wait for the rap on my wall.

I didn't have to wait very long.

WITH YOLANDA on my shoulder, I tapped on Ben's door, and he yanked it open right away with two beers in his hands.

"You've got a cat," he said. "And darn, you're wearing pants. What happened to your kilt?"

To which I replied, "Don't change the subject."

"Whoa!" he said, handing me one of the beers. "Somebody's an anger muffin."

"If you must know, I'm still mad about you barging into my apartment. I was naked. I could have been doing *anything!*"

A sly look, tinged with a goodly dose of intrigue, crept into Ben's blue eyes. "Like what?"

"Like never mind!"

He flapped his arms like he was flagging down a bus. "Okay, okay. I know. I'm sorry. I didn't think you were home."

That made me mad all over again. "Oh, well *that's* okay, then," I snarked, slipping into serious sarcastic mode. "That clears everything right up, that does! Let me get this straight, then. It's perfectly all right to break into someone's home just as long as you know they aren't there. Is that it? Well, gee, I wish you'd told me that before. That makes everything just peachy!"

"That's not what I meant."

"It's what you said."

Ben's ears were so red I half expected them to burst into flames.

"Look, Shiloh, I had no idea where that door would lead. I thought maybe there was a secret hallway between our two walls. It's possible, you know."

"Right. And what made you think there was a secret hallway? Do you think this building has secret hallways and spooky passages and hidden trapdoors and forgotten rooms and revolving staircases and mad scientist laboratories scattered all over the place? Is that what you think?"

We were circling each other like two boxers, each of whom is afraid to throw the first punch. When we got tired of circling, he plopped down on one end of the couch while I plopped down on the other. It didn't improve my mood any when it took my butt less than five seconds to realize his couch was better than mine. I guess it pays to be the landlord's nephew.

Ben sucked at his beer, and while he sucked at his, I sucked at mine. As soon as we were both finished sucking, he said, "Well, yeah. That's *exactly* what I think. Except for the revolving staircases and mad scientist laboratories. That's just silly."

Is this guy for real? I asked myself. Then I decided I'd go right to the source and ask him. "Are you for real?"

His eyes narrowed, and he casually stroked Yolanda's head after she climbed up onto his lap and fell asleep. Our conversation was obviously boring the crap out of her. I, on the other hand, was positively enthralled. I was also enthralled by the smear of dirt on Ben's nose. Somehow that smear of dirt, which he had undoubtedly collected underneath the porch, made him sexy as hell. Butch, you know? Like a farmhand. And we all know how sexy *they* are.

(Look, I'm a city boy. You keep your fantasies; I'll keep mine.)

I was also intrigued by the lump in the fly of Ben's jeans, where Yolanda was resting her head, the lucky bitch. That intriguing lump reminded me of the day Ben broke into my apartment and the glimpse I caught of that delicious thatch of blond pubic hair peeking out from behind his half-unbuttoned fly. I really liked that memory. And I really liked that lump.

Still, I have my pride. "You're certifiable," I mumbled, just loud enough for him to hear.

Ben pretended he didn't hear it at all. "Have dinner with me sometime," he said out of the blue.

"No," I said, wondering if he knew how to cook.

"Then we'll go to a movie."

"Sorry, Ben. I don't want to interrupt your classes in breaking and entering. It's October. You probably have finals coming up."

"Funny. Are you ever going to forgive me for sticking my head through your door while you were standing there with a dripping hard-on?"

"It was only half a hard-on and barely dripping. And as for that movie, that would be another no."

Ben eyed me while he scratched Yolanda's head. There was the teeniest of smiles playing at his mouth, which made me even madder than I already was. It also made my dick twitch. I mean, in a good way. Damn, I was confused.

"I'd like to get to know you, Shiloh. I'd like us to be friends."

"Friends trust each other."

"You don't trust me?"

"No."

He batted blond eyelashes and gave me the old downtrodden-puppy-dog pout. "I saved your life. You owe me."

"That's not fair!"

"In some cultures if you save somebody's life, they belong to you forever."

"I don't think that rule applies in San Diego."

"Dinner. That's all I ask."

"Forget it. What were you doing under the porch?"

"Nothing."

"Tell me the truth. What were you doing?"

He didn't answer. Instead, he tucked Yolanda into his shirt pocket like a pack of cigarettes and clomped off into the kitchen, where he extracted two more beers from the fridge.

"What makes you think I want another beer?" I asked.

"Just hoping is all," he said, handing one to me.

Having just stared at the inviting way his ass fit in his jeans as he walked toward the kitchen, I didn't have much choice. I took the beer. He plopped down beside me again. Yolanda was hanging out of his shirt pocket, snoring.

"I'm sorry I hurt your feelings," he said.

"You didn't hurt my feelings. You pissed me off. There's a difference. What were you doing under the porch?"

"Please have dinner with me."

"Why?"

He took a long pull from his beer, gently twiddled Yolanda's ear, and settled back in his seat. Casually stretching his arm out toward me, he rested it comfortably on the back of the couch close enough that his fingers brushed my shoulders getting there. He propped one ankle on the other knee and swiveled in my direction, giving me an unobstructed view of that lump in his crotch again.

Trying not to stare at it, I gazed around the apartment. It looked about the same as it had when I'd helped Ramon and Barney move their stuff out. It was furnished, but that was it. I didn't see a lot of personal belongings sitting around. No pictures. No books. Nothing.

"You don't have much stuff," I said.

His eyes traveled the same path around the room that mine had just taken. "I like things simple," he finally said. "Besides, I haven't unboxed it all yet."

"Are you looking for work?"

He didn't answer. Not about work anyway. "Have dinner with me."

"No."

"Have dinner with me, and I'll tell you everything."

That caught my attention. "You mean you'll tell me why you're snooping around the Arms?"

"Yeah. I'll tell you over dinner."

I squinted and gave him a leery glance. "And what do you want from me?"

He smiled as if he knew my resolve had suffered its first crack. "All I want from you is a chance to get to know you. And I want you to wear your kilt to dinner. I really love seeing you in that kilt."

"You're nuts."

"You said that already. So what do you say? Dinner? My treat?"

His hand had slipped from the back of the couch and now rested on my shoulder. I wasn't sure when it had arrived there, but I have to admit I liked it. The fact that his big warm thumb had come to rest on the back of my neck was nice too.

I turned toward him to say God knows what when my eyes popped open wide to find him leaning in close. He had a gentle smile on his lips, and his pale eyelashes were framing two seriously hypnotic eyes. A look of unstoppable determination in those eyes froze me in stasis, sort of like a bird in front of a snake.

I sat helpless as he leaned in closer and closer.

Finally I found my voice on a trembling breath. "What are you doing?"

"Nothing," he said, his voice just as trembly.

"Yes, you are."

His lips parted as he cupped the back of my head in one hand, preventing any escape I might be planning. "Shut up, Shiloh. For once in your life, just shut up. Please."

And before I could bite his head off for telling me to shut up, he closed in for the kill. The next thing I knew, our noses were side-by-side, his eyelashes were fluttering over mine, and his lips had trapped my mouth in their sweet heat.

His kiss was gentle and fiery all at the same time. As he tasted me, I watched his eyes close and felt his other hand come to rest on my knee. My heart beat loudly inside my head, the rhythm totally out of whack. Too hurried. Too staccato. Was it about to explode? Then I realized it wasn't just my heart I was hearing. I was hearing Ben's heart too, thundering alongside mine, as frantic and excited as my own.

I closed my eyes slowly when his tongue brushed my lips. When I parted my lips enough to let him worm his way in, he settled closer, his hand on my neck holding me firmly, his fingers on my knee softly massaging me. Massaging me until I began to tremble.

And still the kiss went on. His tongue foraged over mine, and I trembled some more.

Weakened by that sensational kiss, I dropped my head to the back of the sofa and almost thanked God when Ben followed me, our kiss uninterrupted. His breath smelled of hunger and breath mints, his lips were warm, and the sheer size of him hovering over me was such an erotic sensation, I soon found myself kissing back.

"Yes," he muttered around a smile, his lips still on mine. "That's my baby."

"I'm not your baby," I muttered, still kissing. My heart still galloping.

"Not yet," he said.

I wondered what he meant by that.

His hand left my knee, and I tensed, wondering where it would go next. But then it came to rest at my side, his fingers massaging my rib cage now, delicately tracing each rib as he stroked me through my shirt, as if memorizing the feel of me.

Just as my dick started strangling itself inside my clothes—and I was really tempted to set it free and see where that might lead—I let a rush of my old anger take the stage for a second bow. I pressed my hands to Ben's broad chest (God, it felt nice) and gently pushed him away. He eased himself back until our lips were the last to part.

But even then, even after his mouth had left mine, he remained close, staring at me as I gazed back at him. No matter how hard I tried to hold on to it, my anger melted away in the wash of his warm breath flowing over me.

"We're both trembling," he whispered, swallowing hard. "You feel it?"

I couldn't speak. I had no voice. So I simply nodded. He stroked my bottom lip with his thumb as if memorizing our kiss by braille. God help me, I trembled again. And when he felt it, he smiled.

"Promise me something," he said softly.

I managed to gasp out an answer. "What?"

His eyes softened, and his tongue came out to lick his lips as if tasting me all over again.

"Promise me that someday it'll be you who initiates the kiss. Promise me that someday it'll be you who reaches out for me."

It was my turn to swallow hard. Already I missed his lips on mine, but I wasn't about to tell him that. I couldn't. Hell, I was still mad at him. Wasn't I?

"You're crazy." I breathed the words on a shuddering inhale.

"Maybe," he said. "But you still have to promise."

I thought about it, and while I was thinking about it, he dipped his head and pressed his mouth to my throat. My heart started galloping once more. *Good grief*, I thought. *Here we go again.*

"Still waiting," he mumbled against my Adam's apple. "Just say the words. Say 'I promise.'" He was smiling. I could feel it. He was massaging my ribs again, and my dick was so cramped it felt like it was tying itself in a Windsor knot. I shifted around so it wouldn't break its little neck.

"All right, all right. I promise," I finally gasped.

He lifted his head then and stared at me. His grin was a heart-stopper. My God, he was gorgeous. "You're not just saying that under duress?"

It was all I could do not to lift my head and press my mouth to his all over again. "No," I said, my breath as fluttery as a dying bird. "No duress." *Oh, no, not much. My blood pressure must have spiked at three hundred over a hundred and thirty about two minutes back.*

"And you'll have dinner with me?"

"Y-yes."

"And you'll wear your kilt?"

"Y-yes. I'll wear the damn kilt. Now give me my cat back. I want to go home."

His smile was still on high beams. I was a deer, frozen in front of it. His hands still held me in place, one at my ribs, the other at the back of my neck. I felt so tiny and helpless in his embrace. It was a weird feeling. A *good* feeling. He seemed to know what I was thinking.

"You don't want to leave, do you?" he asked, a cocky grin fighting for control of his mouth.

I somehow found my voice, or a weakened version of it. "Yes, I do."

"Liar. You're hard," he said, smiling.

"No, I'm not," I said.

His smile widened. "Liar."

"Stop saying that."

"Have it your way."

With a soft tap of his forehead to mine, signaling farewell, he finally pulled back. His hands slipped away from my body. I hated to see them go.

My pulse was still thudding inside my head. I was barely out of his grasp before I missed his touch already. With trembling hands, I lifted Yolanda into my arms and almost ran for the door.

He followed me there, and just before he opened the door to let me go, he said quietly, "Remember your promise. The next kiss will come from you."

"That's never going to happen."

"Yes, it is."

"You're incorrigible, Ben."

"Only a little," he said with a wink. After unlocking the door, he conducted me out into the hall with an exaggerated bow, like I was the Queen Mother or something.

I knew his eyes were on me, so I tried not to faint as I shuffled off toward my door. Once safely inside my own apartment, I placed Yolanda on the floor, leaned my back against the door, and expelled every ounce of oxygen I was holding in my body. I did it slowly so I wouldn't squirt off through the air like a punctured balloon.

While I was calming my fractured nerves, one part of the evening stayed centered in my mind. Well, two. The kiss, naturally, because no matter how much I didn't want to admit it, that had been one hell of a kiss.

But the other thing I couldn't get out of my mind, the really important thing, were the two little words Ben had spoken *after* the kiss.

"Not yet," he'd said when I told him I wasn't his baby.

Not yet.

As if the memory of those words wasn't disconcerting enough, I looked down and realized I still had a boner.

"What the hell," I groaned, and with trembling hands, I dropped my pants and let the little bugger out.

Party time.

Chapter 6

ARTHUR STOPPED by on Monday night. I knew it was Arthur because what other three-hundred-pound man would be wearing a wee Scottish lass's outfit without waxing his legs, chest, and shoulders first? He had a Rita Hayworth wig on his head—red, long, and fluffy—with a gigantic tartan bow over one ear. He wore a lace-up bodice over a tartan peasant skirt and blouse with gothic sleeves, and a matching tartan shawl. His skirt stood out like an open parachute, thanks to a hoop and what appeared to be several petticoats underneath. To top it all off, he had a bagpipe hanging off his back that looked like Godzilla's bladder after the big lizard hadn't peed for about three weeks.

Arthur stood in my doorway like a Freddy Krueger nightmare brought on by too much haggis and stout, unprotected sex with a wailing banshee, and three back-to-back showings of Brigadoon under the influence of a tab of LSD that had obviously gone bad.

"Holy shit" was the first thing out of my mouth.

Arthur preened, mistaking my shock for appreciation. "Oh," he simpered, sucking in his massive gut and giving me his best profile, which in all fairness wasn't that great. "You like?" he chirped. "This ensemble was inspired by you know who."

"Who?"

"You, sweetums."

"Please God, no."

"I'm afraid so."

He fumbled around behind him, grabbed the mouthpiece to the bagpipe, pumped the bladder up a couple of times with a horrible squelching sound, and blew a long, ear-splitting screech with the thing that made me want to run out to the nearest Celtic Thunder store, buy the biggest shillelagh I could find, run back home, lock myself in the bathroom, and beat myself to death with it.

I looked behind me and saw Yolanda standing on the coffee table with every hair on her body sticking straight out. Between her cute little white legs, which were trembling like crazy, I saw a stream of urine dribbling across my TV Guide, obviously jarred loose by that horrific caterwauling coming from Arthur's bagpipe. Yolanda's mouth was opening and closing like a guppy's. Her eyes were as big as Ping-Pong balls. She was clearly in a state of shock.

As was I.

I banged the side of my head with the heel of my hand and tried to shake the bagpipe music out. It didn't work. I feared it was embedded there forever.

Arthur merely giggled at my shenanigans and slapped me on the chest hard enough to nearly knock me over. "Oh, you kidder, you." Glancing over my shoulder, he added, "What's wrong with your cat?"

"She's allergic to bagpipes," I said.

"Really?"

"Well, she is now."

As if that was her cue, Yolanda dove under the couch.

Arthur wiggled fingertips at her and cooed, "Bye-bye, dear," then stormed past me as if he'd been invited in. I've always admired people who have the balls to do that.

Arthur strode through my apartment, eyeing this, fingering that, and all the while he was fluffing the long red wavy wig that flowed down from the top of his head, across his shoulders, and halfway down his back.

He headed straight for the kitchen, pulled open a couple of cupboards until he found a family-size bag of Doritos, tore them open as he parked himself at the kitchen table, and politely asked for a Coke.

"Uh, sure." I served him a Coke, popped another one for myself, and joined him at the table.

"You're a sweet boy," Arthur said around a mouthful of chips. "Benjie likes you."

"Hmm."

"What's the matter, honey? You don't like my nephew?"

"Oh, well, sure, Arthur. I like him well enough." *Too bad he's so fucking weird*, I wanted to add, but thought better of it. *Excellent kisser, though*, I also wanted to add, but thought better of that too. I had a feeling Arthur was here on a matchmaking expedition as it was. I didn't need to give him any more artillery than he already had.

Arthur flipped the wig off his shoulder and fluffed his bodice. It's always distracting when middle-aged, overweight men do that. "You seem to be settling into the Arms nicely, Shiloh. Everybody likes you. You've got yourself a cat. I guess it feels like home now, right?"

I softened toward the guy at that. He really did care about his tenants. That much was obvious. "I do like it here, Arthur. Everybody's really nice. Pete, Sylvia, Milan, Harlie, Stanley, Roger, Barney, Ramon. Even Charlie and Bruce don't piss me off too much. Not yet anyway."

With a horrendous crunching sound, Arthur chomped and chewed and ground up another fistful of Doritos. "Yeah, well, give them time."

He gazed around the kitchen as if trying to organize his thoughts. Whatever he had come for, I figured he was about to let it out. Surely he wasn't going to raise my rent already. Not after I painted and cleaned and redecorated and—

"I'd like you to help Benjie find a job, Shiloh."

That stopped me short. "Oh. He needs a job, then?"

Arthur sighed. "Well, of course he needs a job. Everybody needs a job. He's living on his savings and unemployment at the moment, but how long can that last? Which reminds me, don't tell him I asked for your help. This will have to be our little secret."

"Why doesn't he go find a job *without* my help?"

Arthur eyeballed me while he downed half a Coke in one long gurgling swallow. "That's a very good question, actually. I don't know why he doesn't go find one himself. Well, yes I do, but I don't want to talk about it."

"Talk about it," I said, narrowing my eyes.

It's hard to blush under a layer of trowel-applied makeup, but by golly Arthur did it. He glowed pink underneath his pancake, sort of like

E.T.'s heart shining through his rib cage. (I loved that movie, by the way. This conversation, not so much.)

"I'm afraid Benjie has other priorities," Arthur said. "I'm afraid it is those other priorities that made him move here to begin with."

My first thought was *Do these mysterious priorities have anything to do with your sillyass nephew poking his nose all over the building and crawling around in the middle of the night like he's on some sort of deranged scavenger hunt?*

But Arthur had such a hurt expression on his face, what I really said was "I think you're mistaken, Arthur. I'm sure he came here to be with you. He all but told me so."

Arthur's mouth made a perfect little bee-stung *O*, and he flapped his eyelashes while patting his heart, creating the *schicking* sound of one or two pounds of shifting quinoa, which I now knew he used for ballast in the tit department.

His eyes teared up. "If only I could believe that. No, Shiloh, I'm afraid little Benjie has fallen into the trap that so many have fallen into before him."

"And what trap is that?"

Arthur tipped the Dorito bag up and poured the remaining crumbs down his throat. He had just eaten six dollars' worth of tortilla chips in under five minutes. Probably a world record.

"Never mind," he said. "It's just a rumor anyway. I don't know why Benjie thinks it's true, the idealistic little imp."

I thought of Ben's broad chest, and his flat tummy with the teeny tiny belly button in the middle of it, covered with blond fuzz, and the bulbous biceps that rolled around like croquet balls every time he moved his pale arms. Then I thought about the tight little ass that beckoned me to go spelunking every time he walked away from me. And of course that brought me back to that one astonishingly sexy glimpse of a thatch of blond pubic hair. with the base of a sleeping cock nestled in the middle of it, I had spotted the day he broke into my apartment.

I'm not quite sure what that memory had to do with what Arthur was saying, but it was a showstopping memory nevertheless.

I extended a gentle query. "Your nephew's a little… strange, don't you think?"

"He's a sweetheart!" Arthur wailed, and abruptly he had tears streaming down his cheeks, and his quinoa was *schicking* as his chest heaved, and a sob erupted, and three seconds later the poor man was hiccupping as he sat there softly crying.

I patted his arm. "Don't cry, Arthur. I'll help him find a job."

Arthur's tears dried up like someone had turned off the tap. "Lovely! Thank you so much, honey!" He leaned in close and gave me a wink. "I hear you boys have a dinner date one of these days. Do I hear wedding bells?"

I narrowed my eyes again. "I doubt it."

Arthur's chin dimpled. Oh Lord, he wasn't going to start crying again, was he?

"What, Shiloh? You don't think little Benjie is cute? You don't think Benjie's hunkalicious?"

I recused myself from answering since I had been beating off to the memory of the man for days. Somehow I didn't think I should impart that information to his uncle.

I glanced at my watch, which I wasn't even wearing at the time, but Arthur didn't notice. "Time for bed!" I said. "Thanks for stopping by, Arthur. Sleep tight. Don't let the bedbugs bite. Have a nice night. Buenas noches. Guten nacht. Seeya."

Arthur apparently knew how to take a hint. He gathered up his shawl and his bagpipe and his quinoa tits and gave me a peck on the cheek before whispering in my ear, "A lady always knows when it's time to leave."

Yeah, right. A lady also knows enough to wait to be invited in. "You owe me a bag of Doritos," I said. "A big one."

Arthur executed a bizarre tinkle of broguish bonnie laughter, being a Scottish lass and all, and once again he smacked me on the chest hard enough to stop my heart for about three beats.

"Oh, you kidder, you," he said. He pulled himself together and sashayed his tartan ass across the apartment and out the door, merrily toodling his good-byes as he went, phony Scottish brogue and all.

The moment he closed the door behind him, Yolanda poked her head out from under the couch.

I looked at her and said, "I wonder what trap it is he thinks Ben has fallen into."

"Meow," Yolanda said. And that was pretty much the end of that conversation.

I HATED to admit it, but I was getting fat.

Sylvia brought me Toll House cookies three times in the ensuing days. Arthur had me down to his apartment twice for eclairs and ice cream. Milan and Harlie, who lived on 2 and were both bakers who worked for Arthur's lover, Tom, at his deli (actually Milan was Tom's son and Harlie was Milan's lover), brought me fresh-baked raisin bread as a housewarming gift. It was so delicious I ate an entire loaf in twenty minutes. Charlie and Bruce, the kleptomaniacs on 3, stopped by one evening with a UPS box filled with saltwater taffy, which I love. Apparently the box had fallen off the delivery truck, and Charlie was merely doing the company a favor by picking it up off the street before somebody tripped over it. Yeah, right. Ramon and Barney thanked me for helping them move their stuff to the sixth floor from the apartment next door where Ben now lived by hanging a three-pound box of chocolates on my doorknob. Unfortunately, I spotted it there (and ate it) before the kleptos did.

So you see, through no fault of my own, the calories kept rolling in.

I had been in the Belladonna Arms three weeks, and I had gained six pounds. If I gained any more weight, I'd have to buy a bigger kilt.

Thus the jog.

I was sweating bullets. My running shorts, which were small to begin with, seemed to be even smaller after all those gazillion grams of sugar and fat I'd been force-fed by my neighbors. The little muscle shirt that had barely come to the top of my running shorts before, now hung two inches above my belly button. I was breathing like a bellows as I clomped my way back up the hill toward the Arms after a five-mile slog through downtown.

It was my day off. Tonight I was having dinner with Ben, since I couldn't seem to think of a way out of it. I was both dreading and looking forward to the dinner, and I was hard-pressed to figure out which conflicting emotion I was feeling more. I also intended to tell Ben I had taken it upon myself to get him an interview with my boss for a job at The Twisted Kilt. There were two reasons for this. One was I had promised

Arthur I would help Ben find a job and the Kilt was the only place of business I was familiar with. The second reason was a little less noble. Basically it boiled down to the fact that I really, really, really wanted to see Ben in a kilt. Well, come on. I mean, who wouldn't?

My overriding thought during the duration of my five-mile run was the Kiss Ben and I had shared the night I found him lurking under the front porch. That's how I was thinking about it now, by the way. In capital letters. The Kiss. Actually the Kiss was pretty much my overriding thought no matter *what* I was doing lately.

I must admit it was without a doubt the best kiss little Shiloh Smart had ever experienced in his miserable love-starved life. Because of that, the Kiss wasn't out of my mind more than three minutes at a pop during the entire week since the night it happened. Nor was Ben. As the days wore on *following* the Kiss, it began to take on mythical status inside my head. And inside my trousers. Or kilt. For sometimes at work, I would freeze in place, usually with heaping plates of clapshots or haggis parading up my arms, and let the memory of that kiss wash over me like a blissful, erotic tide. When that happened, I had to hustle around and shed the memory quickly or Shiloh Junior would swell up like a bullfrog, and then I'd really be in trouble.

I could hear the customer now. "Oh, you there! Waiter with the hard-on. More neeps and tatties, please!"

Cringe.

The worst time to think about the Kiss was when I lay in bed all alone in the middle of the night in my darkened apartment. The fact that the man who gave me the Kiss was only inches away at any given time, just on the other side of my bedroom wall, in fact, had become a bit of torture for me, as much as I hated to admit it. After all, I was still mad at him. He was impossible. And he was still slinking around the Belladonna Arms, tapping on floors and peeking around corners, looking for God knows what, although if he kept his promise I supposed tonight I'd find out. To make matters worse, with the Kiss tattooed on my brain in apparently indelible ink, and the way Ben Moss had felt holding me in those massive arms of his, I'm ashamed to admit I was beating off every time I turned around. For all I knew, I was doing irreparable damage to myself.

And holy crap, even *that* wasn't the worst part of the whole Ben and Shiloh thing.

It was the promise that bothered me most. Not the promise of dinner, but the other promise. The promise I had made to Ben that one of these days when we kissed, it would be I who made the first move.

See, now, even the fact he was assuming there would *be* another kiss made me mad. But what made me even madder was the fact that I knew damn well I *wanted* another kiss. I might even be more than ready to make it happen. And if I did that, then Ben would have been right. Sooner or later a kiss *would* be instigated by me. The truth is, he knew it as well as I did.

The rat.

I showered away the sweat from my run, drank some electrolytes to keep my strength up (just in case I got lucky and ended up needing it later), and dressed as promised in my freshly laundered kilt and kneesocks and sporran and the whole silly tartan outfit. Sucking in a great gulp of air for courage, I knocked on Ben's door at the appointed time.

He answered my knock so quickly, I jumped.

Ben stood in the doorway in pressed jeans, a white dress shirt tucked neatly in, and a smile on his handsome face that knocked the chip off my shoulder before I could drag it through his door.

"Hi," I said shyly.

He reached through the door, took my hand, and tugged me gently inside.

"Where's Yolanda?"

"Left her at home."

"Probably for the best."

He stepped back and studied me from head to toe. Halfway through his examination, he patted his chest as if silencing the beating of his heart. "Wow," he said. "Thank you."

I blushed. "You told me to wear the stupid kilt. I wore the stupid kilt."

He stepped closer and ran his fingers along the edge of the tartan drape that hung from my left shoulder over my white puffy-sleeved shirt. Both drape and shirt were tucked into the belt securing the kilt. Ben pulled his gaze from the drape and centered it on my face. "Wow," he said again.

I tried not to stare at the fluff of blond hair peeking through the neckline of his white shirt. I tried not to salivate over the sinewy, fuzzy forearms that stuck out from his rolled-up shirtsleeves, and I tried not to imagine how his trim waist would feel captured in my hands. I tried not to remember, for the hundredth time, how his smile had tasted. Or how his warm breath had blown across my face. Or how his tongue had gently caressed my own.

Basically, I was trying not to do a lot of stuff, but I suspected I was doing it all anyway.

I watched in horror as he leaned slowly toward me, his eyes burning into mine. His lips parted slightly as he stared at my mouth. He was standing so close I could already smell his clean scent. I could feel the heat of his body. I felt so small in his shadow. So small—and turned on.

The bastard knew it too. I was sure of it. I could tell by the hungry, excited gleam in his eyes. And wasn't *that* sexy as hell.

"I need a drink," I said abruptly.

He blinked and pulled back. If my intent was to kill the moment, I'd succeeded.

Still, Ben didn't lose his smile. In fact, I elicited the first chuckle of the evening. "Then a drink is what you shall have, my wee bairn. Beer, wine, scotch, vodka?"

"Yes," I said, and he laughed.

"Let's get you a beer to start with, shall we?"

He headed for the kitchen while I claimed my old spot on the end of his sofa, pulling my kilt primly over my knees.

I called out to him in the kitchen. "I don't smell dinner cooking!"

"That's because we aren't eating here!" he called back.

Then he appeared with my beer. Another Heineken. I snatched it out of his hand, grumpy all over again. "Jeez, Ben, if I had known we were eating out in public, I wouldn't have worn this damn kilt. So where *are* we eating?" I asked, trying to ratchet down the anger and maybe even shoot for being polite for a change. Before he could answer, I chugged down half the beer. I was a nervous wreck.

"On the roof," he said, gazing down at me with a smile. He was standing so close my knees were brushing his shins, which pretty much put his lumpy crotch smack in my face. Did I mention I was nervous?

"You mean on the roof here?"

"Yes. Fifty feet above our heads. Under the sign. The Belladonna Arms sign."

"Are you crazy?" I asked.

He half lidded his eyes and smiled all the wider. "I think we covered the subject of my sanity the last time we were together."

He tucked his thumbs in his jeans pockets and continued to stand there in front of me. I reached out and brushed a piece of lint from his trouser leg.

"Lint," I explained.

"Thanks."

Ben's smile was making my heart do flip-flops. He sat his ass down on the coffee table, and with our knees resting against each other, he gently scooped my hand out of my lap and tucked it among his cool fingers.

"Thanks for coming," he said.

I took another long slug of beer. I really was a nervous wreck. "Just being neighborly," I said.

He tilted his head to the side and studied my face. "Oh Lord, I hope not."

I stared at his thumb as he stroked it across the back of my hand. The hem of my kilt had shifted, and now Ben's bare wrist rested directly on my bare knee. I didn't mention it and neither did he, but I knew we both knew it. I had the oddest feeling that his skin was burning into mine like a branding iron.

"Shall we go, then?" I asked.

"Don't be afraid of me," he said softly.

"I'm not. I'm hungry."

"One kiss and we'll go," he said. "Just a little one."

"What? No, I don't think that's a good id—"

Before I could finish he stretched himself forward and laid his lips gently over mine to shut me up. God help me, I couldn't stop myself. I closed my eyes and let Ben's kiss rumble through me like thunder.

To my surprise, he immediately broke the kiss, then reached out his hand and gave me a motherly pat on the cheek.

"There now, that wasn't so bad, was it?"

Should I mention the fact that my dick is creeping down my leg? Probably not. "No. It wasn't bad at all. I'd like another beer, please."

"I thought you wanted to eat."

"Beer first." I wasn't about to stand up with a boner. If I did, he'd know he turned me on, and I wasn't ready to cede that territory yet in our little back-and-forth power skirmish. I wasn't sure if I ever would be ready. Well, yes, I would, but I didn't want to think about that now.

He didn't move. He still sat on the coffee table in front of me, our knees touching, his hand still on my cheek.

"What are you thinking?" he asked. "What's going on inside that handsome ginger head?"

God help me, I was tempted to tell him. Something about being in Ben's gravitational pull left me helpless and needy. And really, really aroused.

"Please, Shiloh. Tell me what you're thinking."

I stared down at his hand. It was resting on my knee. His thumb was stroking my kneecap. His other hand slipped from my cheek and he brushed my hair away from my eyes.

"You need a haircut," he said around a lazy smile.

"I know."

I also knew what I was about to say. I didn't want to say it, but I knew the words were coming anyway. There was no stopping them.

"You were right," I said.

"About what?" he asked gently.

"About me instigating a kiss."

His eyes flared hot. There was sudden excitement in them, but there was something else there too. Something that looked like gratitude. "Really?"

"Uh-huh."

"Are you thinking about instigating one now?"

"Now would be good." At that he carefully leaned in, cupped my face in both his hands this time, and laid his lips over mine. We both closed our eyes at the same moment.

As I tasted him again, my heart beat in a frantic flurry of thuds. Quietly, I hoped. Ben knew what I was feeling too much already. I had most certainly blown my imaginary air of mystery. It didn't take a genius to figure that out. I never was very good at being aloof.

This kiss didn't last much longer than the first one. As if afraid of overplaying his hand or wearing out his welcome, Ben pulled back first, licking his lips.

"Was that okay?" he asked. The blue in his eyes was the palest I had ever seen it. I didn't know if it was the light in the room or the heat shining out from their depths burning the color away.

I swallowed hard, nervously aware that my hands were shaking and my dick was still hard.

I nodded. "It was better than okay. Thank you."

When Ben spoke, it sounded like a sleepy morning voice, but the fire in his eyes told me otherwise. "I like being with you, Shiloh."

I looked away. I glanced out at the city skyline ablaze on the horizon. It was the same view I had from my living room window. It was a beautiful panorama, but it wasn't what I wanted to see right then. So I turned back to Ben. That's where my eyes wanted to go. As soon as my vision was anchored to his face, I said the last thing I had intended to say.

"I like being with you too. I didn't want to like it, but I do."

His face split wide in a wondrous grin. His teeth flashed. He blinked, and the graceful way his long blond lashes swept across his eyes made me catch my breath.

"We've got the groundwork in," he said. "That's a good thing."

He lost me. "The groundwork?"

"Yeah. Now that we're friends, we can take our relationship anywhere we want to take it."

"And—and where exactly do you think we should take it?"

The corners of his eyes crinkled as he smiled yet again. "I think you know that already. Are you ready for dinner now?"

I realized suddenly that my boner had flown the coop. I couldn't imagine why, but I was immensely grateful it was gone. I gulped and nodded. "Uh-huh."

He laughed. "Relax. It's just dinner. Come on."

He took my hand and pulled me to my feet.

"By the way," I said, jabbering nervously because I thought I should say *something*. "Your uncle wants me to help you find a job. I arranged for my boss to interview you tomorrow night."

That stopped him cold. It also elicited a laugh. "You're kidding."

"Nope."

"You want me to work with you at the restaurant?"

"Yeah."

"In a kilt?"

"Only if there's a God," I said, regretting the words the second they fell out of my mouth.

Another tiny flash of fire ignited Ben's eyes. He stood there, towering over me, and before I knew what he was up to, he had dragged me into his arms again. Ducking his head, he pressed his mouth to my ear and whispered three little words that I knew would be making return appearances in my psyche from here on out.

"For you," he said, "anything."

Chapter 7

I FOLLOWED Ben up the stairwell to the sixth floor, which was the highest inhabited floor of the building. The stairs, however, did not end there. One flight up from the sixth-floor landing, the stairway disappeared into a trapdoor in the ceiling.

"Worker's passage," Ben explained.

I was so enthralled watching Ben's jeans-encased ass as he climbed through the trapdoor ahead of me, I almost didn't hear what he said. Once he was out of sight, he reached down through the hole in the ceiling to give me a hand up. Ben was so strong he practically lifted me off my feet and pulled me through the opening like I was made of feathers.

I poked my head out into the night and my breath caught. I couldn't believe what I was seeing.

The vast Belladonna Arms sign loomed over our heads. It was rendered in orange neon and cast a fiery glow over the roof beneath it as it winked and stuttered above us with little electric pops and fizzes. Beyond the sign was a sparkling blanket of shimmering stars and one big fat harvest moon that was so bright and beautiful, it might have been hung there by the guys in special effects. The moon and that incredible array of stars were sprinkled across the heavens like spatters of molten silver.

Stunned to silence, Ben and I stood shoulder-to-shoulder, gazing up. We both sucked in great gulps of air at the beauty of that glistening sky. "Golly," Ben said on a sigh, and all I could do was nod in agreement.

It was a warm night. The sky was clear, and a breeze rolled over us from the ocean a mile to the south. The breeze smelled of sea life, shoreline, and pizza.

Pizza? That nabbed my attention. Why did the air smell like pizza?

Gazing around the rooftop, I spotted a card table parked over in the corner, with two chairs tucked under it and a white tablecloth neatly covering the top. In the middle of the tabletop were two unlit candles surrounded by a chimney glass, a bouquet of yellow daisies in a vase, and two table settings in what looked to be fairly decent china and crystal.

Next to the table sat another smaller table. This one had a microwave oven perched on it. The microwave was plugged into an extension cord that trailed off across the floor of the roof to an outlet in the floor about twenty feet away. On top of the microwave oven lay two pizza boxes, which explained the pizza smell, and as I drew a little closer, I thought I detected the scent of pepperoni and Italian sausage. My favorites.

Everything lay in what looked like warm firelight, thanks to all the orange neon glowing directly overhead.

Ben saw me gaping and waved me forward like the snootiest maître d' ever. "Your table is ready, sir."

I had to fumble around to find my voice. "This is… amazing."

Rather than head directly for the table, however, Ben took my hand and led me toward the edge of the roof nearest the city skyline to the west. The lights of the far-off high-rises cast a blushing dome of pinkish-white light over the entire city. From where we stood, the city seemed to be encased in a giant bubble of radiance. Off in the distance, a siren wailed, and only then did I remember the city was peopled with life. It wasn't simply a work of art Ben had laid out there on the horizon for me to delight in. There were actual souls there, living under that shimmering dome of light—hustling, bustling, scurrying around.

Ben's voice was hushed at my side. It was like he was standing in church. "I come up here a lot. I never get tired of this view."

"No," I said. "It's beautiful."

I noticed his hand was still in mine when his grip tightened almost imperceptibly around my fingers, gathering them gently together. "And you look radiant in the light of it," he said, smiling down at me.

Turning to him, I stared up at his face, and I knew immediately what he meant. His features were softened and muted and sweetly paled by the orange light raining down on us. Only his eyes remained untouched, as eerily beautiful as they always were. As blue as a morning sky. Bluer.

My fingers responded to his touch. I moved against him and tucked my head under his chin, resting my forehead on his chest. His arms came up then and held me. I twisted my head, and together we gazed out at the horizon.

Softly, I said, "You're surprising the hell out of me here. I'm even surprising myself."

"Good," he said, and again the silence settled over us. The night was so hushed I could hear his breath as it stirred my hair.

As if in a dream, he asked, "Still hungry?"

I pulled back far enough to gaze up into his face again. He smiled down at me, his eyes sleepy and calm, as if the very beauty of the city laid out in front of us had mellowed his heart and eased his sorrows. If he actually had any sorrows to begin with, which I seriously doubted. It seemed that since the day I'd met him, Ben's face was rarely without a smile. Except when I'd knocked it off with the occasional insult. God, I'm a dick.

"Yes," I said, letting my own smile spring up to join his. "Let's eat." And since I was still a little nervous, I asked, "Is there anything to drink?"

His dimples blinked to life at that. "Funny you should ask—"

He led me back toward the table, and while I stood waiting, he lit the candles from a book of matches he pulled from his pocket. Then he turned to spin a bottle of champagne in the ice bucket it rested in. Funny, I hadn't seen it there before. There was also stemware on the table.

"Boy," I said. "When you invite a guy to dinner, you really invite a guy to dinner."

"Nothing but the best for you." He gave me a wink, and whispered, "Don't tell anybody, but I borrowed all this stuff from Uncle Arthur. He seems to think we belong together, you know."

"I know," I said, fighting the urge to roll my eyes.

Ben popped the champagne cork, poured some bubbly into the two crystal glasses, and handed one to me. Before he released it into my grip, he stepped close and without any warning whatsoever, once again laid his lips over mine.

I stood there basking in the heat of him. Awed by his size. Marveled by his gentleness. Stunned yet again by his ability to put so much emotion into a single kiss. I was also flattered by all the trouble he had gone to in order to make this night a success. It seemed there was more to Ben than I had imagined there might be. Being with him was one surprise after another.

Like now. With this kiss. And holy cow, what a kiss it was!

His hand entombed mine over the champagne glass, and as my fingers grew colder and colder from the chilled liquid in the glass, our mouths grew ever more heated. His breath was like a fire that slipped between my lips and heated me from the inside out.

When he finally let his lips slip away from mine, I was almost breathless.

"I like kissing you," he said.

I waited for my heart to stop tap-dancing inside my chest. "You're good at this, aren't you?"

"Good at what?"

"Seduction."

"Is that what you think this is?"

"I—I hope so."

At that, he laughed. "I told Uncle Arthur you weren't so dumb. Let's eat."

I STUCK two more slices of pizza in the microwave and nuked them for twenty seconds. When the oven beeped, I dragged them back out, slipped one on Ben's plate and one on mine. We had been eating for a while now. The two pizzas were almost gone.

I knew this night would be stuck in my memory for years to come. Dining under the moonlight. Watching the candles flicker in the breeze wafting off the ocean. The occasional sound of night birds trilling softly overhead from the framework of that massive neon sign looming over us as it cast that fiery orange glow around us.

The champagne bottle was empty. We were back to beer. Thank God for the pizza. Since I'm not much of a drinker, without a little food in my stomach, I'd have been on my ass by now.

Or on Ben's.

"Okay, Ben," I said around a mouthful of pepperoni. I was squinting, I noticed. Trying to keep my eyes focused. I was getting drunk. That did not bode well for the rest of the evening. Or maybe it did. "Time for you to fess up. Why the heck are you crawling around the building sniffing at the baseboards and snooping under the porch? What exactly is it you're looking for? Arthur mentioned it, you know. He wouldn't tell me what he thought you were doing, but he thinks you're obsessed."

Ben stared at me sitting there in front of him. There was a merry twinkle in his eyes. As usual, he was smiling. He really was incredibly handsome when he smiled, especially in candlelight. The glow from the sign over our heads didn't hurt either. Nor did the fact he was built like a brick shithouse.

"I am obsessed," he said. "With you."

I tried really hard to look annoyed. "Stop it. We're not talking about me. We're talking about you."

He stared off at the horizon for a second, then took a gander at the stars overhead. Finally, for lack of anywhere else to look, he settled his eyes on me and proceeded to say the absolute *last* thing I expected him to say. And even *that* he said around a smile.

"Ever hear of Captain Blue Eyes?"

I gave him a couple of blinks. "Who's that? A pirate? Don't tell me you're looking for pirate treasure inside an apartment building that was built in the 1920s. I think most of the pirates were out of business by then, dipshit."

Ben faked a snarl. At least I think it was faked. "Do you want to hear about Captain Blue Eyes or not?"

I did the old zipper across the lips routine followed by the old twisting the key in the lock routine, then I did the old throw the imaginary key over the side of the building routine. God, I hate myself when I'm drunk.

"Proceed," I said. Then I hiccupped.

Ben plucked another bottle of Heineken out of a cooler at his feet and plopped it down in front of me, which probably wasn't a smart thing for him to do. Since I wasn't any smarter than he was, I started drinking it.

"You're so cute," he said as his knee nudged mine beneath the table. He might have been drunk too. I couldn't be sure.

"Don't change the subject," I said outwardly. Inwardly I gloated. Playing kneesies under the table with someone who looked like Ben would make anybody gloat. Somewhere in the back of my mind, I remembered I had planned not to have any fun tonight, but now I seemed to be having it anyway. I'm not sure when the old plan petered out and the new plan kicked in, but I was immensely glad it had.

Ben propped his elbows on the table and tucked his chin in his hands as he stared at me dreamily through the candles flickering between us. "Tell me, Shiloh, what do you know about disco?"

"You mean pink-ruffled-shirts and bell-bottom-pants disco?"

"Yeah."

"You mean zebra-striped-platform-shoes and black-lights disco?"

"Uh, yeah."

But I wasn't done yet. "You mean 'Play That Funky Music' disco?"

He laughed. "Okay, now you've gone too far. And that last one is the right era, but the wrong genre. That's soul, but you've got the drift."

"What the hell does that have to do with you snooping around on your hands and knees digging up the floorboards?"

"Everything, actually." He plucked out a beer for himself and settled back in his chair to get comfortable. He also pulled the chair up closer to the table so he could casually—or *not* so casually—lay his hand over mine and leave it there, which I didn't mind at all. Yep. I was drunk, all right.

Ben dragged my hand to his mouth, kissed it, and placed it back on the table, leaving it captured there beneath his own. Then he started talking.

"In the mid '70s, when disco was king," he began with a grin, "there was an old warehouse just up the street from here that had been converted into a gay disco joint called The Cinnamon Cinder. Captain Blue Eyes was the disc jockey there."

"How do you know all this?"

"Don't interrupt. Through most of the '70s, The Cinnamon Cinder was packed every single night of the week. The owners were raking in money hand over fist, overcharging for drinks, demanding a cover charge just to get in the door, and their overhead was low. A little bribe money to keep the cops out, a little rent, a little watered-down booze, a little piped-in music, and that was all the outlay needed to keep the customers happy. That and Captain Blue Eyes to spin the platters for the little dancing queens."

Ben sipped his beer, so I sipped mine. I was dragging my thumb over the palm of his hand because I really liked the way it felt. I was starting to like his story too, or at least I was really starting to like the mellow, sexy timbre of his voice when he *told* the story.

He clapped my knee between his legs under the table, which made my dick jump, and then he picked up where he left off.

"The owners of The Cinnamon Cinder had a gigantic safe in their office where they kept the cash that was rolling in. The safe was as big as a refrigerator. Once a week a Brinks truck pulled up out front to cart the money off to the bank. Captain Blue Eyes became fascinated with that Brinks truck and the whole procedure of transferring the money to the bank once a week. Captain Blue Eyes was also sort of pissed that the managers wouldn't give him a raise, which the managers would later come to realize was a really big mistake."

I leaned in closer. Ben's story was getting good. "I think I see where you're going with this," I said. "But I still don't understand what it has to do with you slithering around the Belladonna Arms like a deranged snake."

Except for continuing to play kneesies under the table, Ben ignored me.

"Captain Blue Eyes hatched a plan to get the combination to the safe. He knew where the numbers were written down, see. He knew because a couple of times a week, Captain Blue Eyes would be invited into the office for a little hanky-panky with the boss. And once, while Captain Blue Eyes was down on his knees in front of the boss's desk, while the boss was sitting there with his pants down around his ankles and getting ready to squirt a load of jism up Captain Blue Eyes's left nostril or down his throat—I can't be sure which since I'm not privy to *every* little aspect of the story—it happened that Captain Blue Eyes was fortunate enough to spot a piece of paper taped to the bottom of the boss's desk. The piece of paper had numbers scribbled on it."

"The combination," I said.

Ben gave me a wink. "The combination."

When I tore a page from Ben's playbook and lifted *his* hand to kiss it, his eyes lit up like crazy. He snuggled his chair up even closer. I sucked his finger into my mouth all the way down to the second knuckle, and he licked his lips and his ears turned red.

"You *really* like my story, don't you," he breathed on a whisper.

"Maybe," I said, easing his finger out of my mouth and laying his hand back on the table. I had an almost uncontrollable urge to reach under the table and readjust my dick, but I fought the urge. I was also tempted to reach under the table and readjust *Ben's* dick, but I had a pretty good idea that would lead to me never hearing the rest of the story at all. "What happened next?" I asked.

Ben sighed as if he now had other things he'd rather be doing than telling the stupid story. Like me. He'd rather be doing me. But he gave himself a shake and continued anyway.

"Captain Blue Eyes wasn't greedy. He didn't want to steal everything in the safe. He just wanted a little spending money, which he figured he was due anyway since they repeatedly refused to give him a raise in pay and since it was because of him that all those thousands of gay disco queens continually flooded the joint. It was also thanks to him that the boss got his rocks off a couple of times a week. So one night when the Brinks truck was due the following morning, Captain Blue Eyes snuck into the office while the boss was off doing something else. Scared to death, but determined, Captain Blue Eyes ducked his head under the desk, memorized the numbers on the little piece of paper, hurried over to the safe and twisted the dial until the tumblers clicked and the door swung open. Inside, Captain Blue Eyes saw more money than he had ever seen in his life. It was all neatly separated into individual bags according to the denomination of the bills. Fighting the urge to break into a jig—Captain Blue Eyes was of Irish descent—he stuck his nose up at the bags filled with ones and fives and tens and twenties and fifties and centered all his attention on the one and only bag stuffed with hundred-dollar bills."

"Good for Captain Blue Eyes," I said.

Ben reached beneath the table and patted my bare knee with his warm hand. I almost fainted. When I realized he intended to *leave* his hand there, I almost fainted again.

"May I continue on?" he asked with a wily smile.

With every BTU of heat in my body heading for the shadows under the table, I stopped chewing on my lower lip, and stuttered, "P-Please do."

Ben's fingers rustled through the hair on my leg. It was all I could do to concentrate on what he was saying. But oddly enough, Ben wasn't saying anything. He was staring at me with wide, excited eyes while his fingers continued to stroke my bare knee.

Finally he did speak, but it had nothing to do with the story. It did, however, have everything to do with me. "I love the way your skin feels," he said.

I swallowed a quart of saliva. "And Captain Blue Eyes?"

Ben heaved a sigh. His priorities had obviously shifted. "Fine. Captain Blue Eyes got away with the money, as you've probably surmised by now. It was never seen again. What you *don't* know is that he died two days later in a freak accident when he was hit by a trolley car as he was crossing Broadway less than three blocks from where we're sitting at this very moment. He had a hundred-dollar bill in his pocket. That was the only part of the stolen money the authorities ever found. End of story."

I blinked. "How sad," I said. Then I said, "Wait a minute. That's not sad, that's annoying! What the hell does that story have to do with you crawling around the building? Are you saying that money is *here*? Why in the world would you think *that*?"

"Because Captain Blue Eyes lived here. He lived in the very same apartment I live in now. 4C."

I studied Ben's face. His hands on my bare leg were almost forgotten. Almost. "You asked for that apartment, didn't you? That's why Barney and Ramon moved up to six. You asked Arthur to move them out so you could have their apartment."

"Yes."

"And you've torn it apart looking. That's why I hear all the hammering and banging going on next door."

"Yes."

"And you've found nothing."

Ben sighed again. This sigh came all the way up from his toes. "Yes. The money isn't there. But it's in the building. I know it is. There wasn't time for Captain Blue Eyes to dump it anywhere else. It *has* to be on the premises."

"Does Arthur know about all this?"

"Yeah. He searched for the money too, back when he first bought the building and heard the rumors. He practically tore the place apart looking for the money. He told my mom about the money in a series of letters back in the '90s. My mom was his sister. I found the letters after my mom died two years ago. That's how I heard the story. Now, of course, Uncle Arthur thinks it was all a pipe dream. An urban legend. He thinks I'm wasting my time. He doesn't think the money ever existed at all."

"But you think it does."

"Yeah, I think it does."

I cocked my head and eyed him sideways. "And you want me to help you look."

He batted innocent eyes that didn't fool me in the least. "Yes."

His fingers were still moving on my knee, and I was finding it harder and harder to ignore them down there. "Wh-why would I want to do that, Ben?"

Less than gently, he hooked his hand under my knee and pulled me closer. When he tugged me forward on the chair, my kilt hiked up higher. His fingers abandoned my knee and stroked a path across my thigh. His fingertips were hot, his eyes lidded and dreamy. "Because we're attracted to each other, Shiloh. Because as soon as we finish our dinner, I'm going to take you downstairs and toss you on my bed."

"You are?"

"Yes."

"And what if I say no?"

He smiled. "You won't."

"I won't?"

"No."

"Why?"

"Because you're nuts about me," he said. "The same way I'm nuts about you."

"Oh."

I watched as he leaned toward the candles on the table. Just before he blew them out, I asked, "How much money are we talking about here?"

Ben gave me one of *those* looks. Sexy, mysterious, hungry. I wasn't sure if he was hungry for me or the missing money or both.

"Apparently they only deposited the hundred-dollar bills every couple of months. At best estimate, there was about three hundred thousand dollars in the bag when Captain Blue Eyes snatched it. Now then, Shiloh. Let's get down to other business, shall we? We've been dancing around each other way too long. Please don't make me wait anymore."

"Wait—for what?" As if I didn't know.

"For you."

Ben stood and roughly flung the table aside. Plates went flying, stemware shattered, candles tumbled through the air and snuffed themselves out. It was probably the butchest, coolest thing I'd ever seen in my life. Movie cool, you know? Romantic page-turner cool. Pulling me to my feet, he tucked a hand beneath my kilt and cupped my ass, pulling me close. That was pretty butch and cool too. Still wearing that sexy, mysterious smile, he ground his hard crotch into mine while his hot breath washed over me.

"You're mine now," he said from a distance of maybe an inch and a half.

My voice had a quiver in it. I couldn't imagine why. "Your uncle's going to kill you for breaking his dishes."

"I lied," Ben said. "I bought them at the thrift store up the street for a buck and a quarter."

"Oh. So you planned on hurling the table aside from the very beginning to impress me."

"Yeah. Are you impressed?"

"No."

"Liar."

Two seconds later, his tongue was down my throat, which seemed to imply dinner was over, and now it was time for dessert.

I had a sneaky suspicion that would be me.

Chapter 8

I COULD have said no, of course. I could have said no the minute Ben pulled his tongue out of my mouth. I would have had plenty of time to bitch about a headache or an issue with an unresolved STD or even heartburn from the damn pizza as he led me down the stairs to the fourth floor, all the while groping my ass and whispering urgent words of lust in my ear along the way. I could very easily have lied through my teeth and told him his hunky body and the luscious pelt of blond hair on his arms and chest and his bulging basket and musclebound biceps and long, lean legs were creeping me out since I really find emaciated ugly guys much more enticing. Or I could have simply told the man I was desperately saving myself for marriage. Like he'd really buy that, considering the fact that my dick was poking out the front of my kilt like a tent pole and my knees were shaking so badly I could barely walk.

The fact that I was tugging his shirt tail out of his pants and clawing at his belt buckle just to get my hands on his body before we ever got to the fourth floor probably didn't add any sense of urgency to the proposition that I wasn't in the mood for fooling around either.

I did at one point come out with the well-oiled excuse "I'm drunk," but all Ben did was laugh and say, "I know. Isn't it great?" for which I was immensely grateful. If he had backed off because of that crappy excuse, I would have never forgiven him.

No, what I *did* do was go with the flow, just like any red-blooded horny American with loose morals would do. I wanted Ben as much as Ben wanted me, and since we were both just drunk enough to dive into each other's crotches face-first, what the heck was the problem anyway?

Ben steered me through his front door, locked it behind us, and none too gently spun me around and pushed me against the wall.

I could have sworn the guy had twelve hands. They were everywhere. He dropped to his knees in front of me and gently stroked my knees with one hand as he tugged my shoes off with the other. After my shoes were out of the way, he eased my knee-high woolen socks down and plucked them happily off my feet, all the while stroking the back of my calves with his hot fingertips.

When I was standing in front of him barefoot and barelegged, he slid his hands up the back of my thighs and ducked his head under my kilt to press his lips to my kneecaps, first one then the other. His tongue dipped lower and slid along my shin while his fingers moved higher through the bristly hair on my thighs until he came to my BVDs. He trailed his fingertips along the elastic of the leg holes, then without getting all sentimental about it or putting in a work order or anything, he took a firm grip on those suckers and tugged them right off, peeling them down my legs and over my feet while my dick boinged up and banged him in the forehead. I stood there bucking and shivering and gasping for breath, with my hands in his hair and my thumb—which he was now sucking on like a lollipop—in his mouth.

The next thing I knew, Ben spit out my thumb and burrowed all the way underneath my kilt to press his nose against my balls. He sniffed and rooted around like a hog hunting for truffles while I jerked and gasped and chewed on my tongue, all the while trying not to pass out cold from hormonal overload.

Jesus God, Ben's nose felt good on my nuts.

It took every ounce of concentration I possessed to squirm out of my shirt, undo my belt, rip my kilt from around my waist, and fling it away until I was standing there as naked as a jaybird. That was when I realized what Ben was really doing.

I gazed down at his snarfling face just as he tilted my cast-iron cock toward his mouth and swallowed it whole. My mouth fell open, my eyes squeezed shut, and I rose up on quivering tiptoe as far as I could go while Ben went to town on my dick.

When his other hand took a side trip to my ass and his fingertip came to rest on my hole in a companionable sort of way, I decided it was time for me to get involved.

I started tugging at his shirt. Not bothering with buttons, I peeled it over his head, almost ripping his ears off in the process.

"Ouch," he said around my dick.

When his shirt was off and I had thrown it as far as I could throw it, the sight and feel of Ben's broad, bare shoulders sent such a rush of desire through me that I cupped his face in my hands and pulled him away from my cock long enough to grab his attention.

"Bed, Ben," I gasped. "I want you in bed."

He smiled up at me, his lips moist, his eyes shining. "Finally admitting it, huh?"

I glared down at him, but I couldn't very well disagree, could I? What with my shiny wet dick pressed against his cheek and his finger still massaging my hole.

I mouthed the word "Please," since I seemed to have lost the power of speech.

Ben rose straight up to tower above me. His chest now bare and smack in front of my face, he flattened me against the wall with his weight. He stooped enough to bring his mouth down over mine, and what followed was a battle of four separate hands all trying to get Ben's pants off at the same time. I finally had to slap his hands out of the way so I could do it myself.

He grunted and groaned and groped and growled, and while his tongue dove down my throat again like an eel, his hands foraged over my body like he was trying to memorize the lay of the land. While he did that, he kicked his shoes off and wiggled his hips around trying to help me remove his pants.

Finally when the belt was undone and the zipper was down and that final button was popped, he shimmied his way out of the fucking trousers and frantically kicked them away, leaving himself in nothing but socks and a ruddy glow.

His heavy cock, as hot as molten steel and a whopper by anybody's standards, pressed against my stomach, and before I knew what was happening, Ben had scooped me off the floor as if I weighed nothing at all. Naked in his arms and with his mouth still clamped on mine, he carried me into the bedroom and tossed me unceremoniously onto the bed. That job finished, he flicked on a lamp and gazed down at me.

Blazing in the heat of his glance, I rose up on my elbows and stared back at Ben. He stood naked at the side of the bed, his eyes afire with hunger, his body just as perfect as I knew it would be. His cock was fat and long and uncut. Huge. It stood straight out from his body, and I wondered, just briefly, if maybe I could do a couple of chin-ups on it. Then I stopped wasting time and got down to business.

Rising onto my knees, I pressed my face to Ben's chest and pulled him into me while he stood there at the side of the bed. His cock nudged my chest as my lips found a nipple. Ben's huge hands kneaded gently at my back. He held me close while my own hands slid over the smooth, broad expanse of his muscled back, then gradually, slowly, slipped downward until I felt the swell of that perfect ass beneath my touch. I had no sooner gotten my hands on his butt when Ben bent over me and glided his own hands down my back until he was stroking my ass too. Ben's fat cock nudged me under the chin, and I smiled and gently cupped his balls. They filled my hand, and I smiled wider when Ben gave a little gasp.

Pressing my mouth to the side of his cock, I moved my tongue upward, easing his foreskin back, and by the time I was in position, every inch of his beauty was there waiting for me. I licked away a crystal drop of liquid shimmering on his slit, then tucked the bulbous head of his dick into my mouth and tasted him for the very first time.

"Oh, man…," he muttered above me.

I took his cock as far into my mouth as I could. I was so turned on, I had to reach down and stroke my own. When Ben realized what I was doing, he gently eased me off his dick and laid me on the bed. Hovering over me, he ran his hands along the length of my body, and as he did, he eased down onto the bed at my side.

Since he'd had the foresight to stretch himself out in the opposite direction from the way I was lying, I found myself exactly where I wanted to be. Crotch to nose, eyeballs to nuts. I again took Ben's heavenly cock into my mouth, and the moment I did, he slipped mine into his, making me cry out and flop around like a fish.

Time was lost as we lay there, absorbed with each other. Ben's mouth kept me trembling, and his hands traveled every square inch of my body, just as mine were doing to his. His skin was hot to the touch, his furred chest as soft as down. While savoring his cock, I also savored the feel of his long, strong legs as I slid my hands down their length as far as I could reach, then back again, over and over. I shuddered with joy as his large hands oh so lightly caressed my ass.

"You're so gentle," I gasped and slipped his cock from my mouth just so I could drag it across my face, the better to feel its weight and girth. Then I slipped it between my lips again, and Ben lifted his hips to bury himself inside my mouth.

We were both trembling like crazy now. Ben took my cock all the way in until his lips were in my pubic hair and my balls were resting atop his nose. I could feel him breathing in my scent even while his mouth pleasured me from above.

Lost in the size and the heat of the man, I was so excited I was going cross-eyed. I knew I couldn't last much longer, and I didn't.

When he slipped my cock from between his lips and pressed his mouth to my stomach for a little change of pace, all the while stroking my cock and pressing it against his face as I had done with his, I felt my upcoming release churning inside me. In preparation for blasting the guy with a torrent of come, my balls drew up so far into my body they were practically in my throat.

Before I could cry out around Ben's swollen cock, which I still couldn't take all the way into my mouth since it was so big, he gripped the side of my head and arched his back off the bed. Only then did I realize Ben was closer to exploding than me.

When he came, he filled my mouth with a surge of heavy, delicious cream. I held him tight in my arms and never released his cock even once from between my lips, eagerly accepting everything he bestowed on me. He bucked and writhed against me as his cock emptied itself, and just as he was beginning to relax back onto the bed, my own release came.

My first jet of come splashed over his face, and when he realized he was in the line of fire and those precious bullets were being wasted, he hurriedly slid my dick back into his mouth to claim the rest.

I gasped and thrashed beneath him, but Ben's broad, strong hands kept me easily within his control as he gently, insistently, milked me dry.

When my flow of come dwindled to a seep, he kept me in his mouth, feeding still. His strong arms circled me and held me close as our two hearts thundered in our ears.

Ben's cock, replete and shiny with Shiloh spit, slipped from between my lips, and he gave one last shudder when I pressed my mouth to his stomach and another splash of come I found there. I kissed it away, and then I rose up on one elbow and gazed down on Ben's face.

His eyes were closed. An exhausted smile played at his lips. His chest heaved as his breath slowed, and seeing how beautiful he was lying there beside me, I let my hands explore his resting body: The strong lines of his thighs, softened by the blond hair that coated them. The rustle of hair, even lighter in color, that splashed across his stomach and rose up in a line to spread over his chest. The pillow of pale pubic hair that offered bedding for his softening cock, which was still magenta with pulsing blood. Ben's foreskin had slipped partially over the corona, leaving only the slit behind for me to bend down and lick one last time, making him shudder and gasp.

I slid my hands farther up the length of his body and felt the bristle of dawning stubble on his chin. The delicate line of his ears. The smooth heat of his temple beneath my thumb. His smile.

His eyes were on me. They never once left my face.

"Kiss me," he whispered.

So I climbed up and laid my mouth to his.

He pulled me over him like a blanket. I lay atop the warmth of him, the massive, solid heat, and closed my eyes to better enjoy the sensation of those heavy, muscled arms trapping me in their embrace. When our kiss sloughed away, he tucked my head under his chin and pressed my face to his throat.

His Adam's apple bobbed against me when he said on a gentle exhalation of air, "I knew you'd be beautiful."

I rose up again and gazed into his eyes. "Not as beautiful as you," I said just as softly.

He once more tucked me under his chin and held me close, then breathed words into my ear. "Stay with me tonight."

I nodded. "All right."

When his lips buried themselves in my hair, I knew he was smiling again.

Lost in his scent and as safely content as I had ever been in my life, I closed my eyes and locked the feel of Ben inside me. I tasted his seed on my tongue and wondered if he could still taste mine.

As if it had all the time in the world, the night settled quietly around us.

We slept.

IT WAS the first dawn I had seen in months. Of course, it wasn't really the dawn I clawed myself out of sleep for. It was the sight of Ben lying naked beside me, hair tousled, sleep-warm, softly snoring into my pillow. Not his pillow, mind you. Mine. That's what pulled me awake.

His arm lay across my chest, pinning me to the bed as if even in sleep he didn't want to let me go. I liked that. I liked it a lot. I also liked the fact that the hair on his forearm tickled my chin. By tilting my head down just a wee little bit, I could press my lips to his silky, bulging bicep, and not only taste his skin yet again, but also better to breathe in his scent. I *really* liked that.

What I *didn't* like was the fact that the man snored like a fucking locomotive. But hell, nobody's perfect.

With or without his snore, Ben Moss was no doubt the sexiest man I had ever bedded. Even now I blushed, remembering the night we had shared. Were still sharing.

Fighting the urge to squirm down under the sheets and sample his juices again, I thought of everything he had told me. About the stolen money. About Captain Blue Eyes. The whole thing was ridiculous. Wasn't it? That all that money could still lie hidden inside the Belladonna Arms? Arthur had searched. Ben was searching now. Probably other people had searched over the years. Surely if there was three hundred thousand dollars laying around the place, someone would have found it by now.

Yet somehow even the thought of buried treasure (God, that sounded corny) was not as mind-boggling to me as the realization that I was lying there in Ben's arms. *And that he was the one who had lured me there.*

Ben stirred, scooping me closer as he mumbled something in his sleep. His mouth came to rest on my arm. I could feel the heat of his breath as he snorted against my skin, and the moment I did, my dick sprang awake. Ben's dick was already awake. I could feel it when he flopped his leg over mine and pressed it into my hip, still snoring like a buzz saw. Jeez, I should wake up at dawn more often.

I thought of the dinner he had arranged for us the night before. All the trouble he had gone to. No one had ever done anything as romantic as that for me. Not in my twenty-six years on the planet. There was something about Ben in his more sincere moments that stripped the breath from my lungs. He seemed to truly be infatuated with me. But how could that be? Look at the guy! He was stunning. And look at me. I was a midget next to him. A midget in a kilt, no less. Closing my eyes, I remembered his hands on my body the night before. So gentle. So driven. And I remembered my own hands exploring him. I had never in my life slept with a specimen of manhood as perfectly scrumptious as Ben Moss.

I turned my head now to study his face as he slept, and to my surprise I saw his blue eyes staring back at me.

"Hi," he said around a gentle smile, his voice heavy with sleep, like his eyes. Since his mouth was on my shoulder anyway, he gave me a kiss there. I could see him breathing in the scent of my skin, and his eyes grew heavier. Not with sleep this time, but with contentment. "You smell heavenly."

I lifted my arm to slide it under his head. He snuggled closer, resting his head on my chest. His broad hand covered my face just long enough to sweep my hair out of my eyes; then he laid it on my sternum while his warm fingers came to rest on my throat. Their touch was as light as the stirring of a breeze.

I tilted my head and planted a kiss on his forehead. He sighed when I did, as if that was the thing he needed most. I felt his eyelashes brush my chin. His cock stirred against my hip.

"Good morning." The words were barely out of my mouth before he cupped my chin in his fingertips and dragged my mouth to his for a proper kiss. In the midst of the kiss, he slid his hand down my torso and rested it on my stomach. He fingered the hair that surrounded my belly button while my cock, engorged with morning blood, settled atop the back of his hand. His thumb came up to test its warmth, and a moment later he abandoned my stomach and circled my dick instead. I arched into his touch, and he snuggled even closer.

I felt small and safe in his arms. Small and safe and incredibly wanted. It was a new sensation for me. Usually I was the one doing the wanting. The feel of his warm, gentle fingers caressing my dick made me fight to lie still. I was wanton enough last night. I didn't want him to think I was *too* easy. Or was it too late for that? So I could really enjoy this spectacular moment, I closed my eyes and hid in the darkness behind my eyelids. I hid there to think, and I hid there to decide what to do next. It didn't take me long to decide. It didn't take me long because I knew right away I had no control over the decision-making progress whatsoever. My dick was in charge now. Maybe it always had been.

I opened my eyes and focused all my attention on Ben's mouth. His lips met mine just as I'd hoped they would. We kissed while our hearts thundered in our chests, and when I broke the kiss, I found myself doing what I had wanted to do since the moment I woke: I burrowed down into the twilight beneath the sheets, where the morning light was dimmer. There, in the shadowy heat of sleep-warmed bedding, I laid my face on Ben's ribs and explored his body again. He twisted onto his side and gathered me into his arms, holding me tight. I heard a sound erupt from my throat like a purr. I was pretty sure I had never made that sound before in my life.

Then, tired of the shadows and hungry for the sight of him, I flung the sheets aside and exposed us both to the light dawning through the bedroom window. When the light fell over us and there was nowhere left to hide, I slipped his cock into my mouth. The moment I did, he flipped me around in the bed as if I weighed nothing at all. I ended up on top of him on my hands and knees, my own cock sliding across his face even as I continued to claim his cock for my own.

He gripped my hips and pulled me down. At the same time, he slid up in the bed and positioned my ass directly over his face. "Sit up," he muttered. "Sit up, Shiloh. Let me taste you."

I tensed. "I-I've never been fucked, Ben."

He kissed the patch of hair at the base of my spine, dragging his tongue through it as if relishing the texture. "I'm not asking you to. I just want to taste you. Relax, Shiloh. I won't hurt you. Trust me."

I forced myself to do as he asked. Releasing his cock from my lips, I rose to a sitting position. With his hands on my thighs, he pulled me down directly onto his face. He kissed me there, sliding his mouth ever closer to the center of me, and when he got to where he wanted to go, he swept his tongue across my hole and buried his face in my ass like he was home.

I cried out and thrashed around like a trout. It felt so good. God help me, I decided to go all out, so I lowered myself onto him even more. I heard him giggle down there while his tongue washed over me and his teeth nipped at the tender skin of my perineum. I was hopping around, gasping and squirming my ass all over his face until it was all he could do to stay under me. He latched on to my thighs to keep me where he wanted me, and I didn't mind one little bit.

"Oh God, Ben!"

He slid his hands up my torso and gripped my shoulders, pulling me down onto him even harder. If we got any closer, they'd have to surgically remove his nose from my colon. His mouth felt incredible. I reached behind me and cupped the sides of his face while I shook all over as if I had malaria. He laved my opening with his burning tongue until I thought if I was going to die, this would be the perfect time to do it. No regrets going out like this. No sir. Take me, Lord. I'm ready.

I fell forward and took his cock into my mouth because I had been away from it too long. I needed to taste it again. I needed to slide my fingers over his balls while I tried to swallow him whole. As I lay doubled over him, my stomach against his chest, my balls against his chin, he gripped my legs and pulled me back to where he could claim my own cock again, sucking it into his mouth while his trembling hands continued to stroke my ass, his fingertips still exploring my hole, still wet from his kisses.

He arched his back and pushed his fat cock deeper into my mouth. He was shaking now as much as I was.

"Come for me," I gasped. "Please, Ben. Come in my mouth."

No sooner had I spoken the words than it was I who came. My body convulsed and my cock erupted, filling his mouth. He slavered over me and drank me down like a milk shake. And just as I began to collapse over him, spent, it was Ben's turn to spill his seed into me.

He groaned, and then he groaned again. He pulled me down onto him and once again buried his face in my ass. The moment his tongue entered me from behind, I felt his cock swell up even bigger than it already was, and before I knew it, I was drowning.

Ben's come shot out of him like a geyser, spraying my throat, filling my mouth. He was trembling so violently I could barely stay on top of him, but even then, as his come kept flying, much to my delight his hot mouth never left my ass. Not frigging once.

It took a while, but Ben finally stopped coming. As soon as he did, we collapsed against each other. I slid to the side, but Ben continued to hold me close. He seemed to have no intention of letting me go. He buried his face in my stomach and left it there, kissing me, still shuddering, hands still roving over my body from ankles to neck, hips still moving with the aftershocks of his explosive orgasm.

I kept his cock in my mouth until even his seepage ran dry. I finally let that delicious appendage slip from between my lips, but even then I didn't move from where I lay. I still rained kisses across his stomach, through his pubic hair, over his balls, never tiring of the taste of him. His hot skin, the soft blond hair that sprinkled his thighs, the continuing taste of his come on my tongue. Loving the way I made him tremble. Loving the way he made *me* tremble. Loving the way we trembled together.

Well, rats. And here I thought I was finished with romance.

With morning sex out of the way, and while my blood pressure ratcheted down to normal—which was a good thing because for a minute there as we were coming I thought our hearts were going to explode like hand grenades—Ben and I dragged a sheet over ourselves and settled in to cuddle. As before, he tucked my head under his chin and wrapped his arms around me, holding me close. His lips moved in my hair as we chatted breathlessly.

"Thank you for coming to dinner," he said. "Oh, hell—" He snorted a giggle. "—thank you for *coming*. Twice."

"Don't be juvenile," I mumbled into his neck, but I was grinning when I said it. His hands slid over my back and those magnificent arms squeezed me just a wee bit tighter, making me wriggle in contentment.

"Do I really have an appointment for an interview with your boss at the restaurant?" he asked.

"Yeah, Ben, you do. Arthur says you need to find a job."

"I know, but do you really want me to work with you?"

"Sure. Why not?"

"Will I have to wear a kilt?"

"God, I hope so."

"Kilts are certainly sexy on you, Shiloh. Not so sure about me."

"Are you nuts? You'd be sexy in anything. Or *out* of anything, for that matter."

His voice was hushed. Almost awed. "You think I'm sexy?"

I tilted my head up to give him an incredulous look. "Don't you own a mirror?"

He dragged his smile across my forehead while one hand dipped to stroke my ass. He seemed to like my ass—a consideration I thought maybe one of these days I should take to an altogether new level. Then I recalled the size of Ben's dick and worried that I might not have the guts to even try. Ben's mumbling interrupted my worrying.

"He thinks I'm sexy." Ben had his mouth in my hair, and he was mumbling to himself, being a wiseass. At least I think he was being a wiseass. Surely he wasn't really surprised to learn I thought he was sexy. No one could be that dumb. Could they?

I shook my thoughts away and ducked my face into his neck again. I planted a kiss atop his carotid artery because I liked the way it was thumping there under his skin, beckoning to me to pay it a little attention. Ducking a little farther down, I slid under the sheet and rested my cheek on his chest while I savored the warm fuzziness of his stomach beneath my hand. He made a little rumbling noise, like a happy tiger. It was a cute sound, so I gave him a kiss on the sternum to show my appreciation.

"Have an affair with me," he said out of the blue.

I tensed. "What did you say?"

"I said have an affair with me. Have an affair with me, and I'll go to the job interview."

"You're trying to extort me into helping you get a job by offering sexual favors?"

"Yeah."

"Ben, we just had sex. Twice. You don't have to extort me to get me to have sex with you. And besides, aren't we already having an affair?"

"No. This is tricking, not affairing. An affair implies an exclusivity agreement."

"What are you, a fucking lawyer? And what do you mean, an exclusivity agreement? You mean like seeing each other and nobody else?"

"Yep. That would be it."

"We practically just met. Are you nuts?"

"You keep asking me that. I'm starting to get paranoid."

"Ben, we've only known each other a couple of weeks."

"Yeah, but I saved your life. That's like adding six months to the acquaintance factor."

"Are you…? Never mind."

I rolled onto his chest and crawled up his torso like I was shimmying up a log. When we were face-to-face, I took a gander into his blue, blue eyes. They were laughing, but they looked kind of serious too. It was a strange combination.

"Have an affair with me, Shiloh," he said, gazing up. "We have fun together."

"But you drive me crazy."

"No, I don't. You're having fun too. You just hide it better than I do."

"I used to think Arthur must have gotten all the crazy genes in your family. I'm beginning to reassess that evaluation."

"Oh, shut up. Have an affair with me. Be my boyfriend. Let the pollen fall where it may."

I blinked. "The pollen." Then I realized what else he said. "Your *boyfriend?*"

"Yeah. Arthur's always going on and on about the Belladonna Arms love pollen. There are boyfriends all over this building. We could just be two more. Nobody would even notice."

"I'd notice."

Ben rolled his eyes. I guess he was still being a wiseass. "Well, I should *hope* you'd notice."

"But I don't love you, Ben. I barely like you."

Ben drew his lips into a sexy smile. With our chests pressed together, I could feel his heart beating in rhythm with mine. A tom-tom duet. "You like me," he said. "You're just too smart to show it."

"No," I said. "You really sort of piss me off all the time. Like now, for instance."

"I'm not pissing you off. You think I'm being romantic. You're just too smart to admit that too."

"You're nuts."

"There you go again with the nuts. Tell me we'll have an affair, and tell me you'll help me search for Captain Blue Eyes's loot. If you'll do those two little things, I'll go to the job interview."

"Now you're trying to up the extortion with an extra clause in the contract before I ever agreed to the *first* condition in your attempt to extort me into helping you find a job."

"It's called the art of the deal."

"Okay, Mr. Trump, let me put it clearly so even you will understand. No. A thousand times no."

"Wrong answer. Say yes."

He took a break in the negotiations to lay his lips over mine. I could taste my come in his kiss. I also felt my heart rate begin to climb again. For some reason, Ben's kisses always jump-started my blood pressure. I wondered what that meant. Like I didn't already know.

"An affair," I mumbled into him.

"An affair," he mumbled back. "Just you and me."

"I... I—"

"Say yes."

"But I—"

"Say yes."

I tucked my face back under his chin and thought about it. Sex on a regular basis would be nice. Sex on a regular basis with someone who looked like Ben would be *more* than nice. It would be great. He hadn't mentioned the L-word, so I wasn't getting in over my head in that direction.

"Ben, you're talking about having a *sexual* affair, right? Not a love affair. Just a mutual arrangement to bring about mutual orgasm and have a little mutual fun without going through all the angst of cruising and schmoozing and acting on our best behavior for weeks on end before we let the person we're interested in find out what we're *really* like."

"You mean dating."

"Yeah. Dating. We won't be doing any of that."

Ben guffawed. "Why should we? We've already found each other. Dating is for people who are looking for someone. We already found ourselves, we did."

"You sound like Yoda."

He lifted my chin and focused his eyes on mine while he cupped my face in his hands. Suddenly there was no humor in his eyes at all. The time for jokes seemed to have ended.

"Please," he said softly. "Just you and me, Shiloh."

I sucked in a great big gulp of air, then let it out in a long, drawn-out sigh. As soon as my lungs were deflated, I dropped my face to his chest. That broad expanse of muscle and fuzz and heat felt heavenly. Ben's words felt heavenly too. I hated to admit it, but they did. I hadn't realized until this moment how much I missed kind words. How much I missed... romance.

I squeezed my eyes shut and inhaled Ben's scent, his gentle, encompassing arms scooping me close.

"Please," he said again, his whisper so soft I could barely hear it.

So I nodded. Just once.

The moment I did, he rolled me off his chest and switched positions before I knew what was happening. Suddenly he was on top, and I was on the bottom. He propped himself up on his elbows so he wouldn't squash me. Smiling down, he planted kisses everywhere he could reach. Big wet noisy ones. On my chin, my ear, my forehead, my nose, my neck.

When I started laughing and sputtering and threatened to kick him in the balls if he didn't stop, he slipped off me sideways, and we lay like that for a while, side by side, just staring into each other's eyes.

"See? Extortion's a good thing," he said, sampling my mouth yet again.

I couldn't think of a single argument to prove him wrong. "I still think you're crazy."

He shrugged and dragged me even closer than I already was. "Eh. Sanity is highly overrated."

Oddly enough, I couldn't think of an argument to that either.

Chapter 9

ASIDE FROM a couple of excursions to Ben's fridge, then to mine, to replace expended body fluids, we spent the day in Ben's bed, which pretty much explains the expended body fluids. Yolanda joined us there for a grand total of five minutes until we started fooling around again, at which time I thought she was too young to witness what was going on, so I carted her back to my apartment before her young morals were seriously compromised.

I never said Ben was the *only* one who was crazy.

We rejoined the world just as evening was coming on. After a lovely joint shower, I dressed for work—once I'd unearthed the kilt I'd thrown behind Ben's TV the night before when Ben had me nailed against the wall with his nose to my nuts. Ben donned dress slacks and a nice shirt for his job interview with my boss, and together we set out.

Before we were out of the building, we ran into Arthur and his handsome lover, Tom. They were coming in as we were going out.

Arthur was wearing men's clothing—a neatly ironed 4X guayabera, brown trousers, and sandals. No earrings, no feather boas, no makeup, nothing. His outfit looked so strange on him, I almost tumbled down the stairs headfirst in shock. In fact, I probably would have if Ben hadn't been holding my hand.

Of course, the only thing Arthur saw was Ben and me holding hands.

He squealed like a piglet. Apparently men's clothing didn't make him any butcher. "You're holding hands! Look, Tom, they're holding hands!"

While Tom stood by patiently watching and smiling fondly at Arthur's antics, Arthur dragged Ben and me into a suffocating embrace that almost killed us both.

"I can't believe it! You boys are an item already!" he trilled.

Ben grinned proudly. "A *big* item! Item with a capital *I*!"

"Ben's exaggerating," I snapped, trying to pull my hand out of Ben's grasp, which he seemed to think was funny so he held on all the tighter. "We're a *small* item, Arthur. With a little bitty *i*. That's all it is. No capital letters here. No sir."

Arthur dragged Tom into the embrace, just because he wasn't cutting off enough oxygen to our lungs already. "Aren't they cute together, Tom? They're arguing about how much of an item they are! How precious is that!"

Tom looked vaguely embarrassed for us both. Or quite possibly appalled. He cleared his throat and tried to gently pull Arthur off our backs. "It's precious as hell, Arthur," he muttered around a sigh, as befit the most patient man in the world. I mean, come on. He lived with Arthur. How could he *not* be the most patient man in the world? "Really, really precious. Sweet as pie, actually. Now back off a little, hon. Let them catch their breath."

Arthur pinched our cheeks, one after the other, all *four* cheeks; then he apologized for his bizarre appearance, being dressed in men's clothing and all. Which in effect means he apologized for dressing normal for a change.

"We've just been to church. I had a sudden urge to confess my sins."

"What sins were those, Uncle Arthur?" Ben asked.

The minute Arthur released us from his bone-crushing embrace, Ben slipped an arm around me and went for bone-crushing embrace number two. I was starting to feel like a big ball of hamburger being kneaded into a meatloaf. Jesus, give these people an opening and they'd hug *anything*.

Arthur gave Ben a limp-wristed smack on the nose, as if telling him not to be so snoopy. "My sins are for the priest to know and for you to find out." He leaned in and whispered in my ear, "That priest was a hottie too. I've never seen a hotter priest."

Tom rolled his eyes, but he was smiling while he did it. "Whatever Arthur told the priest, the poor guy looked shell-shocked when he stepped out of the confessional. He'll probably be working at Walmart next week just to interact with a few normal people for a change."

Arthur blushed. "Oh, he will not. Well, maybe he will. But I hadn't been there in a while. I had a long list of sins to rattle off. See?" And with that Arthur pulled half a roll of adding machine paper out of his pocket, where apparently he had listed his sins so he wouldn't forget any when he came face-to-face with God's rep. The piece of paper was about three feet long and had writing on both sides. I noticed his list was numbered. It went from 1 to 112. Poor priest.

Ben saw it too. He snuggled up against me, and snickered in my ear. "After our last twelve hours in bed, we've probably got a list of sins to confess even longer than that."

I slapped his arm. "Hush." But strangely, I had to smile when I said it. After all, those last twelve hours had been pretty incredible. Even I had to admit that. Big *I* or little *i*, we had most certainly racked up a few no-no's worthy of the confessional.

"We're off to my job interview," Ben announced. "Shiloh's helping me find honest employment."

"How sweet!" Arthur happily wailed. "That's so nice! What a lovely, selfless thing for Shiloh to do without being prodded into it by some nosy relative or other."

He shot me a wink, then suddenly his chin got all crinkly, his eyes teared up, and a drop or two of snot dribbled out of his nose. Nobody could leak body fluids like Arthur. Well, aside from Ben and me. Of course we don't usually *leak*, we *spray*. "You boys run along, then," Arthur said around an emotional hiccup. "I'm glad you're getting a job, Benjie, love. You've wasted enough time with—well—*you* know. That *other* thing."

You almost never hear anybody say "Pshaw," anymore, but Ben said it now. "Pshaw! I'm through with all that. Shiloh showed me the error of my ways. No more treasure hunts for me."

That was a lie, of course, but I didn't figure it was my responsibility to let on.

At the news that Ben was going straight, so to speak, Arthur teared up even more. The next thing I knew Arthur had dragged me into another embrace, this time all by myself. He whispered in my ear, "Thank you, love. Your rent just went down ten bucks."

"Really?"

"No. I'm blowing smoke up your ass. But thank you anyway."

Tom pulled Arthur off my back like he was peeling an orange. "Come on, baby. Let's let these boys go about their business. Nice seeing you, Benjie. Nice seeing you, Shiloh." And with those niceties out of the way, Tom towed Arthur up the stairs, offering us our first opportunity to escape.

We took it.

As we headed out the door into the evening air, I grumped, "We're *not* an item, Benjie."

Ben punched me gently on the arm. "So *you* say."

I sighed and followed him out the door.

BEN GOT the job. He also got an armload of Scottish drag to take home and try on. Including a kilt. That pleased me no end, because now I knew beyond all doubt there really was a God after all. Heaven knows I'd prayed hard enough to see Ben in a kilt. And the minute I saw him in it, I had plans to rip it off him. After all, what's the point of seeing a hunky guy in a kilt if it's not to rip it off his ass the first chance you get?

No, Ben and I hadn't spoken the L-word. No, we weren't living together. No, we had made no lifelong promises of commitment. Heck, we'd only been in bed once (of course that one time lasted twelve hours and entailed numerous orgasms), yet somehow every time I laid eyes on Ben, my heart did a tap dance to see the way his eyes lit up when he saw *me*.

In case you're wondering, yes. I was perfectly aware that my heart was already in trouble.

The day of the interview I began my shift while Ben toddled home with his work uniforms under his arm. Since I wanted nothing more than to see Ben in his brand-new kilt, it was the longest shift I ever worked in my life. It lasted weeks. Well, no, it didn't, but it seemed like it did. Ben's first shift would be the following day, which was the only drawback to the whole plan of getting Ben work in the same place where I was employed. Until they knew he could handle food service without slopping sheep offal all over the patrons and spilling rollmops down their backs, he would be working the less busy day shift while I continued to work nights.

At midnight I rushed home and slipped quietly through my apartment door. I gave Yolanda some whispered endearments, rushed into the bathroom for a quick washup, concentrating on the more personal areas. After drying off, I patted my hair, evened up my kneesocks, blew some air up my nose to test my breath, then slipped back out into the hall and tapped lightly on Ben's door, still in my kilt, hoping for a little tartan-on-tartan action.

"Who is it?" Ben called from the other side of the door. The poor man didn't have a peephole. I did, but I tried not to be braggy about it.

"It's me!" I called back. "Let me in!"

"No!"

"Why the hell not?"

"I look like a fool!"

"Are you wearing your kilt?"

"Yes!"

My dick was getting hard. I pressed my mouth to the crack in the door. "Oh, please, Ben, let me in. I'm having some really incredible fantasies, God help me, and I can't do anything about them out here all by myself or I'll get arrested!"

I heard shuffling at the door. Then I heard Ben's voice again. It sounded like he was just on the other side of the crack I was talking into. How cute was that?

"You'll laugh," he said, his voice a humiliated whisper.

"I won't!"

"You promise?"

"Fuck yeah. Open the door."

"Are we an item?"

The asshole was extorting me again, but I was too horny to mind. "Fine! I admit it. We're an item."

"With a capital *I*?"

"Oh for fuck's sake. Yes! Anything you want!" My dick was so hard now it was starting to ache. I leaned in closer to the crack in the door. I lowered my voice to a delicate wheedle. Well, not too delicate. I was still shooting for butch. "Oh please, baby, let me in. I won't laugh. I swear."

"You called me baby. Say it again."

I rolled my eyes and growled, "Baby."

"Once more."

Okay, enough is enough. My dick was about to snap off. I kicked the door and screamed, "Open this fucking door, you twit!"

Ben opened the door. He stood there with a hangdog expression on his face. He had the blousy white shirt, the tartan shawl over one shoulder, the sporran over his crotch, and kneesocks on his legs like the ones I was wearing. In fact, he had the whole Scottish thing going on.

And the kilt. That glorious, wonderful kilt. While I hated the thing on me, on Ben it was a gay man's wet dream.

He looked so sexy with his bare knees peeking out I almost came on the spot.

Ben's eyes grew big and round when I slammed his front door shut behind me and walked straight into his arms. I laid my hands on his chest and felt those amazing pecs of his. When I slipped my fingers into the vee of his shirt and pressed my lips to his throat, he rested his hands on my hips and tugged me closer.

"I look stupid," he said, but his voice was a little breathless already. "If this kilt offends you, I can take it off." I was pretty sure I detected a tiny smile on his face when he said it.

For some reason, *my* voice was really breathless. "No way. That's my job."

With trembling fingers, I began unbuttoning Ben's shirt. He stood stock-still while I worked my way down his torso from one button to the next, popping them open, spreading Ben's shirt wider with every advance, licking his chest as I went along. When I reached the last button, I tugged the thing out of his belt and, along with the shoulder drape, let the whole shebang slide off his naked back and puddle at his heels.

Now Ben stood there shirtless in just the kilt, sporran, and kneesocks. My heart was beating so fast I was pretty sure I was experiencing arterial damage.

He sucked in a tiny breath of air when I bent and laid my mouth to his belly. Then I dropped to my knees in front of him. I slowly unhooked the sporran from around his waist and tossed it out of the way.

Slipping my hands beneath the hem of Ben's kilt, I gazed up into his face. I slid my fingers along the sides of his muscular, hairy thighs. I thought I detected a slight tremor when I did. I wasn't entirely sure if the tremor came from me or him.

I trailed my hands around to the back of Ben's thighs, and knee-walking a little closer, I once again pressed my face into his bare stomach. His skin felt like heated satin. Already, a bulge had risen in the tartan fabric at about crotch level, and slipping my fingers just a little higher underneath Ben's kilt, I felt his fuzzy ass beneath my touch. His fuzzy ass was naked. The man wasn't wearing any underwear.

"Oh, God…," I muttered while Ben's knees began to shake.

I ducked lower and pressed my lips against that rising lump beneath the kilt. Ben took a tiny step forward and cupped the back of my head, holding me in place while he pressed his tartan-covered dick more firmly against my face.

Ben's voice was a husk of its usual self. He sounded like Lauren Bacall after a three-week drunk and two cartons of Camels. "Maybe this kilt isn't so bad after all," he croaked, trying not to gasp as I slid one hand away from his ass and dragged it around to the front to cup his balls instead.

Ben rose up on tiptoe at the sensation of my cool fingers diddling his nuts. His dick was as hard as a car axle now, and damn near as long. I spotted a tiny stain of moisture leaking through the tartan at about eye level. *My* eye level.

I dipped my head beneath the hem of Ben's kilt and pressed my lips to first one of his knees, then the other. While I did that, I commenced removing my own clothing. Every single thing. When I was as naked as I had ever been in my life, Ben doubled over at the waist and slid his hands down my back to fondle my bare ass.

"Wow, oh wow," he sputtered under his breath.

He took the words right out of my mouth because by that time, my lips had skidded away from Ben's knees and were headed due north, kissing his long furry thighs continually along the way.

When I slid a tongue across his balls, Ben jerked like I'd zapped him with a cattle prod. I pushed the kilt high enough to free his dick and watched in fascination as it sprang straight up into the air while I continued to nuzzle Ben's beautiful nuts.

He wrapped his fist around his cock, but I slapped his hand away. "Mine," I said, my voice so hoarse now I couldn't have picked it out of a lineup.

But still I didn't take Ben's leaking cock into my mouth. I dragged my lips away from his balls and left a snail trail of kisses across his hip. When I reached as far as I could go, I applied pressure with my hands until Ben finally got the hint and turned away to face the wall.

And there it was. That glorious ass.

I pushed my nose straight in, scooting those luscious asscheeks aside as I went.

Ben cried, "Whoop!" and his whole body went into a spasm that really turned me on. Jesus, talk about responsive! I let his kilt fall over my head as I rooted around that beautiful butt like a gopher looking for a home.

Ben giggled and trembled and grunted, so I was pretty sure he enjoyed my attentions. When he reached around to grab the back of my head and press my nose into his ass even more, I knew I was right.

To urge him to lean forward, I applied pressure to his spine. Since he was up against the wall, he spread his arms wide and braced himself, all the while widening his stance to give my nose a little more room to work its magic.

I flipped the kilt up over Ben's back to bring his ass completely into the light, and then I really went to town. I was squatting on the floor directly behind him, so I spread my knees against Ben's ankles and widened his stance even more. With that I caught a glimpse of Ben's hole, and man, it was a beauty. Pink, puckered, sprinkled with blond hair, and twitching in excitement.

I spread his asscheeks a little wider and dragged my tongue across his opening. Ben's knees almost buckled. He grabbed a fistful of my hair, sort of like the reins on a horse, and with a good grip, he pretty much slipped his ass over my face like a Halloween mask. I had never been so happy in my life.

"Oh Jesus. Oh God," Ben stammered.

I dipped my tongue into that sweet hole and really tasted the man. He was trembling so badly now, it was like licking a lollipop while it was running down the street. I gripped his hips and held him in place. He apparently decided I could do better work if he played along, so he smashed his cheek against the wall and spread his arms and legs even wider to give himself a sturdier base.

When I figured he was as still as he was apt to stay, I gave myself up completely to the job at hand.

Ben removed one hand from the wall so he could stroke his cock, but again I slapped it away. Now while I was licking and slavering away in the rear, I dipped a hand between his legs and stroked his fat cock myself. Sometimes multitasking is the only way to go.

He gave a great shuddering breath and reached around to grab a fistful of my hair once more.

"Fuck me," he gasped. "Fuck me, Shiloh. Please."

Well, now, I have to admit I had envisioned a lot of scenarios during the past few days that entailed Ben and I fucking. Most of them were nightmare scenarios in which Ben's enormous cock was tearing through my tiny ass like a freight train, uprooting organs as it went, while I screamed in agony. For some reason, none of my imaginings entailed me being the one doing the grunt work.

"What?" I asked, frozen in shock with my lips still on his hole. "What did you say?"

"Fuck me," Ben said again, so I knew I wasn't hallucinating after all.

"Here?" I asked. "Standing up?"

"Yeah. Fuck me."

I tried to do a quick rundown of the facts involved. I was already in dreamland, what with my tongue up Ben's butt. And I had to admit the idea of poking something else up there was pretty tantalizing too. But logistically speaking, the whole idea was impossible.

I spit out a butt hair and said, "Ben, think about it. You're too tall. I'd need either a dick extender or a chair to stand on."

He pointed across the room. "There's a chair over there."

"I'll fall off and kill myself. I'll land on my dick and snap it off like a twig."

"It's hardly a twig."

"You know what I mean!"

Ben was full of ideas. "Fine. I'll get down on my knees."

"Then you'll be too short!"

"Jesus, you're picky. Then take me to bed!"

I blinked. Of course. Why didn't I think of that?

"I can do that," I said to no one in particular. My Mensa application still hadn't come in the mail, by the way. I couldn't imagine why.

I tucked a hand through the back of the belt still holding Ben's kilt on and dragged him backward through the apartment to the bedroom, where I unceremoniously shoved him down onto the bed face-first. He landed with a grunt.

"Romantic," he giggled.

"Shut up. Where are the condoms? Where's the lube?"

Ben's trembling finger pointed to the top drawer of the nightstand by the bed.

In less than four seconds, I had a condom rolled down my cast-iron cock, and in another four seconds, I had slopped so much lotion on Ben's ass we'd be lucky if we didn't slide right out of the apartment, down the stairs, and end up in the lobby in a greasy, naked, twitching clump of broken limbs.

I reached beneath him and undid his belt buckle. With that task accomplished, I tore his kilt off and threw it across the room. Ever try to get lube out of wool?

Now that he was as naked as I, I climbed onto his back and trailed a line of kisses from the nape of his neck all the way down to his ass. Squatting on the bed behind him, I spread his legs wider with my knees and positioned myself for entry.

Ben felt the first surge of pressure as I nudged my dick to his ass and breathed, "Yes, baby, yes."

He gripped the two posts on the headboard of the bed, and lying there in a well-oiled, trembling puddle of desire, he begged me to hurry.

So I hurried.

I slid into Ben like a butter knife going through a tub of margarine. Before I could stop myself, or even go through the *motions* of trying to be genteel, I was already in as far as I could go. And once I was there, Ben reached around to grab my hip and hold me in place until he grew accustomed to having my dick inside him. I felt like a Chihuahua fucking a Great Dane, but oddly enough the Great Dane seemed to be enjoying it.

"That feels great," he happily groaned, proving my suspicions correct.

I lay over him and peppered his neck with kisses. When he felt me there, he twisted his head around and found my mouth with his.

While we kissed and trembled and gasped and shuddered, I slowly began to move. Ben's tongue shot into my mouth, and I sucked on it while my dick forged a path in and out of his sweet ass.

I was so turned on, I knew right away this was going to be the shortest fuck in history.

"Oh God, Ben. Oh no."

Ben smiled around my kiss. "It's okay, baby. If you want to come, come. I don't mind. But oh Lord, you feel great inside me."

Buried to the hilt, I stopped moving completely. That helped a little. But then Ben gave a really big shudder, and I knew the battle was lost.

My cock swelled up like a toad, and suddenly I was squirting come while Ben bucked and laughed and shuddered beneath me.

"I'm gonna come too!" he gasped.

Before I could flip him over and claim his seed for my own, he exploded into orgasm while I was still buried inside him from the back all the way up to my neck. He bucked and wailed and came and grunted, and then we were lying there, exhausted, with Ben drenched in his own come and me still buried six inches deep in his magnificent ass.

Ben's bed was a sticky mess. After catching our breath, we dragged our funky selves into the shower, lovingly scrubbed each other down, then slipped next door and collapsed on my nice, clean, unlubricated bed and passed out from exhaustion with Yolanda purring at our feet.

Again, Ben never let me out of his arms through the whole, long night, and not once did I mind at all.

I slept with Ben's nipple against my lips, as close to his heart as I could get.

Sometime during the night, I awoke. Ricocheting through my head, I heard the echo of Ben's voice whispering in my ear as I had lain sleeping beside him.

"It's you, Shiloh. It's only you."

Did he really say the words, or did they come in a dream? Unsure, I snuggled closer. I sensed him smile as he pressed his lips to my hair.

In that position, we drifted off to sleep again.

Chapter 10

BEN'S JEANS-CLAD ass was poking out of a hole in the west wall of the basement party room. He was speaking to me, but I was so concentrated on his ass I wasn't really listening. Besides, he sounded like he was talking from the bottom of a well. It was annoying as hell.

We had been seeing each other for a month now. Our vow of exclusivity was still operable, and truthfully, I don't think either one of us had ever considered breaking the vow by going after somebody else. I know I was content, and I'm pretty sure Ben was too. He even seemed to be enjoying working at The Twisted Kilt. Probably because he did really well in tips, looking the way he did.

God knows our sex lives were full enough. I still hadn't found the courage to take the receptive role when it came to anal sex. Ben's dick was so big I was pretty sure it would split me wide open like a cantaloupe. He didn't seem to mind my reluctance. We found plenty of other ways to enjoy each other's bodies. I hadn't told him yet, but I was getting really close to biting the big one (no pun intended) and sitting on that big dick anyway. If it killed me, it killed me. And as far as death went, I couldn't imagine a better way to go.

Still, as a last attempt to retain a little independence, I had left the old chifforobe in front of the secret door leading from my apartment to Ben's closet. He wanted that roadblock gone, I knew, but for some reason I was afraid to sever that last tie with the person I had sworn to be when I moved into the Belladonna Arms—the person who had chucked romantic commitment forever in favor of a loveless existence.

By mutual agreement, the L-word was still tucked away somewhere inside my psyche where I couldn't get at it. It was on the tip of my tongue a hundred times a day, and I had seen Ben bite back what I suspected was the mention of it a few times too, but so far the word had remained unsaid.

And that silence was beginning to grate.

Following Ben around the Belladonna Arms searching for his stupid treasure was starting to grate too.

Ben sneezed with his head still inside that stupid hole in the wall, and I imagined a flurry of cockroaches raining down on the back of his neck.

"You all right in there?" I called out, rapping my knuckles on his ass at the same time.

"I see something in the distance!" he bellowed around a cough.

I swallowed back a sarcastic comment. I had heard this line before when we were searching for Ben's imaginary buried treasure. "Something's up ahead!" "Something's shimmering in the shadows!" "I found some coins!" (That time he had found two quarters tucked under a baseboard in the lobby. Not exactly three hundred thousand bucks by anyone's standards.)

I slid my hand between Ben's legs and cupped his balls. He jumped, and I heard a horrific *thump* inside the wall. "Ow! My head," he groaned.

I guess I took him by surprise. "Sorry!" I sang out.

Ben mumbled something that sounded like "moron," but I couldn't be sure.

The party room looked exactly the way it had the first time I saw it after I'd moved into the building and stumbled on it in my search for the laundry room next door. Wide open space, a rickety stage at one end of the room, dusty tables and chairs scattered around, and a big fat disco ball hanging from the middle of the ceiling.

By all accounts, Pete and Sylvia had been married in this room. Not that I cared. I just wanted to go home.

"I'm getting discouraged," Ben called out from his echoey hole in the wall.

Thank God.

"Then come out, and I'll take you upstairs, and we'll find something else to do. Hee-hee. What the heck is that hole anyway?" I yelled, tapping him on the butt again. "Why is it here? What did it used to be?"

"It was a dumbwaiter," Ben hallooed from the other side of the wall, and I could hear his voice echoing straight up the side of the building.

Must have been the shaft leading up from the dumbwaiter to whatever floor it ended up on.

"Does it still work?" I asked, trying to poke my head in alongside Ben's so I could see too.

Ben grunted, "No. The cables are shot. Rusted all the way through. There's an old bagel in here, though. You hungry?"

"I think I'll pass."

"Thought you might."

With a series of grunts and groans, Ben dragged his head out of the wall and trained his 1000-watt smile on me. His teeth were blindingly white, mostly because his face was coated with dirt.

"Miss me?" he asked. He had a big hammer in one hand that he had been banging around with in the dumbwaiter, listening for hollow spots in the walls where the stolen money might be stashed. He was about to lean in and either give me a kiss on the nose or bonk me in the head with the hammer, I wasn't sure which, when he looked over my shoulder and jumped. "Well, hello there, Pete!"

I spun around to see Sylvia's Pete standing there watching us. As usual, when Pete wasn't going to or from work, he had little Artie strapped to his chest. The baby was barefoot, and his fat little legs were swinging like pendulums. He had a rope of slobber dangling off his chin like a bungee cord.

"Somebody should check that kid's O-ring," I said, and Pete grinned.

"Permanent leak. Can't be helped." He moved forward and stuck his head in Ben's hole in the wall, but not going in nearly as far as Ben had. Pete had common sense. "What's in there?"

Ben frowned. "Nothing, dammit. Just a fossilized bagel."

"Your treasure's still a no-show, huh?"

Ben blushed. He hated it when people talked to him about his treasure. Mainly because they always talked to him about it like they were talking to the village idiot. No surprise there.

I tossed my own contribution into the conversation. "I'm Ben's treasure. You'd think he'd be happy with that."

Ben laughed and jumped at me, dragging me into an embrace while a great cloud of soot and dust and hundred-year-old crap billowed up around us. Jesus, the guy was filthy. And now so was I.

Pete coughed and little Artie sneezed. Then he farted. Artie, I mean. Pete was too much of a gentleman to fart.

"Yikes," Ben said, staring at the kid after dragging his tongue out of my ear. "It's about to blow."

"God, I hope not," Pete whined. "If baby poop were money, I'd be richer than Midas." Then he took another appraising look at Ben and me. "You guys appear to be made for each other."

Ben smiled through the muck on his face. "Yeah, we get along like bacon and eggs."

"Bread and butter," I chimed in.

"Chicken and dumplings."

"Drunk and disorderly!"

Pete simply stared at us fondly. Bored with the conversation, little Artie looked up, saw the bigass disco ball hanging over Pete's head, and started flapping and cooing and snorting as he threw his fat little hands around trying to reach it. All he managed to reach was Pete's nose, which he smacked like a prize fighter.

Pete went cross-eyed for a minute, then gave his head a shake like Bugs Bunny after Elmer Fudd whaps him in the noggin with a skillet.

Ben gave a sympathetic cluck. "Kid's got a killer left hook."

A cell phone started beeping in Pete's back pocket. He fished it out and checked the readout. "Oops," he said. "The little woman. Gotta run."

He gazed at Ben and me still standing there in each other's arms in a cloud of crap, dribbling gunk all over the floor, and said, "Um, have fun, boys." And shaking his head, he took off for the door, with little Artie still goo-gooing and gurgling and kicking his daddy in the nuts with his fat little feet.

"Poor bastard," Ben muttered, watching him go. He turned to study my face. "Remember when you grabbed my balls a few minutes ago?"

"Yeah."

"It gave me an idea."

"I'll bet it did. In fact, it's probably the same idea I had."

Ben reached down and with a come-hither look in his eye, popped the top button on his jeans.

I did my best Artie impersonation and started flapping my arms around like a pissed-off monkey. "Are you crazy? You're filthy. This room is filthy. The only thing I'd put in my mouth in this room is the barrel of a shotgun so I could blow my brains out!"

Ben looked hurt. "Well, that's not very romantic."

I schmoozed up close and laid my mouth to his ear—after I crawled up on tiptoe since that was the only way I could reach it. "Come upstairs with me, and we'll take a nice long bubble bath together. How would that be?"

"Will you wash my back?"

"I'll even wash your front."

"Ooh."

He gazed down at the hammer in his hand. "Where should I put this?" he asked.

"If you had any brains at all, you wouldn't ask me that question."

He smacked me with his hip, and arm in arm we headed for the door. Before we ever got there, he dragged me to a stop and cornered me against the wall. Moving in close he brushed his mouth over mine. Crud and all, it still turned me on.

"I've decided to tell you something," he said.

"What's that?" I asked, sliding my crotch over his.

"I'm tired of biting my tongue."

"What does that mean?"

"It means I love you, Shiloh. I can't not say it anymore. I don't want to not say it anymore. And if there's the least little chance that you might love me back, this would be a good time to let me know."

I saw red. At least I think I did. I narrowed my eyes and felt my mouth go into a straight little slash across my face. "I thought we weren't going to do this."

"Like I said, I changed my mind."

"So now you expect me to say I love you back."

"I hope you will."

I eased myself out of Ben's arms, stepped away, dragged a chair out from under the nearest table, and dropped into it and sat there all slumped over, staring at him. There was an arrangement of dead flowers in a vase on the table from some long-forgotten party. The party was so long ago, all the water had evaporated from the vase, leaving a film of brown scum behind. When I jarred the table with my knee, brown petals drifted down to sprinkle the tabletop like autumn had just set in. A cockroach scurried out of the mess and did a swan dive off the side of the table. Greg Louganis with antennae and six legs.

Ben did a little tap dance around the roach, then pulled up a chair opposite me. He propped his elbows on the table while he stared across at me. "I guess I shouldn't have said it," he said sadly. "I'm sorry, Shiloh."

I sucked in a huge breath of air. My heart did some sort of awful wrenching somersault inside my chest as I leaned across the table and took Ben's hand. "You just surprised me is all."

He cupped my hand in both of his and pressed it against his mouth. When he spoke, I could feel his lips moving on my skin.

"I know you've been hurt before," he said. "I know you didn't want to fall in love again. But please, baby, don't you think it's time to do what our hearts tell us is right? I'm crazy about you, and unless you're the best actor in the world, I think maybe you're crazy about me too. Please don't push me away anymore. Please don't make me keep my love for you behind a brick wall like I've been doing."

"I've never pushed you away," I said.

"No. But you've never let yourself completely go either. I don't just want the part of you you're willing to share, babe. I want all of you."

"Is this about the anal sex thing?"

There were tears standing in his eyes. "No, Shiloh. This is about the commitment thing. I want you to tell me you love me."

My breath caught to see such need in the man I cared so much about. His usual good humor was gone. Like an insensitive clod, I had knocked it right out of him. "You know I do, Ben."

"Then say the words. If you care for me at all, please say the words."

I felt a burning in my throat and a pressure behind my eyes. Suddenly my vision blurred in a rush of tears. When I tried to speak, my voice was almost gone. I had to clear my throat to get the words out. Basically, I was a fucking mess. "What if you leave me? Everybody does."

"I won't leave you."

"What if you get tired of me?"

"Never."

I swallowed hard and noticed my hands were shaking. "I've been happier with you, Ben, than I've ever been with anybody."

"Me too," he mumbled into the palm of my hand.

He sat watching me, still kissing my hand. A tear slid over his golden lashes and skittered down his face. I stroked his cheek with my thumb and brushed the tear away, leaving a swath of clean skin behind in the dirt.

I stared at that stupid disco ball hanging above us while I tilted my head back to make the snot run in instead of out. The last thing I wanted to do was look like Artie with a rope of mucus dangling from my nose.

In my imagination that dusty globe of mirror chips hanging motionless above our heads suddenly sprang to life. I pictured it glittering and spinning and casting shards of light over a raucous party, with flowers and ribbons and balloons and streamers and music and laughing carefree faces twirling on the dance floor below. Instead of what it hung over now. Two guys sitting in the shadows, both of whom needed a bath, and one of them not quite knowing how to tell the other he loved him back.

"You won't leave me, Ben? You promise you won't leave me?"

Ben dragged his chair closer and reached across the table to stroke his fingers through the hair on my arm. "Baby, I will *never* leave you. I've never felt this way about anybody. You're all I want. You're all I need. You're all I *crave*, Shiloh. You're *everything* I crave. Come on, let yourself go. Trust me. I trust you completely. All I'm asking is that you trust me back."

I swiped across my eyes with the heel of my hand to squeegee off the tears. I felt a smile trying to twist my face. My heart was beating so hard I could feel the pressure of it in my temples.

Shyly, in the softest whisper, Ben muttered, "Tell me, Shiloh. Please. Say the words. You won't be lying. I know you won't. You love me. Admit it."

I stumbled from my chair and dropped to my knees in front of him. Wrapping my arms around his waist, I pushed my face into his lap and held him as tight as I could. He stroked through my hair. His heart was thumping. I could hear it beating out his love for me.

Just like mine was beating for him.

I lifted my eyes and gazed up at Ben's handsome face. I let out a trembly breath. "It's true," I said. "You know it's true. I've loved you since the first night we slept together. I've wanted nobody else since. Everything about you turns me on. I don't know why I couldn't say the words before. I'm sorry. They've been on the verge of spilling out a thousand times. But something always held me back. Forgive me, Ben. I do love you. I always have. I—I think maybe I always will."

Ben doubled over and held me in an unbreakable embrace. I could feel his tears on the side of my face, his hands stroking my back, soothing, comforting. His breath blew hot on my neck as his kisses ruffled through my hair.

I stretched my body out to reach his lips with mine. His tears were warm on my cheek.

"I love you," I said again, choking out the words through a sob. "I do."

Ben eased himself away from my kiss. Brushing my hair out of my eyes, he swiped another batch of tears from my cheek and gave me the last thing I expected to see at that moment—a devilish grin.

"Thank you, baby," he said, laying his forehead to mine. "Thank you." He pulled back just far enough to focus on my eyes. "And now that that's cleared up, I think it's time I meet your mother."

I froze. Then I dropped my head in his lap like a load of laundry. Stammering into his crotch, I mumbled, "Shoot me, Ben. Just shoot me now."

"Such a comedian."

Laughing quietly, he draped himself over me and inadvertently slobbered on the back of my neck.

God help me, even that was a turn-on.

BEN NAGGED me for two weeks about meeting my mother. Finally, in a fit of lust brought about by four vodka tonics and Ben's tongue up my ass, I had given in. Now here we were, standing on my mother's front porch.

Mom had answered my knock and was peeking around the edge of the door, which was barely ajar. She looked suspicious, like maybe we were home invaders come to steal her brand-new slow cooker.

When she spotted me, she looked immensely relieved, although I had told her a dozen times we would be there at exactly six o'clock. It was now a minute to.

"You're early," she said, pulling the door the rest of the way open. When she spotted Ben standing there looming over her, she tilted her head all the way back and shielded her eyes from the sun like Sir Edmund Hillary gazing up at the peak of Mt. Everest just before setting out to conquer that fucker. My mom stood five two, and Ben was six five, so her reaction was understandable.

"Ben," I said. "Meet my mother, Ila Smart."

Mom stuck out her hand, and Ben gave it a gentle shake with his massive paw. "You're a big one," she said.

I felt a sudden rush of desire for the man standing next to me. Jeez, since Ben and I had finally admitted we loved each other, I was having those sudden rushes of desire at some of the most inopportune times. Like now.

"You have no idea how big he is," I mumbled under my breath, which made my cheeks go red and prompted Ben to elbow me in the ribs.

My mother missed the innuendo. "Why are you mumbling? And what do you mean I have no idea how big he is? I'm standing right here looking at him, silly." She stepped aside and ushered us in. As we passed, she said to me, "You're flushed. Maybe you should have your blood pressure checked."

I didn't answer because I was too busy staring at the Kiss the Cock apron she was wearing. While Ben walked in ahead of us, I leaned in and hissed, "I told you not to wear that apron!"

"I *love* this apron."

"And what the hell happened to your hair?"

"It's Clairol Intense Red. You like it?"

"No. You look like a headshot revolutionary," I hissed. "And what the hell is that bristly thing sticking out of it?"

"It's a sprig of baby's breath," Mom hissed right back, patting screaming red hair that looked like Mae West doused in ketchup. "I was trying to look nice for your friend."

I plucked the tiny clump of white flowers from her hair like I was weeding a garden and dropped it in a vase on the sideboard. "You're killing me here. Take off that apron."

"I will not, Mr. Bossy Pants!" She fished around in the vase, pulled out the baby's breath, and stabbed it back in her hair.

I sighed. "What's that I smell? A dead possum?"

"We're having stuffed bell peppers for dinner."

"But I hate stuffed bell peppers. You *know* I hate stuffed bell peppers."

"I thought I'd give you one last chance to change your mind. Besides, I'll bet your friend just *loves* stuffed bell peppers."

"But, but…."

Mom threw her nose in the air and flounced off after Ben, who was standing in the middle of the living room looking uncomfortable, like maybe he was waiting for a bus and had suddenly realized he was standing on the wrong street corner.

Taking Ben by the hand, Mom leaned back to just short of falling over because that was the only way she could see his face hovering so far above her head. Once she homed in on him smiling down at her, she said, "Tell my persnickety and easily embarrassed son you like stuffed bell peppers, Benjamin."

It must be said that Ben knew how to take a cue far better than I. His face lit up, and he looked like he had just won the Publisher's Clearing House grand prize of five thousand bucks a week for life.

"I *adore* stuffed bell peppers!" he exclaimed, doing everything but jumping up and down, waving pom-poms and clapping his hands in glee. "It's my absolute favoritest thing to eat in all the world!"

Mom rolled her eyes at me as if to say, "See?"

Ben gave me a wink behind her back, and I fell in love with him all over again—although I still hated stuffed bell peppers.

"Your hair is lovely," Ben said, making my mom simper like a little girl. "It's so bright! And those peppers smell heavenly."

The house reeked with them. I still thought they smelled like an oven full of dead possums. And my mother's hair color *sucked*. Was Ben blind?

Ben rattled on, the most obsequious house guest ever, which my mother was lapping up with a spoon. "I hope you didn't go to too much trouble just for me, Mrs. Smart. I just wanted to meet you. I didn't expect you to cook me dinner, although a home-cooked meal sounds wonderful. Thank you."

Ben knew we were here for dinner as well as I did.

Mom patted him gently on the chest and coughed up a virginal giggle. "Oh, pishposh, Benjamin, dear. It's no trouble at all."

I wasn't sure, but I thought I saw her hand linger for a second when she squeezed Ben's left pec as if she were testing melons at the market. I was left with the unnerving realization that even my sixty-year-old Jewish mother was not immune to such a gorgeous hunk of manhood and didn't mind the feel of a muscle or two now and then. I could have happily gone to my grave without coming to that realization.

My mother's head came to about fourteen inches above Ben's belt buckle. "So you're my Shiloh's new friend. You're certainly a handsome fellow."

Ben blushed.

I moved in to set the record straight. Taking Ben by the hand, I sidled up beside him while my mother looked innocently on, beaming up at the two of us like a lighthouse. She was still smiling from the compliments Ben had sprinkled her with earlier. Even my snuggling up to Ben in the middle of her living room didn't seem to bother her much.

"Ben's not just my friend, Ma. He's my boyfriend. We love each other. That's why we wanted you to meet him."

Mom looked first at me, then Ben. Finally her eyes wandered back to me. "So this whole gay thing you're always prattling on about wasn't just a phase after all?"

"I never prattle. And no, Mom. You know it wasn't a phase. I've been gay since I was nine. Good grief, you caught me wearing one of your dresses once when I was in the fourth grade. Remember?"

"All little boys play dress-up."

"Why did you think I had a crush on my sixth grade teacher, Mr. Witt?"

Mom blinked. "Role model?"

"No. He had a nice ass."

"Oh."

"When you caught me beating off in the bathroom on my fourteenth birthday, why do you think I was holding a copy of my yearbook, and why do you think it was open to the page that showed the school's swim team posing in their little Speedos?"

"I thought you were getting interested in sports." Then she grinned. "I mean *really* interested in sports."

Ben released my hand and stepped closer to carefully scoop up one of Mom's tiny paws. He held it like it was the daintiest of birds and he was scared to death he would startle it. "I love your son very much, Mrs. Smart. You don't have to accept me into your family or anything. All we ask is that you be happy for us."

Mom's eyes skidded to my face once again, then back to Ben's. She patted his hand. "What makes you think I won't be happy for you? I want my boy to be happy as much as the next mother. And if you're the one it takes to make him happy, then you are most certainly a member of our family from this day forth."

Ben's eyes misted over, which wasn't surprising considering the fact that his own family of Indiana hillbillies were so unaccepting of homosexuality they practically drove him out of the state. The pricks.

"You have no idea how much that means to me," he said with a sniff. It was an honest sniff too. There was nothing insincere about it. Ben was deeply touched by my mother's reaction.

And I had never been more proud of her.

I scooted in to spread around some of my own gratitude for my mom's willingness to accept Ben into the family. Pulling my mother into my arms, I held her close and gave her a peck on the cheek.

"Thank you, Mom."

"Oh, please," she muttered, accepting my embrace as if her actions were nothing, really nothing.

"And I love your hair."

Her eyes lit up at that. "Really?"

"Really."

While I had her in my grasp, I slipped my hands down her back and sneakily untied her apron strings. Peeling them carefully from around her waist while she was busy accepting our thanks, I tossed the Kiss the Cock apron behind the couch. She was so overwhelmed by my praise of her new hair color, she didn't notice a thing.

"Thank you, Mrs. Smart," Ben said at my side.

Mom pulled him into the hug as well, making it a three-way. She ratchetted her head all the way back as far as it would go so she could gaze up at Ben's face again. "You call me Mom too," she said. "We're family now. But I'll warn you right now, if you do anything to hurt my boy, I'll come after you with the garden shears, and you'll never see another stuffed bell pepper for as long as you live. An irritated Jewish mother is nothing to sneeze at. Remember that."

I laughed. Ben did too, but he looked a little uneasy when he did, as if the very idea of a five-foot-two, pissed-off Jewish mother with Intense Red hair going on a homicidal rampage with a pair of garden shears and cutting off access to her kitchen had always been two of his greatest fears.

Before I could explain to him she was kidding—at least I *thought* she was kidding—we heard the kitchen timer ring in the distance.

"The possums are done," Mom happily sang out, and the next thing we knew, she was hugging us again.

When she at long last released us, even my mother's eyes were misted over. She blew her nose in a hanky while feeling around for her apron, which she suddenly realized was gone.

Shaking her head at her own absent-mindedness, she finally announced, "Come on, now. Let's go eat."

"Okay, Mom," Ben said, casting a shy glance at me.

"Okay, Mom," I echoed softly.

My mother eyed us proudly, one after the other. "My sweet boys," she said on a sigh. Then humming softly, she patted the baby's breath in her hair and led us to the dining room table.

Chapter 11

THREE WEEKS later, Ben was promoted to the night shift at The Twisted Kilt, which was a win-win situation for everybody involved. Ben and I were now able to work the same hours, which gave us more time to be together. It also gave him better tips than he made working days. Of course, I laid claim to Ben right off the bat, just so the other waiters, who were all a bunch of horny sluts, wouldn't be trying to put the moves on him while I wasn't looking. If I've learned anything in this life, it's that you can never trust a horny gay slut around a handsome hunk in a kilt. Especially when that hunk looked like Ben.

Some of our favorite moments together took place during our late-night walks when we were heading home from work. It was then that Ben and I would hold hands and bump shoulders and speak softly of romantic things as we strolled along the deserted streets.

While our relationship progressed, Ben's relentless search for the Captain Blue Eyes loot managed to hit a few snags. For one thing, Ben was running out of places to search. For another thing, he wasn't getting much support from the man who loved him. (In case I've lost you, that would be me.)

The truth is, poor Ben never did have much support from me when it came to his obsession with the stolen money. I thought his search was a waste of time. More than that, I agreed with his Uncle Arthur in thinking the whole story was just an urban legend, and nothing more.

I was sitting at my kitchen table with Ben one day in November, sipping sun tea and petting Yolanda, who was purring softly in my lap. Yolanda was getting big. She was almost a cat now, no longer a kitten, and except for Ben, she was the best thing that ever happened to me. I loved her to pieces. In case you're wondering, I loved Ben to pieces too. In fact, I told him so continually.

That's right. Shiloh Smart was no longer afraid of uttering the L-word. Nope. Not one little bit. Ben Moss had cured me of that. Now I did everything but shout it from the rooftops like a lunatic every time I had a spare minute.

Ben's bare toes were twiddling the hair on my shins underneath the table, and all the time he twiddled the hair on my shins, his eyes kept getting sexier and sultrier. I was just wondering how much longer it would be before I threw the cat off my lap, leaped across the table, and started ripping Ben's clothes off. Or maybe if I was lucky, he'd rip mine off first. It had been known to happen. We were both in a celebratory mood, you see, for only the night before we had dragged the chifforobe away from the connecting door to Ben's apartment, doing away with the last obstacle to our complete and utter commitment to each other. Now that the secret door was propped permanently wide open, we found ourselves with one big apartment instead of two little apartments, and that was perhaps another reason behind my wanting to celebrate by ravaging Ben's body right there on the kitchen floor. Not that I ever needed a reason before.

I was about to set my tea aside and jump Ben's ass because I was tired of waiting for him to jump mine, when there came a knock at our door. Dammit.

I peered through my peephole and spotted Barney Teegarden standing in the hall with another young guy I had seen around but didn't really know. I peeled open the door and offered my friendliest smile, all the while hoping they wouldn't notice the remnant of my hard-on angling down my pant leg.

I greeted them with a smile I hoped wouldn't look *too* phony. "Hi, Barney. Who's your friend?"

Ben came up behind me, slipped his arms around my chest, hugged me close, and rested his chin on the top of my head. I imagined him up there offering his friendliest smile too. It was probably handsomer than mine, but I didn't mind. I didn't mind that the remnant of *his* hard-on was poking me in the butt either.

Barney grinned to see us so happy. At least I think that's why he was grinning. He tugged his friend forward and said, "This is Lester. He lives on the sixth floor next to me and Ramon."

Lester was cute in a prim, yardstick-up-the-ass, bookish sort of way. His dress shirt was perfectly ironed and buttoned all the way up to the top button where a snooty little bow tie was neatly fastened beneath his chin. His hair was crisply parted and slicked back off his face with what looked like about a pound of Crisco. He had really thick glasses propped up on the end of his nose, and the glasses had a chain attached to the ear pieces that wrapped around the back of his neck so that even if he fell out of an airplane, he still wouldn't lose his specs. He also had a big bulge behind the fly of his dress pants.

He looked like a librarian. With a really big dick.

As if to prove me right, he stuck out his hand and said, "Hi. I'm a librarian."

I waited for him to prove me right about the other thing too, but he didn't.

What he did say was "I work at the main library over on Park Boulevard."

Ben and I did the neighborly "that's nice" and "happy to meet you" thing, and as soon as that was out of the way, Barney leaned in, pressed his finger to his lips, and made a shushing sound like there were simply spies *everywhere*. "Can we come in for a minute?" he whispered. "It's *important*."

"Uh, sure," I said, wondering what the furtiveness was all about. Ben and I ushered them inside, offered them each a glass of tea, which they refused, and waved them down onto the couch.

Only then did I notice Lester was holding a book. *Wow*, I thought. *This guy's really a librarian. He even carries his books around with him.* I waited for Lester to pluck a dater from his pocket and stamp my arm. Either that or tell me to shush and proclaim my sorry ass overdue.

Ben and I got comfortable on the floor on the other side of the coffee table from our guests. Even with company in the apartment, Ben scooted up snug behind me and wrapped me in his arms while we waited to see what was going on. Yolanda flew up to the back of the couch and settled in to watch from there. Yolanda was nosy.

Barney plucked the book out of Lester's hand and waved it in our faces.

"Know what this is?" he asked.

Ben's chin dug into my shoulder when he answered, "A book?"

"Yes, wiseass," Barney snorted. "But do you know what's *in* this book?"

I was ready to elbow Ben in the gut if he dared to say "Words?" but he didn't. Instead, he and I merely shook our heads.

"Crime stories," Barney said, looking pleased as punch. "*True* crime stories."

"That's nice," I said, wondering what the heck Barney was getting at.

My obtuseness, apparently, was enough to cue Lester into impatiently snatching the book back from Barney's grasp. He cleared his throat, straightened his bow tie, used the tip of his pinky to slide his geeky glasses a bit farther up his nose, sucked on his teeth as if maybe the last residue of his breakfast was still lodged in there somewhere, and slammed the book down on the coffee table, making Ben and me jump.

For a librarian, Lester was kind of dramatic.

He flipped open the book and ruffled through it until he came to a dog-eared page. Then he spun the book around and slid it under our noses, all the while tapping it with his fingertip. *Tap, tap, tap, tap, tap.* For a librarian, Lester was *really* dramatic.

Barney gave an impatient groan and snatched the book away, slapped it closed, and tossed it on the couch. "They don't need to read what it says. I'll *tell* them what it says."

"So what does it say?" Ben asked. He was obviously bored. He was too polite to say anything, but I suspected our guests had strained his patience. I could tell by the way his finger was surreptitiously reconnoitering my ass, poking around beneath the waistband of my shorts. I would have slapped his hand away, but I didn't want to. I liked Ben digging around back there. If I had had access to Ben's ass, I would have been doing the same thing. My patience was strained too.

Our company apparently didn't notice what Ben was doing. Either that or they didn't care.

"It's all true!" Barney declared.

"Every word of it!" Lester agreed.

Ben and I just sat there staring at them. "That's nice," I said.

"Lovely," said Ben. "Glad to hear it."

My turn. "Umm, what is it we're talking about exactly? *What's* true?"

"Aren't you listening?" Barney and Lester declared together. "It's here! We found proof! Ben's not as nuts as everybody thinks he is."

I glanced over at Ben. I was pretty sure he'd just been handed a compliment, but by the look on his face, you'd never know it.

"Excuse me? Who said I'm nuts?"

Barney waved his words away like he was shooing away a gnat. "Oh, everybody, but I'm not going to sit here and name names. It would take all day. Besides, that doesn't matter. What matters is that you try to keep up with what my literary friend here is about to tell you."

He slid his arm around Lester's shoulder and snagged him close, giving the librarian a good shaking while he was at it, like they were best buds. "Lester here has been doing a little research."

"Research on what?" I asked. "The fact that Ben is nuts? I could have told him that and saved him a lot of time."

Ben bit my earlobe, making me flail and scream. Then he smacked his lips. I guess I tasted pretty good.

Barney eyed us up and down and sighed, like he might have done if he was a teacher and we were his two dumbest students.

Before Barney could say something snippy, we were interrupted by a knock on the door.

Ben was homing in on my earlobe again, so I slapped him away, making him giggle. I answered the door to find Ramon, Barney's lover, standing on our doorstep.

"Am I too late?" he asked.

"Too late for what?" I was about to respond, but Barney beat me to the punch, yelling from across the room, "Ramon! Get in here! Close the door behind you."

Ramon eyed me as if asking for further permission, but since I didn't know what was going on anyway, I just shrugged and waved him in.

Ramon squeezed himself between Barney and Lester on the sofa while Ben picked up where we'd left off.

"Would somebody please tell us what you all are talking about?"

Lester banged his hand down on the coffee table. A candy jar filled with jelly beans tumbled off the edge and jelly beans scattered everywhere.

"Jelly beans!" Ramon exclaimed, diving off the sofa and scaring Yolanda, who took off running. She'd obviously had enough. Crowds always did make her fidgety.

Everyone in the room watched Ramon gather up jelly beans, one right after the other, and pop them into his mouth as he went along. There was a general all-around eye roll before Lester banged his hand down on the coffee table again, making everybody jump.

"I heard about the crazy guy crawling around the Belladonna Arms looking for a fortune in stolen money, so I started doing some research in my spare time. I am, after all, a *librarian.*" He said it like he was an astronaut, not a librarian. But who was I to mock? I was a fucking waiter.

Ben dug his chin into my shoulder again, staring forward, and by that I assumed Lester had finally said something to grab his attention.

"And…?" Ben asked, trying not to growl but sounding intrigued nevertheless.

I decided to answer for Lester myself. "And you found out it was all a myth, right, Lester? An urban legend? There is no money to be found. Never was, never has been. Not a penny. Tell me I'm wrong."

Lester, Barney, and Ramon (who was talking through a mouthful of jelly beans) all answered in unison. "You're wrong!"

Now it was Ben's turn to bang his hand down on the coffee table, and he cried, "I knew it!"

Caught up in his own drama, Lester was so excited his eyes were bugging out. "I looked everywhere. I researched back issues of the *San Diego Union* from 1976 on. I read every news article there is that came out at the time of the robbery. Newspapers, magazines, police reports, transcripts of local news shows—both television and radio. Everything!"

Ben was squeezing me so tight in his excitement, I was turning green. "So there really *was* a robbery!" he bellowed, his voice trembling with excitement.

"Yes!" Lester bellowed right back, although his bellow wasn't as butch as Ben's. But I didn't hold it against him. Ben was six five. Lester was a runt like me.

Runt or not, Lester opened his mouth to prattle on, but before he could get any momentum going, there came another knock at the front door.

"Well, poop," I groused, "What is this, the train station?" Extracting myself from Ben's grip, I headed for the door. I yanked it open to find Milan and Harlie, the two bakers, standing on my stoop.

They were dressed in their baker outfits. White pants, white shirts, white aprons, big fat poufy white hats. Harlie even had a smear of flour on his cheek.

"Has the meeting started yet?" Milan asked.

"Is that what this is, a meeting?" I asked right back.

But when Milan and Harlie looked over my shoulder and saw Barney and Lester parked on the couch, they hustled right past me as if I wasn't there and pulled up a couple of chairs to make a bigger circle around the coffee table. What started out as a little neighborly get-together had grown into a conclave. A big gay conclave.

Ben was looking mightily confused by now. So was I. Lester just looked determined.

"As I was saying," Lester continued on as if he hadn't been interrupted at all. "It's all true. The Cinnamon Cinder reported a robbery of approximately three hundred thousand dollars on May 12, 1976. Two days later, Captain Blue Eyes, the disc jockey at the disco joint, was hit by a trolley just up the hill from the club. Three blocks from here. He died instantly. Actually he was cut in half, so death was pretty much a given. In his pocket they found a single blood-soaked hundred-dollar bill. The money was obviously part of the stolen loot, so Captain Blue Eyes, whose real name was Cedric Weaselton, instantly became the prime suspect in the caper."

"And that's all they found?" Ben breathlessly added. "A single one-hundred-dollar bill?"

Lester nodded. "That's all they found. The authorities suspected more of the stolen money had been spent, however. The night before he died, good old Cedric Weaselton, aka Captain Blue Eyes, threw a party for his friends here at the Belladonna Arms. By all accounts, booze flowed freely and private orgies popped up all over the place." Lester sighed. "Oh, those hedonistic seventies! Cedric held the party in the party room downstairs, by the way." Lester gave me a wink, which startled me, then said, "You might be interested in knowing that good old Cedric lived in 4C, right next door."

I'm afraid Lester didn't get the reaction he was expecting. "So we've heard," I said, faking a yawn just to piss him off. Lester was getting on my nerves.

While everybody was soaking up that last tidbit of information, there came another rapping on the door. This time I just stomped across the room, yanked it open, and stomped right back to drop myself into Ben's arms without so much as a nod to whoever the hell it was standing outside my door.

Roger and Stanley followed me in. They headed off to the kitchen, grabbed a couple of kitchen chairs, and dragged them back into the living room. The conclave had now become a summit meeting. Roger and Stanley parked their chairs side by side next to Ramon, who was still crawling around searching for more jelly beans on the floor. I guessed Ramon really liked jelly beans.

Ben whispered in my ear, "Told you Captain Blue Eyes lived next door."

I sighed, staring at all the excited faces around me. Every one of them, including Ben's, wore an expression like their owners had just won the lottery. A couple even had drool dribbling off their chins like little Artie. I was pretty sure if I looked up the word "avarice" in the dictionary, I would find a group snapshot of their greedy faces placed right alongside it.

I hated to be the one to burst this massive bubble of bullshit, but I did it anyway. What choice did I have?

"Okay, so there was a robbery," I said. "There was a robbery, the robber died, and no one ever found the money. That doesn't mean the loot is still inside the Belladonna Arms."

Several sets of eyes rained a flurry of pitiful looks down upon me. Clearly they thought I was as dumb as a stump.

"Well, where else would it be?" Milan asked, which pretty well summed up the general consensus of opinion concerning the matter. There were also a couple of glares of outrage directed at me personally, as if they thought I was being a traitor to the cause.

"What about my uncle?" Ben asked. "Did anybody think to ask him about all this?"

Barney shrugged. "Arthur thinks it's a fairy tale. You know that."

"He's not the only one," I mumbled to myself.

Since the front door was still open, nobody said a word when Charlie and Bruce wandered in, sucking Big Gulps and grazing from two humongous bags of candy. Probably stolen. One was filled with Goobers, the other Raisinettes. No wonder Charlie had a zit problem and Bruce was pudgy. Chomping away, they perched themselves on the arms of the sofa, one at either end. Klepto bookends.

Following along right behind them came Pete and Sylvia. Pete had little Artie harnessed to his chest as usual, sort of like a terrorist with a strapped-on bomb. (If you've ever witnessed little Artie in the midst of a bowel movement, you would fully appreciate the simile.)

Pete and Sylvia waved hellos around the room while little Artie burped and spit up a glob of white crap that dribbled down the front of his onesie. Jesus, that kid was a mess.

It was official. The summit meeting was now a full-fledged convention. We even had a kiddie section.

Ben's arms were around me again. He was gazing from face to face, and at the same time, all those faces were gazing back at him.

"So what do you think?" Barney finally asked, his eyes darting excitedly to Ben.

Ben gave him an empty stare back like he was speaking Swahili. "What do I think about *what*, exactly?"

Barney coughed up a great put-upon sigh. "What do you think about all of us chipping in together and finding that damn money? There's plenty to go around, you know!"

"I think it's great!" a booming voice barked from the open doorway, making everybody jump.

Heads spun to find Arthur standing there. He was dressed in bunny slippers, a chenille housecoat with more bunnies on the pockets, and a white snood covering his big bald head. All he needed was big fluffy bunny ears to top off the ensemble. His face was slathered with what looked like vanilla icing. He had his fists buried in his hips, and he was furiously tapping one size-twelve bunny slipper against the floor like he was royally irked.

"I was just having a mayonnaise facial—they're wonderful for the pores, don't you know?—when I heard everybody sneaking up and down the stairs. Now I find you all holding a clandestine meeting, and not one of you had the common decency to invite your Auntie Arthur to participate. I'm crushed!" He didn't look crushed. He looked mad. "Just when were you sneaky Petes going to tell me about your plan to retrieve the stolen Belladonna Arms treasure? It's only my building, after all. I've only been searching for this treasure since most of you were sprouting pubes! Answer me, you ingrates!"

And with that, everybody jumped again. It was Barney who looked the guiltiest, but even he didn't know what to say.

Arthur waited about three seconds for an answer that didn't come. Acting like he expected no less, he huffily gathered his chenille housecoat around him, swooped through the doorway, and headed straight for the kitchen, calling out, "Where are the canapes? Where are the hors d'oeuvres? Don't you people know how to entertain? If we're going to tear this building apart looking for poor old Cedric's treasure, we need food to keep up our strength!"

His voice was still booming, but it was also echoey because he had his head buried in my refrigerator. While everyone else sat around looking shell-shocked, Arthur continued mumbling to himself as he rattled through the contents of my fridge.

"Never heard of such a thing. Not even a bowl of peanuts set out. What's this? Dill pickles? No, no, no. That won't do. Oh, I do so love a treasure hunt! I gave up the search because I ran out of places to look. Oh, but now that we have some young, fresh minds on the case, we'll find it. I know we will. This is going to be fun! Oh, lookie. Radishes!"

Ben just sat there blinking. He looked at me snuggled up in his arms shaking my head, and then he looked through the kitchen door at Arthur's big chenille butt poking out of the fridge, and then he gazed back at me and blinked some more.

I hated to say it, but Ben looked a little shell-shocked too.

"Congratulations," I said, nuzzling his neck in surrender. "You're contagious. Now everybody else in the building is just as nuts as you are."

BEN AND I lay naked in each other's arms. The bedroom lights were on, and Yolanda was in the kitchen chomping away at a bowl of Meow Mix, sounding like a cement mixer full of gravel. Country music played softly on the clock radio beside the bed. Ben liked country music. It irked me to admit it, but I was starting to like it too. I was probably an embarrassment to city boys everywhere.

Love certainly does strange things to people.

Ben's warm breath washed over me as he touched his mouth to mine and whispered, "Turn around." His words were so jam-packed with hunger, I felt my heart start thundering inside my chest just listening to the guy.

Without too much trepidation, I eased myself around in his embrace until my back was pressed against his chest. With his mouth laid to the nape of my neck, he slid his hands gently down my rib cage. He softly prodded every rib as if he was counting them as he went along. Finally his hand came to rest on my hip, and he dragged my ass closer against him. As always, we fit together perfectly. His steel cock lay snug against the small of my back. With his other hand, the one attached to the arm that had wormed its way under me, he circled my dick and simply held it there in his tender grasp. As he did that, he stroked back and forth across my slit with his thumb, spreading my precome around. Somehow when I was with Ben, I always seemed to be dripping. Thanks to that damn thumb, which felt terrific, I started shaking like a leaf.

I could feel his smile on the back of my neck. He knew exactly what his thumb was doing to me.

"You're getting all trembly," he crooned in a sexy, mellow baritone.

I tried not to gasp. "I know."

"Are you going to help me and the guys look?" he asked, nibbling at my ear now, making me shake even more.

I found my voice, but it was a little fractured, I was so turned on. "Oh, are you all looking for something?"

"Don't be a wise guy."

I tilted my head back, and the hand that had previously been resting on my hip began to move. He brushed it along my stomach, then my chest, and all the way up to my throat, where he gently cupped my Adam's apple in his fingertips. With the gentlest of pressure, he twisted my head just enough to lay his lips to my ear. He dipped his tongue inside and sent shivers shooting down my spine.

I found my voice again after a quick but frantic search. This time, just to be *more* of a wise guy, I did my world-famous Judy Garland impersonation, which I had perfected during countless nights of watching old MGM musicals on the Movie Channel, back before I had Ben to occupy my evenings. "I know!" I sang out, all virginal and perky and sarcastic. "I'll get Mickey Rooney and the gang and we'll put on a show out back in the barn! We'll have singing and dancing and *everybody* will come! It'll be great!"

Ben chuckled. Then he started rumbling in a lascivious growl. "Keep that up and you'll be sorry. Judy Garland turns me on."

"And why would I be sorry if you got turned on?"

"Consider where you're lying, my love. Consider which way you're facing. Consider what's nestled up against your ass. Consider how powerful I am and how helpless you are. Consider—"

"Jeez. Okay. I get the picture. You're right. There'll be no more Judy impersonations from me." While my words were joking, I did indeed discover an all-new appreciation for the delicacy of my position. That's not to imply I hadn't been thinking about it already.

Inundated with a sudden surge of bravery, I scooted my ass a little farther back, pressing it against his cock and wiggling it around a little bit, just because I figured I wasn't driving him crazy enough already.

His strong fuzzy arms held me close. He gave a tremble as he arched his back to push his dick against me just a wee bit harder. I closed my eyes and loved every second of it. After all, it was all innocent flirtation, right? Nothing *invasive* was about to happen. Was it?

"So are you going to help us search or not?" he asked while his tongue slipped back in my ear.

I wiggled and squirmed and dripped a little more precome onto his thumb. "Wherest thou goest, I goest."

He gave a happy sigh. "I like the sound of that."

With a lapse in the conversation, Ben must have decided to go exploring. His lips slid a gentle trail along my spine, beginning at the spot where my head attached and working his way south to where my ass attached at the other end.

I immensely enjoyed the entire duration of his trip from one destination to the other, although by the time he arrived at the final stop, I was a bundle of shattered nerves indeed. I mean that in a good way.

The moment Ben's tongue grazed a path through the little patch of hair at the base of my spine, I was a jumble of exploding synapses.

"Hmm," he moaned, as his tongue slipped farther south. Rolling over onto me, Ben slid his hands beneath my thighs and hoisted my hips in the air so that my face was crammed into the pillow and my ass was aiming straight for his nose. As he lifted me a little higher, I felt my buttcheeks spread wider, and by that time I was sure I had few secrets left.

I knew this was true when Ben's hot mouth came down on my hole and his tongue shot out, seeking a home. I gasped when his warm tongue slid across my opening, oh so slowly. In fact, it was lingering more than moving.

It felt so wonderful, I stuffed the pillow in my mouth to keep from screaming.

"Hmm," he said again, as he lifted my ass even higher and his tongue traveled from my hole on a southern side trip along my perineum to pay a short visit to my balls. Ben had my butt lifted so high in the air by this point, he was up on his knees, and I was almost standing on my head.

He had barely said hello to my nuts when he was already kissing them good-bye and ambling along on the return trip to my hole. His tongue arrived there and slipped right in without knocking or ringing the doorbell or anything. Next thing I knew, I had two inches of tongue up my ass, and I was flailing like a grounded mackerel.

I slithered around on the end of his tongue, gasping and snorting and having the time of my life. Ben seemed to be enjoying himself too. With a trembling hand, I reached around behind me, grabbed a fistful of his short blond hair, and dragged his mouth down on me even harder.

"My baby likes this," he muttered into my ass. I wasn't sure, but I thought I heard an echo.

I couldn't very well deny the truth of his statement. "I do! I like it—oh God—I like it a lot!"

I liked it even more when Ben slipped his hand between my legs, and while still slavering away at my ass, scooped up my dick and gave it a couple of gentle strokes. You know, in case it wasn't hard enough already. I flopped around with my face crammed in the pillow, humping his fist and still yanking his mouth down onto my ass, and while I was doing all that, I was also making an executive decision.

"Fuck me," I gasped into the pillow.

Ben's mouth froze on my hole. His tongue made a couple more passes across my tender opening, and then it froze too.

"What did you say?" Ben asked, his voice weak, his diction blurred since he still had his tongue in my ass.

I swallowed back my fear and spoke the words again. "Fuck me."

Ben lifted his mouth from me and laid his face to the side of my hip, peeking around to where I was still practically standing on my head because of the way he had me propped up and doubled over in midair. He was still languidly stroking my cock while my balls bounced around on his wrist.

"Are you sure, baby?" he asked. "You've never done it before. I don't want to hurt you."

I slipped my other hand behind me, found his mouth, and poked my thumb inside it, just because it seemed the right thing to do. Ben started sucking on it, so I guess he thought it was the right thing to do too. After waiting for my answer for a moment, Ben spit my thumb out, moved his mouth back to my ass, and worshiped it a little more. I trembled, shuddered, gasped, and spread my legs as far as I could get them. I thought I heard a couple of hamstrings snap like rubber bands, but I wasn't sure. If it had been Thanksgiving, Ben could have yanked me apart and made a wish. Not that I would have cared. All I wanted was that hot mouth and that extremely talented tongue to continue doing what they were doing. And for the first time in my life, I wanted more too. I wanted much more.

It took a minute, but I finally found my voice again. "Fuck me, Ben. Use a lot of lube. It'll be all right. I don't want to be a virgin anymore. I want to feel you inside me. Please, Ben, do it now before I chicken out."

Once again he moved around to lay his cheek to my hip and gaze at my upside-down face in front of him. "I'm too big," he said.

"No. You're perfect. I want you inside me."

"Maybe we should try a vegetable first. We could start with a gherkin and work up to a cucumber."

"Oh, shut the hell up and just do it."

Ben flipped me over onto my back and crawled up to stare me straight in the eye. His hot breath flowed across my face like a summer wind, making me want him all the more.

"I've dreamed about this, baby," he said, his voice as brittle as parchment. "Promise me you'll stop me if I hurt you. All right?"

I snarled. "Hell yes, I'll stop you. I'm horny, not stupid. Now hurry. Please, Ben. I want you inside me *now*."

"You da boss."

He reached over the side of the bed and pulled open the nightstand drawer to fish around for what we needed. While he did that, I circled his cock with my hand, gauging the size of it—as if I hadn't done that a million times already. I swallowed hard and shot a brief prayer skyward.

With the implements he needed in hand, Ben slid his mouth over mine one last time before easing himself back on his haunches between my legs, which I had folded back like chicken wings until my knees were at my ears. He dipped his head to take my cock into his mouth, as if he needed another wee taste before getting down to the real business at hand. He then rose up again, ripped the condom wrapper open, and slowly and carefully rolled the rubber down his long, fat cock.

I could feel my eyeballs bulging out the front of my head. "My God, it's a bratwurst."

Ben growled. "Shut up."

Scooping me up with his broad hands, he lifted my ass again, this time while I was facing him, and when he had me where he wanted me, he covered my hole with his mouth once more.

I cried out and tugged at his hair, and when Ben rose up in front of me at last, he was smiling.

He popped the cap on a bottle of lotion and poured a big glob in his hand. After holding it there between his great paws for a minute to warm it up, he slathered it over his cock. Satisfied, he slopped another squirt of lotion onto my hole. When that job was finished, he wiped his hands on a corner of the sheet. I guess he didn't think I was lubed enough yet. Pushing my legs higher and wider, he spat a long stream of saliva, hitting my asshole dead center. I had to admit the guy had excellent aim.

Oh so gently he slid a finger into me. Then another. Sliding them in and out, I felt my jaw go slack. It felt so good. As I relaxed more and more, he slipped a third finger in. I arched my neck back and wondered if this was what it felt like to be an apple on a stick.

Opening my eyes, I smiled up at him in case he needed reassurance, which he didn't seem to. So then I cupped his face in my hands anyway, just to let him know I was still there. Like he didn't know that already. He slipped his fingers free, then got all squinty eyed and serious as he positioned the bulbous head of his cock to my teeny tiny opening. At his first gentle push inward, I squeezed my eyes shut and forced myself to relax.

"Baby," he muttered softly.

"Do it," I gasped. "Please, Ben. Do it."

To my utter amazement, I felt my anal ring open up and offer Ben the entryway he needed. It surprised me so, I gave a tiny cry. But it wasn't a cry of pain. It was a cry of joy. Ben knew it too. I could tell by the happy little guttural sound he made.

He lifted my ass higher, and gripping my hips, he carefully slid the head of his cock into me, one silly millimeter at a time.

"Yes," I sighed. I had expected pain, but this wasn't pain. This was *great*.

Ben continued to gently push. With half his length inside me, he stopped and let me grow accustomed to his girth. When I opened my eyes to stare up at him, he ever so gently eased himself deeper inside me.

"All the way, Ben," I gasped. "Don't stop. Take me all the way."

"My little trooper," he said. His voice was barely a croak by now. He stooped over me and covered my mouth with his as his cock slid ever deeper.

I sucked Ben's tongue into my mouth while I lay there impaled. It was the most erotic moment of my life. And the pain was minimal. I couldn't believe it.

Trembling above me, Ben breathed in my ear. "You did it, baby. You did it. It's all the way in."

I nodded against him, the stubble on our cheeks rasping together. "It is," I said. "It really is."

I gasped when his cock swelled inside me. But still it wasn't a gasp of pain. It was pure, unadulterated pleasure. "Now!" I said, breathless. "Do it, Ben. Please."

Ben slid his lips from my mouth, and taking a firmer grip on my hips, he lifted me higher as he himself rose up onto his knees.

Gently, still being careful, he began to ease his cock in and out of me. I fondled his arms and stroked his chest and pulled him closer with every thrust. I couldn't get enough. It was an incredible feeling. But my God, Ben's cock was so big! I felt like a Volkswagen with thirty-six people inside.

When I clutched his ass and tried to drag him even deeper, Ben must have decided my virginity was most assuredly a thing of the past, and he was finally convinced I didn't mind parting with it *one little bit*.

With a manly grunt, he began to move faster.

"Oh, God," he gasped. "You feel like honey."

He pierced me now as deeply as he could. Every stroke went straight to my heart. I felt his pubic hair tickling my hole. I felt his heavy balls slapping against my ass. I laughed out loud when his cock stroked through me and brushed my prostate. I liked it so much I grabbed his ears and almost ripped them off.

"Yeowch!" he cried, but he kept on pumping.

When he slowed his pace and leaned in to press his mouth to mine again, Ben's heart was hammering like crazy.

"I love this!" I gasped into his kiss. And almost before the words were out of my mouth, Ben gave a lurch and his cock swelled up inside me until I thought I would surely burst wide open.

He groaned and arched his back. His rhythm went haywire as he bucked and lunged uncontrollably against me as the come exploded from his body. Then he simply collapsed on top of me. One minute he was humping away, and the next minute he was a throw rug. He buried his face in the side of my neck, and with his pulsating cock still buried to the hilt inside me, he expelled every ounce of breath from his body, making himself even more of a throw rug.

Slowly, his cock began to wilt as well. We were both covered in sweat. We lay like that as if waiting to see if our overworked hearts were going to go kablooey and kill us dead. I was surprised when they didn't, and maybe Ben was too, because he suddenly opened his eyes and gazed down at me. A drop of sweat slid from the tip of his nose and landed on my lips. I hungrily licked it away.

"Oh, man," I mumbled, and I lifted my head and laid my mouth to his throat.

His Adam's apple bobbed up and down as he strove to speak, but words wouldn't come. He simply collapsed over me yet again, burying me in his heat and his strength and his gentleness. His scent was hypnotic. I closed my eyes and breathed him in, loving the feel of his softening cock inside me. Remembering how it felt when it was iron as well. Wondering how soon I could get it that way again.

Jesus, I thought. *I really am a slut.*

When his cock slid free of my grasp and I found myself empty beneath him, I wrapped my arms around his strong back and refused to let him move.

Slowly, he began to stir, his gentle fingers once again beginning to stroke, to touch, to savor. While his heartbeat slowed, and his panting ceased, I gently caressed the contours of his face and whispered loving words into his ear. Thanking him, thanking him.

He tasted my mouth for a brief moment, then played his kisses down my stomach until he found my cock, still hard and hungry. Still waiting. He slid me into his mouth and less than a minute later I was exploding beneath him. He drew my come from me like drawing water from a well. As I bucked and arched beneath him, he smiled around my cock, watching my face with those loving, azure eyes. He savored me until I had no more seed to spill.

Both of us exhausted at last, he let my dick slip from his lips and pressed his face into my stomach, holding me there against him. Calming my trembling. Calming his own.

When our hearts had finally stopped galloping, Ben slid upward and pulled me close against him. With his mouth to my ear, he spoke in such a breathless, tender voice, I could barely hear the words leaking from him.

"We have no more secrets, Shiloh. Now we know everything there is to know about each other. Please, baby. Tell me it's enough. Tell me it's enough to keep you happy."

"It's more than enough," I whispered back, still seeking my voice, still gasping for a breath of air. "Everything about you is more than enough."

A tear leaked from my eye, and Ben was right there to kiss it away.

He gathered me into those heavenly strong arms and kept me there as the night settled silently around us. The familiar feel of his skin and the gentle strength of his arms comforted me. They were the ship that carried me toward a lazy, contented sleep.

Each of us breathed in the air the other expelled, and in that effortless back and forth of love and commitment, we melted together. We became one. Stronger joined than we were apart. Stronger with every hour we were together. Stronger with every touch we shared.

Even amid all the romantic mooshy ponderings, it still crossed my mind as I snuggled into Ben's embrace that perhaps my ass would never be the same again. I couldn't see it, of course, but I suspected my hole was still so stretched out of whack, one could easily have driven a bus through it.

Then I blushed in guilty contentment, remembering how I'd enjoyed every single thing Ben had done to me. I bit back an embarrassed laugh and burrowed my face into Ben's armpit to hide myself even from me.

The most annoying thing about being in love is that your partner always knows what you're thinking.

"Don't worry," Ben whispered in my ear. "Your back door will close up again. I promise. Just give it a little time. And stay away from the Scottish curry until it does."

Chapter 12

THE NEXT morning all the treasure hunters gathered together in the lobby of the Belladonna Arms. Myself and Ben, Tom and Arthur, Barney and Ramon, Milan and Harlie, Charlie and Bruce, Roger and Stanley, Pete and Sylvia, and even little Artie, who was gumming one of his mother's Toll House cookies and had a slimy stream of chocolatey spit dribbling down his chest like an offshore drilling rig leaking crude oil.

Lester the librarian, in his little bow tie, was there too. He was on the arm of a brand-new tenant I had seen move in a couple of weeks earlier. The new tenant's name was Dan, and he too was sporting a bow tie and had his hair slicked back with a pound of Crisco. Clearly, the Belladonna Arms love pollen was still as potent and as shrewdly selective as ever. Golly, that stuff was a matchmaking powerhouse!

Dan even had a chain around his neck securing his glasses to his head, just like Lester. Maybe they shopped for accessories together at Geeks "R" Us.

Aside from Lester and Dan, the two resident neat freaks, everybody else was dressed in their rattiest clothes, obviously prepared to get down and dirty digging around for that three hundred thousand bucks.

Except for Arthur, of course. There was nothing ratty about Arthur. Ensemble-wise, Arthur had truly outdone himself.

He was wearing a woman's khaki safari ensemble, with shin-length culottes, brown leather boots with a four-inch heel that made me hurt just looking at them, and some sort of deadlyass riding crop in his hand that looked like a freeze-dried donkey dick. He also had a jaunty pith helmet that perched on his head like a UFO sitting atop Mount Baldy. The pith helmet had streamers of ribbons wrapped around it. The streamers draped down Arthur's back in an explosion of color and actually looked quite fetching. Strapped to his shoulders, for some bizarre reason, Arthur sported a pair of opaque angel wings, which flapped every now and then seemingly of their own accord. He looked like the first drag queen ever to set forth in search of the source of the Amazon dressed by the Looney Tunes wardrobe department.

Arthur's lover, Tom, was carrying a huge pink box packed with what must have been two hundred dollars' worth of donuts and various other assorted pastries, which everybody was dipping into like they hadn't eaten for a month. Thanks to the pastries, I suspected several of the attending asses would be considerably larger tomorrow than they were today.

And speaking of asses, mine was feeling just fine after my premiere adventure with anal sex the night before. My heinie had never felt better in fact. Or happier. Or more imbued with future purpose. I admit I was walking a little funny, but that had nothing to do with penetration. I was walking funny because I'd pulled something in my back while hanging upside down so Ben could go spelunking through my ass with his tongue.

Ben was being very solicitous this morning, by the way. The fact that I had entrusted him with the demise of my virginity seemed to mean a lot to him. His hand rested on my butt continually in a proprietary sort of way, which I thought was really romantic. In fact, I already had plans to give him another tour of the premises the first chance I got.

For somebody who had avoided anal sex for twenty-six years, now I couldn't go twenty-six *seconds* without longing for it again. Yes, I'm afraid a monster had been born, and Ben was the one who brought it to life. With a bang. (No pun intended.) Pastries were not the only commodity being offered. Arthur had a box of walkie-talkies he was passing out. Heaven knows where he got them, but judging by his ever-extensive wardrobe, frugality had never been high on Arthur's list of personality traits.

"I have no idea how to work these things," he said as he handed out the walkie-talkies, "but I'm sure there's somebody in this crowd of fruit cups butch enough to figure it out. We'll be able to communicate with each other, see? It'll be lovely. Sort of like a great big get-together where everybody is in a different room."

Ben groaned and whispered in my ear, "A great big get-together where everybody is in a different room? That makes a lot of sense. I can't believe I'm related to this guy."

"I know," I said. "Lucky you." The funny thing was, I meant it. "Your Uncle Arthur is the greatest guy I've ever met, Ben. I love him to death. You *are* lucky to be related to him."

His eyes softened and he stroked my ass. "Do you love *me* to death?"

I snuggled into his neck. "No, baby. I love *you* to infinity."

I slipped a hand under Ben's shirt to brush my fingers across his fuzzy, flat belly. Simply knowing what I was about to say made the blood rush to my face, but I didn't care. I said it anyway. "Let's sneak away from these people. I want to feel you inside me again."

Ben's eyes turned smoldery as all six feet five of him loomed over me, purring in my ear, "You don't have to ask twice. Come on. We'll be home and greased up before they know we're gone."

We were about to slip away when Arthur barked, "Where do you two think you're going? Get back here! I'm about to pass out assignments."

Ben frowned, but a frown wasn't good enough for me. I got downright testy. "Assignments? What is this, grade school?"

Apparently, nobody was allowed to mess with my new sex life without me getting snippy about it. Even I didn't see that one coming. Obsession was a new experience for me.

Ben patted me on the butt and cooed, "Later, baby. I promise."

Then he snagged us both a donut. It was no substitute for Ben's dick—hell it wasn't even cream filled—but it was better than nothing.

Arthur approached, all smiles. His wings were flapping like he was about to take off.

When he saw me staring at them, he leaned in and whispered, "Solar powered. They'll flap for three weeks if it doesn't rain. It's the latest technology."

I tried really hard not to twirl my finger at the side of my head to indicate he was crazy. Some people don't like that. "Well, golly, Arthur. What'll they think of next?"

Arthur had donut glaze on his chin, a sprinkling of coconut on his shoulder, a dollop of custard on his boot, and powdered sugar all over his tits. God knows how many donuts he'd eaten. With a wink, he passed me a walkie-talkie. Still grumpy about the sex thing, I growled and snatched it out of his hand.

He didn't notice. He was too busy wagging a finger in Charlie the Klepto's face, telling him he wanted that walkie-talkie back the minute the search was over. No sneaking off and selling it on eBay, to which Charlie looked guilty, disappointed, and mortally offended all at the same time.

Charlie was a conflicted soul.

Then Arthur spun back to me. "Yes, Shiloh, assignments! We're going to do this floor by floor. There's no other way to cover the building properly." He reached over and dragged Ben into the conversation. I mean, literally dragged him. "I want you two boys to cover the basement." He gave me a wink. "Your boyfriend here has darn near torn the place apart anyway. I might as well let him finish. The little scamp."

I suspected if Arthur ever found himself on the end of Ben's dick, he wouldn't be calling his nephew little *anything*.

While everyone fiddled around with their walkie-talkies, trying to figure out how they worked, Arthur tapped a bright red, three-inch-long fingernail (obviously a press-on) against a sheet of paper he had taped to the bank of mailboxes on the lobby's west wall.

When everybody blithely ignored him, occupied as they were with fiddling with their new walkie-talkies and snarfing down donuts, Arthur smacked the wall with his riding crop, and everybody jumped.

"Okay, girls," Arthur announced. Then he straightened his pith helmet, giggled, and gave his lover a wink, "You too, Tom." Here, Arthur's wings went into a little spasm of excited fluttering, like he'd just had a power surge. The sun must have coughed up a sunspot. Arthur went on. "I've posted everybody's search assignments. Like I said, we'll be doing it by floors. From the basement, right up to the roof." He flapped a limp wrist at Lester and Dan, the newbies. "You two will be searching the grounds."

The two bow-tied geeks gazed shyly at each other while their ears turned red. Yep. They'd definitely been love-pollened.

Arthur scanned all the faces. Then he adjusted his tits, causing a cascade of powdered sugar to rain down and sprinkle the blob of custard on his boot. "If Captain Blue Eyes really did plant three hundred thousand bucks of stolen cash on the premises, one of us is bound to find it! By my calculation, if we split the loot sixteen ways, we'll each come out with a little less than twenty thousand bucks apiece. A nice piece of change by anybody's reckoning."

Excited looks were swapped around. A few greedy mumbles could be heard. Little Artie burped. Then he screamed loud enough to make everybody clutch their hearts. A couple of donuts hit the floor. Muttering apologies to her startled neighbors, Sylvia poked another Toll House cookie into the kid's mouth, and he immediately quieted down.

The horde swept in to check the list on the wall. Everyone except Ben and me. We already knew we would be searching the basement.

I wasn't sure which *part* of the basement we would be searching, since Ben had already turned it upside down looking for the money on his own. But I knew there was no way out of this. Arthur was on a tear, brooking no opposition, and even Tom looked wearily resigned to the inevitable.

Ben, on the other hand, wasn't resigned at all. Ben was actually trembling with anticipation, eager to begin. He tried to hide it from me, but I saw the excitement in his eyes.

God help me, I still thought the whole enterprise was a waste of time. But I also knew I was in love with Ben, and loving him, the least I could do was overlook this one little obsession of his. After a few hours of misery, crawling through the bowels of the Belladonna Arms, I could then drag Ben upstairs, rip his clothes off, and have my way with him. That was my goal. That's all I cared about. Everybody else saw monetary gain at the end of this fiasco. All I saw was a Ben-induced orgasm and another chance to stretch my—horizons.

I jumped when Ben exclaimed, "It works! The walkie-talkie works!"

While everybody abandoned the list on the wall and swooped in on Ben for a quick lesson in the dynamics of wireless communication, I just stood back and watched the show.

Arthur took the opportunity to snatch up a caramel log and a chocolate donut.

BEN AND I were alone at last.

I rubbed my hands together and, overriding my better judgment, tried to appear determined.

"The quicker we find the money, the quicker we can fool around," I announced.

Ben came up behind me, tucked a finger in the neck of my shirt to drag it down out of the way, and slid his tongue across my second vertebrae, causing my sphincter to contract. Who knew one erogenous zone led directly to another?

"My baby's feeling amorous," he mumbled against my skin.

"You're not helping," I griped.

Ben laughed, and to my utter dismay, exclaimed, "You're right. Let's get down to work."

With his hands at my waist, and his chin digging into my shoulder, the two of us stood there surveying the laundry room. It was probably the last place in all the world I wanted to be.

"Maybe the money is hiding in that bigass pile of filthy lint wadded up in a disgusting ball over there in the corner. Doesn't anybody ever clean this place?"

"Uncle Arthur expects the tenants to keep it clean on the honor system."

"Well, that's working out well."

Ben gave me a commiserating pat on the ass, causing my sphincter to contract again, then pulled open the broom closet door and peered inside. As far as I could determine, the broom closet was the only part of the building actually filthier than the laundry room.

I pointed to a row of shelves above a utility sink. "What's that louvered thingie on the wall up there?"

"Wow," Ben said, ruffling my hair, "Good eye. I've been in here a dozen times and never noticed that before."

He climbed into the sink and, standing on tiptoes, peered at the object I had pointed out.

"It's a ventilation shaft."

"Open it up," I said. "Let's see what's inside."

"Good idea," Ben said. He pulled a screwdriver from his back pocket (how butch was that?), crammed it through the vent, and pried the plate loose from the wall with a screech.

A torrent of cockroaches spilled out.

I screamed and took off running while Ben started flailing in front of the sink, trying to knock the creatures off his clothes, all the while flapping his arms around and bellowing like a bull.

Two seconds later, he raced through the door to join me in the hall. His eyes were as big as ostrich eggs and a cockroach was perched on his shoulder looking around like he was on a tour bus.

I finger-flipped the cockroach in the head, and he went sailing through the air.

Ben watched him go. "Thanks," he said to me.

"I think the laundry room's secure. Let's move on."

Ben still looked a little bug-eyed, but he was obviously braver than I. "No. We still have to search it. Come on. I need your help."

So I helped. Still tap-dancing around a scurrying parade of cockroaches, we checked everywhere. Around the baseboards looking for loose panels, beneath the washers and dryers in case Captain Blue Eyes was crazy enough to bury his loot under the floor beneath the appliances. Everywhere.

An hour later, sweating bullets and peeling the dust bunnies off our shoes, we gave up.

The furnace room was next. It wasn't really a furnace room anymore, of course. The Belladonna Arms had been built over eighty years ago. Electric wall heaters had been installed in the apartments along about the time Hula-Hoops hit the stores, leaving the monstrous coal-burning furnace to gather rust and probably go condo for throngs of some disease-bearing vermin or other. Even disease-bearing vermin like a nice place to live.

We both cast a leery eye at the furnace door.

"Have you looked in there?" I asked.

He shook his head. "Not yet."

"You want me to do the honors?"

He gazed at me, stunned, but hopeful. "Really?"

"Hell no. I'm not looking in there."

He sighed. "That's what I thought."

Taking a deep breath, Ben lifted the handle on the furnace door and yanked it open. A rat fell out and landed on his foot.

I was hard-pressed to determine who looked more surprised: Ben or the rat.

Two seconds later I was standing out in the hall waiting for Ben to join me again.

When he did, he didn't appear as bug-eyed as before, but he didn't seem particularly calm either.

"Good grief, Ben, you're jumpier than I am. How did you search this building when you were doing it by yourself?"

"Simple. Before, when I was sneaking around searching for the money, I was trying to look butch to impress you. Now that I've actually won you, I don't have to look butch anymore. I can be myself."

"You're as big a coward as I am."

He grinned. "I know. Who'd have thunk?"

"It's a good thing God gave you a big dick."

"I know. It was quite a boon."

"Where'd the rat go?" I asked.

"He got all snooty and started mumbling to himself. Then he crawled back into the furnace."

"I hate it when rats do that."

I pulled a flashlight from my back pocket. Ben wasn't the only one who had tools on his person. Of course, my flashlight was pink and had Hello Kitty on it. Frankly, I'd rather have had a Hello Kitty shotgun. "Maybe we'd better just take a peek inside that furnace, shall we?"

Ben bent low and gave me a salami-salami-baloney bow to wave me forward. "Absolutely, dearest. Feel free to do all the peeking you want. Love the flashlight, by the way. Very manly."

"Oh, hush," I muttered.

Ben followed me back into the furnace room, where I very carefully poked my nose through the furnace door and, in the flashlight beam, gave a cursory glance inside.

"Nope," I said. "No bags of money in there."

"Well, poop," Ben said, peering in beside me and sounding even jitterier than I did. "I see that rat, though. He's back there in the corner. See him? He looks like he's loading an itty bitty Uzi. Or that could be my imagination."

"You think?"

The walkie-talkie in my back pocket came to life with a staticky *screech*, and Ben and I jumped straight up into the air, banging our heads on the furnace door.

"Shiloh? Ben? You there? Come in? Come in? How do you work this fucking thing?"

By sheer, blind luck I found the proper button and pushed it. "We're here. Charlie, is that you? What's up?"

Charlie's voice was all squelched and distorted. He sounded like he had his head up a cow's ass. "Bruce and I are on the second floor. We just tore out the trap in the utility room sink."

"Find any stolen cash?"

"No, but we found out why that sink never worked."

"Why's that?"

"It had two socks, a dishrag, and a bunch of used condoms crammed in it."

"How the hell did the condoms get in there?"

"Don't wanta know," Charlie said. "Don't wanta think about."

We heard another voice in the background. Charlie came back on and said, "Bruce wants you to know we may have inadvertently flooded the building."

"Okay, then," I said. "Thanks for the update. Gotta run." With that, I clapped the antenna shut and hastily stuffed the walkie-talkie back in my pocket.

"Probably for the best," Ben mumbled. "Floods are biblical. I don't do floods. And somebody else's used condoms just flat-out freak me out. Oh, look. The rat's back."

I turned and saw the rat peering over the edge of the furnace door, staring directly at us.

Two seconds later I was panting in the hall. This time Ben actually got there first. Was it my imagination, or was I beginning to see a pattern here?

There was a fat round air shaft that traversed the entire length of the basement corridor, and it was hanging right over our heads. The pipe started rattling somewhere off in the distance, and then the rattling noise came rushing down upon us like somebody had rolled a bowling ball through the thing. As soon as the bowling ball reached us, it turned into an ear-splitting scream.

It sounded terrified.

It sounded human.

It sounded like Arthur. In fact, it *was* Arthur. Suddenly we could hear him ranting and raving one floor up.

"Kittens? More kittens? That slutty Wilhelmina has gone too far this time! Her other kittens are barely weaned! What did she do, post an Open House sign on her twat? Doesn't she have any sense of restraint? Doesn't she have any morals?"

I grabbed my walkie-talkie. "Arthur? It's Shiloh. What's happening?"

"Kittens!" he screamed. "There's a litter of brand-new baby kittens under the stairs coming off the lobby. We barely found homes for that hussy's last litter of kittens. There'll be cats all *over* the place now! Barney and Ramon are in big, big trouble. Heads will roll for this. Heads will roll!"

Somebody said, "Uh-oh," on the open line. It sounded like Ramon.

"Now, now," we heard Tom crooning in the background. "Look how cute they are. Their little eyes aren't even open yet. And there's only eight of them."

"*Eight?*" Arthur screamed. He ranted on for a minute—cussing, bellowing, threatening. Then the ranting abruptly stopped. "Oh, darn," he muttered calmly. "Look at this. I broke a wing."

With that, the walkie-talkie switched off, and I glanced over at Ben to see him rolling his eyes so far up into his head he almost fell over sideways.

"Auntie Arthur. The schizo queen." He looked me square in the eye and groaned. "I guess I'll be adopting a cat."

"Yeah, well. Join the crowd," I said. "Shall we proceed?"

"Yes, let's."

Next to the furnace room, we found a room I had never been in before. It seemed to be sort of an all-around depository for everything anybody didn't want. Broken bed frames, stained mattresses, assorted pieces of mismatched furniture, antique ovens and refrigerators, bags of clothes and bedding and old drapes, a couple of bicycles that looked like they had seen better days, and books. Tons and tons of books.

Ben sifted halfheartedly through a pile of kitchen pots and pans. "This must be where Arthur dumps the stuff people leave behind when they move out."

I heaved up an exasperated sigh. "Plus all the furnishings and appliances that don't survive from one tenant to the next. Good Lord, Ben, we could search in here for a month and never find what we're looking for, even if it was right under our nose."

The walkie-talkie *screeched.* I was getting used to the damn thing. I only jumped about an inch this time.

"This is Milan and Harlie. Anybody listening?"

Several people spoke up in various levels of electronically distorted gibberish. As did I. "Ben and Shiloh here. What's up?"

"Watch out for rats!" Milan announced. "We just found a nest of the little bastards behind the electric panel on the third floor! There must have been a gazillion of them!"

Someone else piped up. "Oh yeah? Well, we found rats in the trash chute off five. Big, fat monsters as big as guinea pigs!"

And yet another person got in on the act. "The utility closet on six is packed with them too. Arthur really needs to stop buying ball gowns and eyeliner and spring for an exterminator instead. This place is Rat City!"

Arthur's booming falsetto couldn't be mistaken for anything but Arthur's booming falsetto. He sounded insulted to the core. "Who said that? Who said that? I *need* my ball gowns! I *need* my eyeliner!"

We heard a series of "Seeya's" and "Gotta run's" and "Over and outs," and then the walkie-talkie fell dead in my hand. Suddenly it was so quiet I thought I heard crickets, which wasn't surprising. The Belladonna Arms had every other kind of vermin. Why not crickets?

Ben snickered. "Nobody wants to aggravate the landlord. Probably wise."

He was still surveying the wasteland of discarded objects in front of us. "Look, Shiloh. Most of this stuff looks too recent to have been around in 1976. If crazy Captain Blue Eyes stashed any money here, I'd be really surprised. Let's search somewhere else."

"Fine," I said, more than relieved. "I don't want to dig through this crap either."

Ben breathed a sigh of relief. "Good. Want to take another gander at the party room?"

"Another gander at the party room sounds lovely. After you, my love."

"No, no. After *you*."

Arm in arm, we toddled off to the party room.

Nothing had changed, of course. The party room looked the same as it had the last time we were there: Dirty tables decorated with dead flowers. A plethora of mismatched chairs scattered around. A decrepit stage in front of a dusty dance floor. Dust bunnies sliding around as Ben and I stirred the air. Drooping garlands of limp crepe paper swagged across the ceiling. And in the middle of it all hung that bigass disco ball, looking like the Death Star powering up to obliterate Alderaan.

Once again, the walkie-talkie roared to life in my back pocket.

"Skunks!" somebody screamed. It sounded like Lester the librarian. "Dan and I just ran into a family of skunks inside the toolshed at the back of the building! *Aaackk*! What do we do? What do we do?"

Ben snatched the walkie-talkie out of my hand. I guess he figured since he was the only country boy in the building, he was the one who should be passing out skunk advice.

"Did one of them spray you, Lester?"

To which Lester and Dan *both* screamed, wailing right over each other and gasping for breath. "No! They all sprayed us! The whole damn family. The mama, the papa, and the three little black and white brats. We're dripping with skunk piss! Oh God, I think I'm going to barf."

Ben *tsk*ed, looking all professorial and annoying. God, he was cute. "Well, now, it's not actually skunk piss, you know. It's actually a mixture of chemicals called mercaptans that are exuded through the skunk's anal glands and used as a defense mechanism against predators. One fascinating side note, Lester, it's actually strong enough to ward off grizzly bears, so I suppose—"

Arthur barged in, sounding both impatient and embarrassed. "Oh, shut up, Ben. What are you, the skunk whisperer? Lester, Dan, I'm sorry, boys. I meant to warn you about those skunks, but in all the excitement, I forgot. On the bright side, don't you think it's lovely to see a little bit of nature here in the big city? Don't you think it's refreshing to know that wild animals can still live free among—"

Lester didn't sound refreshed; he sounded mad. "*Lovely*? You think it's *lovely*? Dan and I are ruined for life! You come down here and smell this shit, Arthur, and see how lovely *you* think it is!"

The poor guy sounded like he was talking underwater. His salivary glands must have kicked into hyperdrive.

"Well, it's not actually skunk shit either—" Ben interrupted, but that's as far as he got. This time *I* snatched the walkie-talkie away to shut him up. In emergency situations, cuteness only goes so far.

It was Arthur's Tom who finally came to the rescue. "Okay, guys, don't panic. And whatever you do, don't come inside the building! I'll run to the store for a fifty-gallon drum of tomato juice, and we'll get you both deskunked as soon as possible. Just hang in there. And you might want to take your clothes off. That'll help."

There was a spate of silence, and then suddenly Lester didn't sound quite so mad. "Both of us? Naked? In the toolshed? I guess we could do that if it's the only way."

"Okay by me," Dan said around a snort. It wasn't a "holy cow, I've been sprayed by a skunk" snort. It sounded more like an *intrigued* snort. "In dire straits you have to do what you have to do, right?" Then I heard a smile enter Dan's voice. "Ooh, thank you, Lester, love. That's a *big* help."

"So I see," Lester crooned right back. "And it's getting bigger all the time."

"You ain't seen nothing yet. You know, you don't smell so bad naked."

"Neither do you. Since both of us stink, one sort of neutralizes the other. Oh golly, Dan, do that again."

Ben whispered in my ear, "Boy, that love pollen is powerful stuff. It even works through skunk juice."

"Well, it's not actually skunk juice—" I began, but Ben groaned and flapped me to silence.

Arthur came on and announced, "Tom is on the way! He'll toss you a couple of blankets on his way out. Just hang in there, boys. Did you get those smelly old clothes off? Are you naked, Lester?"

"Just about," Lester mumbled. It sounded like he had something in his mouth. "Getting naked as we speak."

"Me too," Dan mumbled. A moment later he was pleading. "Oh, wait, Lester. Leave the bow tie on. Just the bow tie."

"I will if you will."

"Deal." There was a short pause interrupted by the sound of grunts and groans and a gentle gasp or two. Then Dan gulped and said, "Oops, maybe we'd better turn this thing off."

"Oh my," we heard Arthur say when Lester's walkie-talkie went dead.

To my surprise, Ben scooped me into his arms. Snuggling into my ear, he whispered, "You'd look good in nothing but a bow tie too."

I blushed. "Thanks."

"Okay, back to work," Ben announced, rubbing his hands together. The next thing I knew, he was crawling around the floor, tapping on the floorboards yet again, listening for hollow spaces where a big glob of stolen money might be stashed. Since I was feeling guilty just standing there watching him, I started halfheartedly banging on the walls so I wouldn't appear as worthless as I really was.

Suddenly Ben jumped up and pulled me away from the wall and into another one of his spectacular embraces.

"You're bipolar, aren't you," I commented drily. "Or at the very least, attention deficit."

"I'm worse than that," he said. I thought he appeared troubled for some reason, but it must have been my imagination. Ben wasn't *that* crazy, was he?

But just in case he was crazy and I had simply never noticed it before, I came up with a plan to take his mind off it. Still cooing, and still snuggling, I decided to twist around in Ben's arms to present my ass to him in the hopes that it might give him a few ideas other than knocking on floors and walls. (That's what monkeys do to instigate sex, and since I was a primate too, I figured it might work for me as well. What's the point of having monkey ancestors if you're not going to tap into the monkey genomes now and then?) I was about to do exactly that, when lo and behold, Ben breathed into my ear, "I have an idea."

Was I good, or what? I hadn't really presented my ass to him yet, and he already had an idea. My heart did an excited patter, and I snagged Ben's belt buckle to drag him closer.

"What idea is that, baby?" Like I didn't know. "What'd you have in mind? Huh? Just tell me what you want. I'm up for it, whatever it is. We've been searching for hours. I'm hungry. I'm sweaty. I'm stinky. A change of pace would be great." I shot him a sexy wink, just to let him know I really *was* as slutty as he might be hoping I was.

Ben slid his tongue in my ear. "That's my boy. Since I'm too big to get all the way inside—"

"Don't be silly, you big galoot. You got all the way inside last night."

But Ben hadn't finished yet. "—like I was saying, since I'm too big to get all the way inside, why don't you climb into the dumbwaiter and see if you can stand up."

That wasn't the suggestion I'd expected. "Say what?"

"Climb into the dumbwaiter."

"With the bugs and the rats?"

"Yeah. The money might be hidden up there."

"What about sex?"

"Who said anything about sex?"

I peeled myself out of his arms and stuck my fists on my hips like Mrs. Butterworth on her fake-maple-syrup jug. Not butch, I know, but it was the best I could do on the spur of the moment.

"It's filthy in there!"

"You can buy a lot of soap with twenty thousand bucks."

"Fine," I growled. "I'll climb in the dumbwaiter."

"Good man."

Sputtering insults, I turned my back on Ben (not like a horny monkey but more like a huffy boyfriend) and headed for the stupid dumbwaiter. Avoiding the fossilized bagel at all costs, I crawled through the hole in the wall with my trusty Hello Kitty flashlight held out in front of me like a light saber. Taking a deep breath, I stood up on trembly legs and looked around with considerable trepidation.

Ben's hands were clutching my ankles as if he was ready to yank me out of there at the first sign of trouble. If I wasn't so mad at him, I would have allowed myself to feel comforted by that thought. As it was, however, I just found it annoying.

"You're cramping my style," I said. "Let loose of my feet."

Blowing a cobweb out of my face, I tried to follow the flashlight beam straight up the dumbwaiter shaft to see what I could see. It didn't take me long to realize there wasn't much there except filth and spiderwebs and really creepy shadows, some of which even my flashlight wouldn't penetrate.

"I want to talk to you," Ben said down below, clutching my ankles all the tighter.

A spider skittered across my face and I stretched my mouth wide in a silent scream, too startled to make a sound. I did manage to start puffing air like a locomotive, though. I was up for that.

"You're hyperventilating," Ben said. "Don't be upset. It's nothing bad."

To my amazement, I found my voice. "Jeez, you have a high opinion of yourself, Ben! I'm not hyperventilating because of *you*! A spider just ran across my face!"

"And you were afraid it was poisonous?"

"No, but I am now! Thanks a lot. I'm coming out."

"No! Stay in there. I want to talk to you where you can't see me."

I was in no mood to argue. "Why the hell don't you want me to see you? If you want to talk to me, you can do it to my face. I hate this place! I'm coming out."

"Oh God," Ben murmured, more to himself than to me, but he released my ankles.

Another spider chose that moment to dangle down in front of my face on the end of a spiderweb and wave hello, so I thought now would be a really good time to freak out. Which I did. Slapping the spider away with a shriek (I found my voice that time), I dropped onto my ass and wiggled out of the dumbwaiter so fast I raised a cloud of dust. I accidentally kicked the fossilized bagel and it went flying across the room. I shot out of that hole in the wall in full hysteria mode, dancing around, shuddering, flapping my clothes. When I was finished with all that, I finally centered my attention on Ben, who was standing there looking even more uncomfortable than I did.

"What's wrong with you?" I asked. "I'm the one having a panic attack."

He didn't answer, but he did reach over and pluck a cobweb out of my hair. I noticed his hand was shaking, which surprised me.

"Thanks. Spit it out, Ben. What were you talking about while I was in there?"

"I was talking about what I wanted to talk to you about."

"Well, now, there's a wonderful sentence."

"Don't be mean."

He dropped to his knees in front of me, which surprised me even more.

"What the hell are you doing? Are you nuts? Get up."

"No. I want to talk."

"On your knees?"

"Yes!" he yelled, as if he'd suddenly snagged a little gumption out of midair.

"Fine!" I yelled right back. I had already found my gumption. In fact I was packed to the gills with it. "So talk already!"

His fingers dipped under the cuff of my pant leg and he gently cupped my calf muscle, rustling through the hair on my leg with his thumb. If he had done that in the dumbwaiter, I'd have probably fainted, thinking it was a rat. But doing it here, with Ben on his knees in front of me, it gave me goose bumps. They weren't the nervous, scary, dumbwaitery kind of goose bumps either. They were the other kind. The sexy kind.

"Why are you touching me like that, Ben? I thought you didn't want to fool around."

"I love you," he said.

I heaved a sigh. Taking a teeny step closer, I cupped his head in my hands and pulled his face to my stomach, holding him there against me. I softened my voice. You almost have to when your heart is melting.

"Fine, baby. You want to get romantic, we'll get romantic. I love you too. There, now. Is that what you wanted to hear?"

He gazed up at me with pale, stricken eyes. "You're the best thing that ever happened to me, Shiloh."

I stroked his cheek with my filthy hand, leaving a smear of dust behind. "What's wrong?" I asked gently. "What are you trying to say? Why are you looking so scared?"

Ben's face softened in a guilty smile. He inhaled a great gulp of air while his eyes never once left my face.

"I don't want to be lovers anymore, Shiloh."

"You—*what*?"

"I don't want to be lovers anymore. It's not enough. I want more."

I suddenly heard my pulse thudding inside my head. I stammered out an answer. "I—I don't understand. Ben, I don't know what you're trying to say."

He pressed his face to my stomach and sucked in another barrelful of air. When he tilted his head back and gazed up at me again, there was a shimmer of tears in his eyes.

"I want us to get married, baby. I want you to be my husband. I want us both to be husbands. Legally. I'll be yours, and you'll be mine."

I expelled the word on a breath of air as if I'd never heard it before. "Husbands—"

"Yeah. Husbands."

"You mean like honest-to-God marriage? Like, you know—*marriage*?"

Ben reached up and laid his hand over my hammering heart. "What we have isn't enough anymore, Shiloh. I want everything. I want it all. I love you so much I can barely function on a day-to-day basis. Last night when you trusted me enough to—you know—make love to you the way I did, it meant a lot to me, baby. It was as if we had torn down the very last barrier to us sharing everything we could be to each other. I didn't think it was possible, but it made me love you even more than I already did. Shiloh, I didn't know I had this much love in me. I didn't. But I know it now. I also know what I have to do." He took another long shuddering breath. "So—so here I am, doing it."

With that final sentence out of the way, he smiled a guilty smile and simply clammed up. But even clamming up, his eyes never once left my face. Those big, solemn, scared-to-death eyes.

I stood there, gazing down at him, my mind a blank. My throat had clogged up. It felt like somebody had stuffed a beach towel in there. I couldn't have said another word if I wanted to.

I was just about to try anyway, when the walkie-talkie in my back pocket crackled to life.

Arthur's booming falsetto wail, shredded with emotion, tore through the party room. "Say yes, Shiloh! Good Lord, man, what the hell are you waiting for?" Then there was a great honking sound like someone had stepped on a duck. Arthur was blowing his nose.

Ben still knelt there staring up at me, his eyes as full of pleading as they had been before. Yet even in the middle of that pleading gaze, he still managed to make a joke. "Uh-oh. The landlord's involved. Now you have to say yes."

I stroked Ben's upturned cheek for a moment and stared into his worshiping eyes. As if someone had yanked a rug out from under me, I collapsed to my knees and pressed my face to Ben's chest. His arms circled me, making me feel safe and loved, just as they always did. He kissed my hair, briefly turned his head to spit out a cobweb, then kissed my hair again.

Ben, the room, the walkie-talkie, everything fell silent for a minute while my mind raced around trying to figure out what I was actually thinking. It felt like I was in a time warp. For the life of me, I couldn't think of one single reason to say no. Not one.

"I love you too, you know," I finally breathed.

Ben's eyes were suddenly alive with hope. The fear fell away. "I know."

"I love you more than anything."

"I know that too."

"So, I guess, uh—yes," I said softly. "I'll be your husband. As long as you're the one who tells my mother."

"Hell, I'll tell everybody!" Ben yelled, dragging me into such an embrace a bunch of cartoony stars and canaries started spinning around my head. When he saw me gasping for air and looking stunned, he relaxed his hold, and said, "Breathe, baby, breathe."

Arthur asked anxiously in a staticky voice from somewhere over our heads, "Is he still alive, Ben, or did you scare him to death? Are we having a wedding or a funeral? Which is it?"

Ben was still laughing. "A wedding, I think. He's looking like I beaned him with a shovel, but he's still alive."

"And he said yes?"

"He said yes."

A chorus of cheers erupted through the walkie-talkie. Pete, Sylvia, Stanley, Roger—they were all laughing and hooting. Even little Artie broke into his ambulance wail, but I doubt if my sudden betrothal had anything to do with it. He probably wanted another cookie. Ben squeezed me tight *again*, and this time I thought I heard a lung pop. Then, laughing, he cupped my face in his hands and kissed me everywhere he could reach.

Blinded by tears and smothered with kisses, I felt Ben's warm, gentle mouth brush my ear. He whispered the words I thought I had heard in a dream months before, when I lay sleeping in his arms. Back when we barely knew each other. I knew now I hadn't been dreaming that night at all. He had truly said the words then, just as he was saying them now.

"It's you, Shiloh. It's only you."

I squeezed my eyes shut, letting the words burn through me like a cleansing flame, freeing me of doubt, bathing me in contentment. Making me whole. Making *us* whole. Making us one.

"Thank you for wanting me," I said.

"Thank you for wanting me back."

"Love pollen," I murmured, and Ben smiled.

"We're going to get married," he whispered in my ear.

"Husbands," I whispered back. "I'll be yours, and you'll be mine. It's meant to be, Ben. I know it is. But you can still be the one who tells my mother."

Chapter 13

LEANING BACK in Ben's arms, with my head tucked under his chin, I stared out at the setting sun as it hovered low on the city skyline. The sky was dressed in tangerine streaks. Seagulls swooped down the hill toward the bay, probably hoping for a fish dinner. Ben took my hand and held it alongside his. Our new silver wedding bands shone in the last gasp of pastel sunlight streaming through the bedroom window.

"Look at 'em sparkle," Ben said.

I wiggled my finger around and the fiery light danced across my hand. "They're beautiful."

Ben checked his watch. "It's almost party time."

We were decked out in our Scottish work drag. Not for work, but for the party. If for no other reason than we loved to see each other in kilts. Kilts, sporrans, white fluffy shirts, kneesocks, and boots. As usual, the sight of Ben in Scottish Highlander garb made my hormones ignite. My God, he was a handsome man.

No, wait. He wasn't just a handsome man. He was also a handsome husband.

We had married at the courthouse that afternoon. Not in kilts, mind you, but in suits and ties and freshly shined shoes, our neckties crisply knotted, our cheeks flushed with love. The only witness to the ceremony was my mother, who, in honor of the occasion, wore *two* sprigs of baby's breath in her hair. Arthur had pleaded to attend too, but we politely turned him down. We suspected my mother would have enough on her plate, what with it being her only son's gay marriage and all. She might not have the emotional wherewithal to also handle a three-hundred-pound weeping drag queen.

Either that, or she would have scared Arthur to death. Ila Smart was a powerful entity.

Oddly enough, my mother was clearly fascinated by the whole gay marriage experience. Her only comment was a haughty, "Liza Epstein's son married a woman. How boring is that?" Then she leaned in and whispered in my ear, "Are you sure this is legal?"

"It's in the Constitution now, Ma," I whispered back. "Even the Supreme Court said it's legal."

"Oh, good. I'd hate for you to get arrested. Liza Epstein's son was arrested once, you know."

"What'd he do?"

"Played with himself on a city bus. At least you had the foresight to do it in the bathroom."

"I was fourteen, Ma. I played with myself everywhere. You only *caught* me in the bathroom. Besides I didn't have a bus pass."

My mother huffed. "For good reason, apparently."

Ben hushed us to silence when the clerk bustled in to perform the ceremony.

Before the clerk could begin, my mother edged her way between Ben and me like a carving knife slicing through a roast. She cleared her throat to get the clerk's attention, and said, "These boys are gay, you know."

The clerk bit back a grin and said, "I suspected as much."

To my surprise, Ben reached over and planted a kiss on my mother's cheek, making her face blossom to the exact same shade of red as her hair. Clairol Intense Red. Apparently she had the same reaction to Ben's kisses as I always did.

"Oh my," she said in a fluttery voice as she stepped back out of the way to let the ceremony begin, all the while flapping a hand in front of her face like she was having a hot flash.

I smiled now at the thought.

Still standing at the bedroom window with our wedding day winding down behind us and that gorgeous tangerine sky splayed out across the horizon, Ben pressed his lips to the palm of my hand.

"We're going to be very happy, you know. Even your mother said so."

"Then we're safe. Jewish mothers are never wrong."

"Liza Epstein seems to have made some mistakes."

"Liza Epstein's a poor example. Her son's a pervert, and her stuffed bell peppers suck."

We scoped ourselves out in the closet mirror. Ben—blond, pale, and beautiful, and a head taller than me. Me—shorter, red-haired, and happier than I had ever been in my life. Even staring into the mirror, Ben did not actually study his own reflection. His eyes were centered solely on me.

"I love you," he said for the hundredth time that day.

And for the hundredth time that day, I almost swooned at the words. "You know I love you too."

Ben clutched my hand a little tighter. "Yes," he said. "I know."

It was two weeks after the big treasure hunt. Ben seemed to have finally lost all interest in the enterprise. He hadn't snooped around the Belladonna Arms, poking in dark corners and prying up floorboards, since he proposed to me in the party room amid a sea of cobwebs and dust bunnies. I presumed he was too wrapped up in our upcoming nuptials to worry about hidden treasure. We still spotted a few other tenants crawling about the building, lurking among the shadows and hoping to strike it rich, but I figured I had my treasure right there beside me already, so why look for more? Ben simply clucked his tongue at the treasure hunters and, shaking his head, looked the other way, as if disbelieving people could be so gullible.

No one is more pious than a reformed hooker.

I nuzzled Ben's neck. "Thank you for last night. And this morning. And two hours ago right after the ceremony."

Ben nuzzled back. "My baby can't get enough."

"It's amazing I can still walk. God, I love it when you're inside me."

Ben slid his fingers through my hair, and held me close. Even now, I could feel our two cocks lengthening against each other beneath the kilts.

He groaned. "We'd better go before I start ripping your clothes off. If we're late for our own party, Uncle Arthur will kill us. He's gone to a lot of trouble. The party room looks incredible."

"I know. And he invited my mother. Probably not the smartest thing he could have done, but at least it will be interesting."

Ben snickered. "Has she ever even *seen* a drag queen?"

"Well, certainly not one of Arthur's caliber."

"Who's picking her up?"

"Arthur's other half. Tom actually knows her. She buys knishes at his deli."

"Oh, good, the sanest man in the building. Maybe he can help ease your mom over the hump."

"I don't know. Arthur is a big hump to ease oneself over. Especially since this is a special occasion. God knows what your uncle will be wearing."

"No kidding."

Since being guests of honor at a party is a nerve-wracking business at best, and since we were already in Scottish drag anyway, Ben and I tossed back two shots of scotch each to help calm our frazzled nerves. Thus braced, we kissed Yolanda good-bye and headed for the door.

Just before we reached it, the phone rang. It was my mother.

"I'm wearing the dress I wore to your bar mitzvah."

"You mean it still fits?"

"What the heck is *that* supposed to mean, Mr. Snooty Britches?"

"Sorry I spoke. Just please leave the flowers out of your hair."

"I'll do no such thing. Will there be other queer boys there?"

"Gay, Ma. We prefer to be called gay. And yes, everybody in this building is queer—I mean gay—except for Sylvia, who recently had a sex change and is now a woman, and little Artie, who's six months old and hasn't come out one way or another yet. Apparently he's still on the fence."

"I saw a special on PBS about sex change operations. It's really quite fascinating. I wonder if Sylvia will show me her newly constructed doodah."

"Oh God, Ma, please don't ask."

"I suppose you're right. It might seem nosy."

"You think?"

On an afterthought, she added. "Little Artie. What a cute name. I do so love babies."

"I know you do. But take my advice. Stay downwind."

"Gotcha. You were stinky at that age too." She hummed a couple of bars of the *Leave it to Beaver* theme song. Don't ask me why. After that, she got back on track. "Did I tell you? That nice man from the deli is picking me up. I can't wait to meet his other half. She sounds wonderful."

"She's not a she, she's a he. She's Ben's uncle."

"Oh, no, dear. I'm sure you're mistaken. Tom told me she spent hours deciding what dress to wear to the party."

"Yes, well, that's our Arthur."

"Her name is Arthur? Funny name for a woman. Sort of like Glenn Close, isn't it? Oh well, I'll see you later, love. Kiss Ben for me." With that she hung up.

"I'll kiss him every chance I get," I said to the empty line.

THE PARTY was already in high gear when we arrived.

I don't know how they did it, but Arthur and whichever tenants he coerced into helping him decorate the party room did a fabulous job. The place was gorgeous. Everything was spotless, which must have been a major undertaking in and of itself.

There was a bar along one wall, manned by a bartender wearing nothing but a sombrero, passing out drinks as naked as the day he was born. I noticed right away that his tip jar was already overflowing, not that I was surprised. I was tempted to sneak over and drop a couple of bucks in it myself. He looked really good in that sombrero.

I wasn't sure how my mother would feel about a naked man in a sombrero mixing up her customary pink lady with his ding-dong (as she called it) flopping around in plain sight, but I guessed we would find out. At least the guy was circumcised. For an older Jewish woman eyeballing her first naked bartender, at least that was a step in the right direction.

Tables and chairs were placed neatly around the perimeter of the room, leaving the area in the middle as a dance floor, and even that was scrubbed clean with not a dust bunny in sight. Above the dance floor hung the huge disco ball, just as it had hung for decades. Freshly cleaned, it was spinning now, shooting swirling sparks of crystal light around the room.

Circling the disco ball hung three piñatas. Arthur had chosen a Mexican theme for the party. It might have had something to do with the fact that the only band he could book on such short notice was a mariachi band consisting of five old men and a young Hispanic singer who looked gayer than anyone else in the room, which was saying a lot. Ben and I wove our way among the tables while the singer, in bullfighter pants and a ruffled shirt, flounced his way through "La Bamba" on the little stage at the far end of the room. His bullfighter pants were so tight I could have read every vein in his dick like braille. Of course, now that I was a married man, I was above all that.

The stage had been adorned with swags of crepe paper in red and green and white, the colors of the Mexican flag. Huge paper sunflowers, obviously bought in Tijuana, were arranged as centerpieces for the tables. Somehow they managed to look both cheap and festive at the same time. In everything but his own wardrobe, Arthur was a master at working on a shoestring budget.

Aside from the young singer, the musicians in the band had a median age of approximately eighty-five, give or take a decade or two, but the music they produced with their three guitars, one fiddle, and one trumpet was actually quite nice. I could have lived without the noisyass trumpet, but hey, we can't have everything. Unless it was my imagination, I thought I saw several of the old geezers gazing fondly at the young singer's perfectly outlined pecker, not to mention his cute little Mexican butt, which prompted me to suspect the singer got the job for more than his vocal talents alone.

As soon as people spotted Ben and me, a stampede of friends, the majority of them already drunk and pretty much incoherent, gave us a rousing cheer and swarmed in like a pride of lions attacking a couple of goats.

We were dragged from hug to hug to hug while drinks were forced into our hands. More than one pair of eyes focused hungrily on Ben's kilt, obviously wondering what delicacies might lie beneath it. I tugged Ben close and kept a protective hand around his waist, just in case one of the drunken louts decided to do more than speculate.

We were in the midst of a throng of raised glasses and hearty pats on the back, all congratulating us on our recent union, when Arthur swept through the crowd like Moses parting the Red Sea.

In honor of the party's Mexican motif, Arthur wore a flamenco dancer's ensemble. Always extra large and extra gaudy anyway, Arthur had squeezed himself into a frilly, flouncy red flamenco skirt that reached midshin, with a slit up one side that exposed a humongous leg sheathed in black nylon with a red garter strapped above the knee. He wore black clunky high-heeled shoes with big red bows on the toes and metal taps on the soles, which made it sound like he was typing eighty words a minute every time he moved. He had also donned a red, crinkly peasant blouse, which showed Arthur's bulging bosom to full effect, and he carried a castanet in one hand that he clacked in people's faces if they didn't get out of his way quick enough.

He had decked himself out in a long black flowing wig, clipped back on one side with a big spit curl glued to his cheek, and on that one exposed ear, he wore a round, dangly earring as big as a Frisbee. His makeup was pure Mexicana. Ruby-red lips, black painted eyebrows arched halfway up his forehead, and to top it off, his stick-on Gloria Swanson mole, as big as a blueberry, plastered to the side of his face, which, had it been real and on my cheek, would have prompted a spate of dermatology appointments.

He also had a red rose clamped between his teeth. When he had to speak, he plucked the rose from his mouth and tucked it down between his tits for storage, where it bobbed around beneath his chin.

Just before Arthur swooped in and gathered Ben and me into a rib-crushing embrace, Ben whispered in my ear, "Your mother's going to love this."

Ben's whispered words were lost in Arthur's tsunami of enthusiasm. "My boys!" He squealed. "My legally married boys! How happy you look! How sexy you are in your kilts! Oh Lord, you're so handsome I can't stand it!"

Arthur ratchetted down the glee and murmured in Ben's ear. "I'm so proud of you, son. I'm sorry your family back in Indiana can't appreciate this wonderful day, the homophobic twits. But screw 'em. I'm your family now, and I think it's *fa-a-a-abulous*!"

Ben had been emotional all day. I watched his eyes tear up as he hugged Arthur back and murmured his own thank-you for everything Arthur had done for him. Then they both turned to me, and their faces lit up so, it prompted *my* eyes to fill with tears. Once again Arthur dragged us into his arms and clamped us to his massive, heaving, bulging, Opium-scented bosom, leaving Ben and me gasping for breath and trying not to blubber like babies.

"Oh my!" Arthur exclaimed, looking off in the distance. And without so much as a "Toodles," he dumped us like an afterthought after spotting the naked, circumcised bartender doling out drinks in nothing but a sombrero over by the far wall. Red skirt flying, Arthur clickety-clacked straight for the guy, snapping his castanet this way and that to clear a path for himself through the crowd, giving Ben and me a chance to catch our breath, straighten our clothes, and take in the surroundings.

Everyone we knew was there. Pete and Sylvia were snuggling in the corner with little Artie strapped to Pete's chest again. As always, the kid was flailing around and slobbering and kicking Pete in the nuts every two minutes. Poor Pete looked rather like John Hurt when the baby monster came tearing out of his chest at the dinner table in the movie *Alien*. The resemblance was even more disconcerting since the kid was sucking on a pacifier that was jokingly painted to look like a mouthful of false teeth.

Oblivious to the actual beat of the music being played from the stage, Stanley and Roger, looking as handsome and devoted as ever, were dancing a slow dance in each other's arms on the dance floor. Also on the dance floor were Milan and Harlie, Milan as tall as Ben, and Harlie as short as me, kissing a long slow kiss while barely moving to the rhythm of the mariachis.

Charlie and Bruce were hanging around the bar, eyeing the naked bartender and sipping beers with their hands tucked in each other's back pockets. They were either being cuddly or trying to steal each other's wallets. One could never be sure with Charlie and Bruce.

Ramon and Barney sat at one of the tables, laughing uproariously at Arthur, who had abandoned the naked bartender and had now struck a dramatic flamenco pose onstage. As soon as he was sure he had the entire room's attention, he began clacking and flouncing his way through a lively *cante chico* number while the horrified band looked on. I wasn't sure, but I thought even the singer's dick wilted in shock.

"Here's your mom," Ben said, and I turned to see Arthur's Tom escorting my mother through the door like the queen of England being bustled in to tea. She was indeed wearing the dress from my bar mitzvah. I thought it seemed a little tight around the middle, but who was I to judge? I was still packing a few extra pounds myself, thanks to Sylvia and her goddamn cookies.

I cringed to see my mother had also gone overboard with the baby's breath, having several sprigs of the stuff poking out of her hair in a dozen different directions. God forgive me for saying so, but she looked like she had just clawed her way through a stand of frozen brambles to get here.

Clearly fascinated by her first gay wedding reception, my mom's eyes were as big as tennis balls. Her glance lingered first on the boys cuddling on the dance floor. Then she froze and batted her eyelashes in amazement for a moment when she spotted the naked bartender in the stupid sombrero, prancing around with his dick flying, passing out drinks. But even that didn't hold her attention long once she spotted Arthur onstage, stomping and clacking his way through the fandango, ruffled skirt flying, castanets clacking, his three hundred pounds of monumental momentum shaking the building around us. Even the paper flowers in the centerpieces were trembling as Arthur stomped his way around the stage.

Tom delivered my gob-smacked mother into our capable hands like a UPS package he couldn't wait to get rid of, and the first thing she said was "That flamenco dancer is quite something. You don't see a plus-size flamenco dancer every day of the week, now, do you?"

"Thanks," Tom said. "That's my lover."

My mother gave Tom a sympathetic moue. "Well, she certainly is energetic, being so—*voluptuous* and all. It can't be easy flinging three hundred pounds of womanhood around like that."

Ben and I stared at my mother as if she might have suffered a stroke en route and was now talking out of her brain-addled ass.

Ben leaned in to clarify the situation. "That woman on stage is my uncle," he said.

My mother slapped his arm and laughed. "Oh, you kidder."

Tom opened his mouth to speak, then thought better of it and slapped it shut again like a mailbox.

Mom barely noticed me standing there in front of her at all, making me feel a bit like an unwanted order of brussels sprouts nobody had ordered. Instead she said to Ben, "I think I'll go get myself a drink from the bar. I've always loved sombreros." And with that she was gone. My dear mother, off to cruise a naked gay guy. Jesus.

"Care to dance?" Ben asked.

"No. I need another drink."

"I thought so. Here. Have mine."

"Thanks." I drank it down in one gulp.

"I'll get us two more as soon as your mother stops monopolizing the bartender."

"You may have to wait awhile."

Suddenly Arthur was at our side again. He was dripping sweat, his Gloria Swanson mole had slid six inches south to the side of his neck, and his tits were crooked. I glanced up to the stage and saw the mariachi band looking relieved. The little Mexican singer was back, swinging his ass in front of the fiddle player's face, which might have had something to do with the old geezer's happy expression.

I was also pleased to note the building had stopped shaking.

"That flamenco shit is a real workout, huh?" Ben asked, trying not to laugh.

Arthur was too out of breath to answer. He simply stood there panting and nodding.

Tom brought the three of us drinks and passed them out. To me he said, "Your mother is talking Jewish history to the bartender. They're planning on visiting the synagogue together next Saturday. Let's hope the kid wears more than a sombrero. I heard your mother tell him he had a lovely penis. She was sipping from the biggest margarita I've ever seen in my life."

I groaned. "Oh God."

Arthur slurped down his drink in three seconds flat, then pulled a lace handkerchief the size of a tablecloth out of his bodice and patted himself dry. He was still sweating like a longshoreman.

Reasonably pulled back together, he caught my eye and motioned to the piñatas hanging from the ceiling by the disco ball. "Your wedding gifts are in there," he said.

"Really?" Ben and I turned to stare at the piñatas.

"No toasters or waffle irons, I hope," Ben commented. "We don't want to kill anybody when they fall out."

"Silly," Arthur tittered, and punched him in the arm hard, catching Ben off guard so he almost toppled over like a tree.

Several drinks later found Ben and me swing dancing on the dance floor, our kilts swirling around our bare legs while the crowd cheered and wolf-whistled us into a frenzy. My mother was on the dance floor too, doing the Black Bottom with Tom, who it turned out was a pretty good dancer, although his repertoire of dance moves, like my mother's, seemed to hail from the age of Busby Berkeley musicals. The fact they were dancing the Black Bottom to mariachi music was so bizarre I didn't even want to think about it.

I caught a glimpse of Lester the librarian and his friend Dan, snuggling together in a cozy little waltz. They had been inseparable since the day of the skunk attack. Apparently that afternoon they'd spent reeking and naked in the toolshed had been a game changer for both of them. Once again, they were decked out in bow ties, spiffy sport coats, and matching white pants with bright red sneakers. Judging by their shared fashion sense, they were obviously made for each other, and I was thrilled to see them so clearly smitten. Even Ben gave a gentle smile when I pointed them out to him. Nobody appreciated a blossoming romance more than Ben.

The evening wound on. Entire crates of alcohol were consumed. Police officers arrived twice after reports of excessive noise were called in by neighbors. Both times the police took one look around, shook their heads, and left arm in arm, chuckling to themselves.

By eleven o'clock, poor Arthur was so drunk his wig was crooked, and he was fanning himself with a bag of quinoa he had plucked from his cleavage, leaving himself one-breasted. A few minutes earlier, he'd wobbled onto the dance floor in his clickety-clacking high heels to tell me if my mother didn't give him his boyfriend back pretty darn soon, Arthur was going to "rip all the weeds out of her hair." I assumed he was joking.

By this time, the party room was so loud no one even tried to carry on a conversation, which in no little part was due to the trumpet player, who also appeared intoxicated. At the moment, the little gay singer was bent over on stage with his matador pants down around his knees while the trumpet player, in the midst of a rousing mariachi number and blowing that fucking horn for all he was worth, was using the boy's left asscheek for a trumpet mute. I wasn't sure why the band was howling with laughter. The trumpet player sounded better than he had all night.

The party was quickly spiraling out of control when Arthur finally stuffed his tit back in his blouse and started clacking his castanet and screaming his head off to get everyone's attention. It took a minute, but he finally succeeded.

"Shut the hell up, everybody!" he wailed like a foghorn. "It's time to present the wedding gifts to the groom and groom!"

A stomping, clapping roar ensued, so Arthur had to yell and clack his castanet to shut them up *again*.

"Let's make them work at it, shall we?" he bellowed over the heads of the crowd. And with that he pulled a fat stick from behind his back. The stick was about four feet long and looked like it was heavy enough to pack quite a wallop.

"Oh Lordy," Ben whispered in my ear. "I have a bad feeling about this."

"Don't worry," I whispered back. "I'm sure Arthur has everything under control."

As soon as the words were out of my mouth, Ben and I gaped at each other and burst out laughing. We laughed so hard, we collapsed in each other's arms, barely able to stand.

Just when I was about to pee in my kilt, Arthur's booming voice shocked us back to reality. Apparently there were rules to this game Arthur wanted us to play.

"Listen up! There are three piñatas, as I'm sure you've all noticed! One piñata is a donkey. One is a cat. And the last one is a marvelous replication of Donald Trump's ugly head, weirdass hair and all." Here Arthur leaned toward my mother, who was standing at his side, and in a drunken whisper loud enough to be heard three blocks away, boasted, "The Donald Trump piñatas were on sale for thirty pesos. That's like a nickel and a half. Do I know how to shop, or what?"

My mother, clearly inebriated and wearing the naked bartender's sombrero, leaving the man *completely* naked behind the bar, shot Arthur a thumbs-up. Nobody appreciated a bargain more than Ila Smart. She appeared not only drunk, but also fairly insane, what with the baby's breath smashed down around her ears by the humongous sombrero perched on her teeny tiny head, but I decided not to mention it. It was my wedding day, after all. I didn't want to die quite yet.

Arthur pulled a tit out of his blouse and blotted the sweat from his face. When he was finished he stuffed the tit back in. I guess he forgot he had a handkerchief. Since his tit was still crooked, my mother reached over and straightened it for him. Don't ask me what was going through her mind at that moment. I don't have a clue and probably wouldn't want to know anyway.

"Let's give my nephew a crack at the first piñata, shall we?" Arthur cajoled the crowd. And when the mob of caterwauling drunks stomped and screamed their support, Arthur hooked a finger at Ben, urging him forward.

Ben made that face one usually makes when it's time to climb the scaffold steps just prior to meeting the hangman and climbing onto a chair with a rope around your neck. I gave my hubby a reassuring pat on the back and pushed him forward. I wasn't sure, but I thought I heard him growl when I did.

Ben turned bright red when Arthur planted a big lipsticky kiss on his forehead, leaving the perfect imprint of his puckering mouth just over Ben's right eye. "Okay, my wee Scottish laddie," Arthur beamed. "Take this shillelagh stick and kill that donkey. Let's see what's lurking inside. Everybody, stand back!"

Pulled along by forces clearly beyond his control, Ben gripped the stick in his big, lovely paws, took a batter's stance, and in one swift blow, smacked that donkey in the keister with all the force he could muster. Mickey Mantle couldn't have done it better.

The donkey didn't stand a chance. It exploded into clumps of tissue and paper-mache, leaving nothing but the poor little decapitated donkey's head dangling from the ceiling, swaying madly alongside the bigass disco ball. Tiny packets of assorted colors flew through the air, and snatching one in midflight, I saw they were condoms, neatly packaged. The condoms were prelubricated and extralarge, which I thought was fortuitous, knowing Ben the way I did. In the biblical sense, I mean.

There must have been three hundred condoms inside that donkey. Everybody ended up with a handful or two.

I was crawling around on the floor, gathering up as many condoms as I could find and stuffing them in my shirt while Ben stared down at me grinning like a fool.

"Your turn," he said, handing me the stick. "You can kill the cat."

Ben took me by the hand and yanked me to my feet, dribbling condoms everywhere. He watched while I spit in my hands and rubbed them together like Paul Bunyon, then grabbed the shillelagh stick and took a stance.

It was a cute little kitty piñata, and I hated to kill it, but like Ben, I was swept up in the heat of the moment. To save face there was no other way out.

"I'm sorry, pussycat," I murmured, and with every ounce of strength I possessed, I swung the stick at the piñata's orange fluffy head and knocked it clean off its neck. The head flew all the way across the party room and hit the trumpet player smack in the nuts. His eyes crossed and he doubled over like a pocketknife.

The rest of the cat hit the floor at my feet and exploded in a cloud of paper-mache dust, shreds of colored tissue paper, and teeny bits of cardboard.

Among the wreckage, I was surprised to see a bunch of index cards scatter across the floor on impact. Dozens of them. Confused, I snatched one up and read it. It was a gift certificate for dinner for two at Tom's deli down the street, signed by Tom and Arthur. Another card was a coupon for a free haircut from Ramon. Another was the offer of a brand-new widescreen TV from Charlie and Bruce, the resident kleptomaniacs. The TV must have fallen off a truck like everything else Charlie and Bruce gave away to friends.

Ben and I stood there for a couple of minutes, grabbing cards and reading what they said. Both of us were beginning to tear up by the generosity of our friends. A new toaster from Lester. A waffle iron from Sylvia. A Swiffer from Roger and Stanley. Another free kitten from Barney. (We both snarled at him for that one.) Groceries. A case of beer. A roll of toilet paper. (That one wasn't signed, the cheap bastard.)

Several people crawled around at our feet, gathering up the rest of the cards and stuffing them in our socks to be perused later. Arthur had tears streaming down his cheeks. Tom stood beside him, his arm around Arthur's waist, looking on proudly. My mother was nowhere in sight. I glanced over toward the back wall and saw her sitting on the bar, legs crossed like a torch singer perched atop a baby grand, sipping from another huge margarita while the naked bartender, still circumcised and wearing his sombrero again, sat at her side and rearranged the baby's breath in her hair. For some reason, my mother was wearing a feather boa. I had no idea where she got it.

Ila Smart, party animal. Who knew?

With one piñata left hanging, Arthur snatched the shillelagh out of my hands and offered to do the honors himself.

In a stage whisper, slurred from the twenty or thirty cocktails he'd consumed, Arthur declared to Ben and me, "There's really nothing in this one, *hic*. I've just always wanted to hit Donald Trump in the head with a stick."

"Then be our guest," Ben said, grinning.

Arthur flipped his long black wig away from his face, hoisted the shillelagh over his shoulder, and with eyes squeezed shut, which probably wasn't a good idea at all, Arthur swung that club with every ounce of drunken muscle power he could conjure up.

It became quickly apparent that when flailing away at a piñata with a shillelagh stick, clearly, a score of cocktails is not conducive to pinpoint accuracy.

Arthur missed Donald Trump's paper-mache head completely, and with a horrifying *crash* smacked the disco ball instead. Shards of mirrored glass rained down upon our heads like an exploding supernova. Arthur screamed in fright, and the entire room froze in horror.

Suddenly, amid the tinkle of glass, a chorus of astonished gasps filled the air. Drifting down around our heads in a wafting, fluttering cloud, came a flurry of hundred-dollar bills. Floating past our noses, lighting on our shoulders, slipping down our legs in papery whispers.

"It's Captain Blue Eyes's treasure!" Arthur screamed. "It was hidden in the disco ball!"

A moment later his eyes rolled up in his head, and with a resounding crash that shook the building all the way down to its foundations, he passed out cold at Tom's feet. Meanwhile, even more hundred-dollar bills wafted down upon him as he lay snoring on the floor.

Ben turned to me, his eyes bright with excitement, his snow-white teeth peeking through a radiant smile. He brushed a hundred-dollar bill off my head and plucked another off my shoulder. "Still think I'm nuts?"

"Nope," I said. "I admit it. My honey was right. The treasure was here all along."

He gazed up at Donald Trump's head still hanging from the ceiling looking kind of pathetic. The disco ball was gone, of course, smashed to smithereens, never to be seen again.

"The exploding disco ball had to be the high point of the evening, don't you think?" Ben asked.

I gazed down at poor Arthur, unconscious on the floor, his head bald because he'd lost his wig in the fall. "I do indeed. Nobody can top that. Not even Arthur."

Ben stroked his thumb across my lips. "Then how about another dance, oh husband of mine?"

I snuggled close, slipping into Ben's arms as easily as a key sliding into a lock. "Another dance sounds lovely."

Stepping over Arthur like he was a speed bump, we waded through the sea of hundred-dollar bills and headed for the dance floor. Seeing us coming, the mariachi band tuned up their instruments, the singer pulled up his pants, and they broke into a mellow Mexican love song, which, considering the circumstances, was absolutely perfect.

With his gentle lips to my ear and his strong arms holding me tight, Ben led me around the dance floor while everybody else scrambled about on their hands and knees, snatching up the stolen loot.

I closed my eyes, breathing in Ben's scent and whispering in his ear. "No more treasure hunting for you, I guess."

"Don't need to," he whispered back. "I've got my treasure right here in my arms."

My heart gave a happy thud, and I watched in considerable awe as the rest of our lives began to slowly unfold before our very eyes.

They would be happy lives too. I didn't doubt it for a minute.

Epilogue

APPARENTLY CEDRIC Weaselton, aka Captain Blue Eyes, hung the gigantic disco ball in the party room the day after the robbery in order to celebrate with his friends his successful foray into the wonderful world of crime. Also apparently, he got the bright idea of stashing the stolen money inside the disco ball, and there it had lain hidden until a drunken drag queen (Arthur) nailed it with his shillelagh stick.

Two weeks after the nailing, Ben and I, naked and slightly flushed from recent activities, found a fat manila envelope without a postmark slipped beneath the apartment door. The envelope was addressed to us in Arthur's lumberjacky handwriting, and the envelope was damp. Our names were smeared and blotchy with beads of moisture.

"Uh-oh," Ben said. "Tears."

Expecting the worst, we tore the envelope open and a sheaf of hundred-dollar bills fell out. There appeared to be three or four hundred of them.

"My God," Ben said. "It's our share of the stolen money. Arthur's finally settling up."

"Cool. But what's with the tears?"

"Oh, wait. There's something else in here."

With the money out of the way, Ben extracted a note from the envelope that we'd almost missed completely. The note informed us Arthur and Tom would be married two weeks from today in the party room downstairs. We were told in no uncertain terms that Ben and I would be giving the bride away and that kilts would be required.

"So they're happy tears, then," Ben mumbled to himself.

We stared at each other. I tried to ignore the splash of come on Ben's cheek. We had been busy when the envelope arrived. At least I had been. Ben was supposed to be the second course, but then we got interrupted.

"Tom must have proposed," I said around a grin.

Ben looked as happy as I did. "I knew he would someday."

We turned our attention back to the note in Ben's hand and read on.

Shiloh, your mother thinks I should wear an empire-waisted gown. What do you think?

Ben and I stared at each other again.

"What's an empire-waisted gown?" Ben asked.

"Beats me. So what do we think?"

"Beats me."

We gazed back at the note.

Ila and I are shopping for the wedding gown and invitations, ordering the cake, and arranging the bridesboys' outfits this afternoon.

Ben stared at me again. "Bridesboys' outfits?"

"Beats me," I said again. Then I went one better. "He's shopping with my mother? That can't be good."

Ben threw the note over his shoulder and bent down to bury his face in my neck. "I can't deal with this now. Let's go back to bed. While you may have carried our little liaison to fruition"—here he pointed to the smear of come on his cheek—"I, on the other hand, have not. And frankly I'm ready to explode."

I gave a shudder of anticipation. "Marriage is good. Arthur and Tom should enjoy it thoroughly."

"I know *I* do," Ben said, scooping me off the floor and carrying me to the bed.

JOHN INMAN has been writing fiction since he was old enough to hold a pencil. He and his partner live in beautiful San Diego, California. Together, they share a passion for theater, books, hiking and biking along the trails and canyons of San Diego or, if the mood strikes, simply kicking back with a beer and a movie. John's advice for anyone who wishes to be a writer? "Set time aside to write every day and do it. Don't be afraid to share what you've written. Feedback is important. When a rejection slip comes in, just tear it up and try again. Keep mailing stuff out. Keep writing and rewriting and then rewrite one more time. Every minute of the struggle is worth it in the end, so don't give up. Ever. Remember that publishers are a lot like lovers. Sometimes you have to look a long time to find the one that's right for you."

E-mail: john492@att.net
Facebook: www.facebook.com/john.inman.79
Website: www.johninmanauthor.com

Serenading Stanley

THE BELLADONNA ARMS

JOHN INMAN

A Belladonna Arms Novel

Welcome to the Belladonna Arms, a rundown little apartment building perched atop a hill in downtown San Diego, home to the city's lost and lovelorn. Shy archaeology student Stanley Sternbaum has just moved in and fills his time quietly observing his eccentric neighbors, avoiding his hellion mother, and trying his best to go unnoticed... which proves to be a problem when it comes to fellow tenant Roger Jane. Smitten, the hunky nurse with beautiful green eyes does everything in his power to woo Stanley, but Stanley has always lived a quiet life, too withdrawn from the world to take a chance on love. Especially with someone as beautiful as Roger Jane.

While Roger tries to batter down Stanley's defenses, Stanley turns to his new neighbors to learn about love: Ramon, who's not afraid to give his heart to the wrong man; Sylvia, the trans who just wants to be a woman, and the secret admirer who loves her just the way she is; Arthur, the aging drag queen who loves them all, expecting nothing in return—and Roger, who has been hurt once before but is still willing to risk his heart on Stanley, if Stanley will only look past his own insecurities and let him in.

Work In Progress

THE BELLADONNA ARMS

JOHN INMAN

A Belladonna Arms Novel

Dumped by his lover, Harlie Rose ducks for cover in the Belladonna Arms, a seedy apartment building perched high on a hill in downtown San Diego. What he doesn't know is that the Belladonna Arms has a reputation for romance—and Harlie is about to become its next victim.

Finding a job at a deli up the street, Harlie meets Milan, a gorgeous but cranky baker. Unaware that Milan is suffering the effects of a broken heart just as Harlie is, the two men circle around each other, manning the barricades, both unwilling to open themselves up to love yet again.

But even the most stubborn heart can be conquered.

With his new friends to back him up—Sylvia, on the verge of her final surgery to become a woman, Arthur, the aging drag queen who is about to discover a romance of his own, and Stanley and Roger, the handsome young couple in 5C who lead by example, Harlie soon learns that at the Belladonna Arms, love is always just around the corner waiting to pounce. Whether you want it to or not.

But tragedy also drops in now and then.

www.dreamspinnerpress.com

Coming Back

THE BELLADONNA ARMS
JOHN INMAN

A Belladonna Arms Novel

Barney Teegarden knows what it's like to be alone. He knows what it's like to have a romantic heart, yet no love in his life to unleash the romance on. With the help of a friend, he acquires a lease in a seedy apartment building perched high on a hill in downtown San Diego. The Belladonna Arms is not only filled with the quirkiest cast of characters imaginable, it is also famous for sprinkling love dust on even the loneliest of the lovelorn.

At the Arms, Barney finds friendship, acceptance, and an adopted family that lightens his lonely life. Hell, he even finds a cat. But still true love eludes him.

When his drag queen landlord, Arthur, takes it into his head to rescue a homeless former tenant, he enlists Barney's help. It is Barney who shows this lost soul how to trust again—and in return Barney discovers love for the first time in his life.

It's funny how even the hardest battles can be fought and won with laughter, hugs, friends, plus a little faith in the goodness of others. All it takes to begin the healing is the simple act of coming back.

www.dreamspinnerpress.com

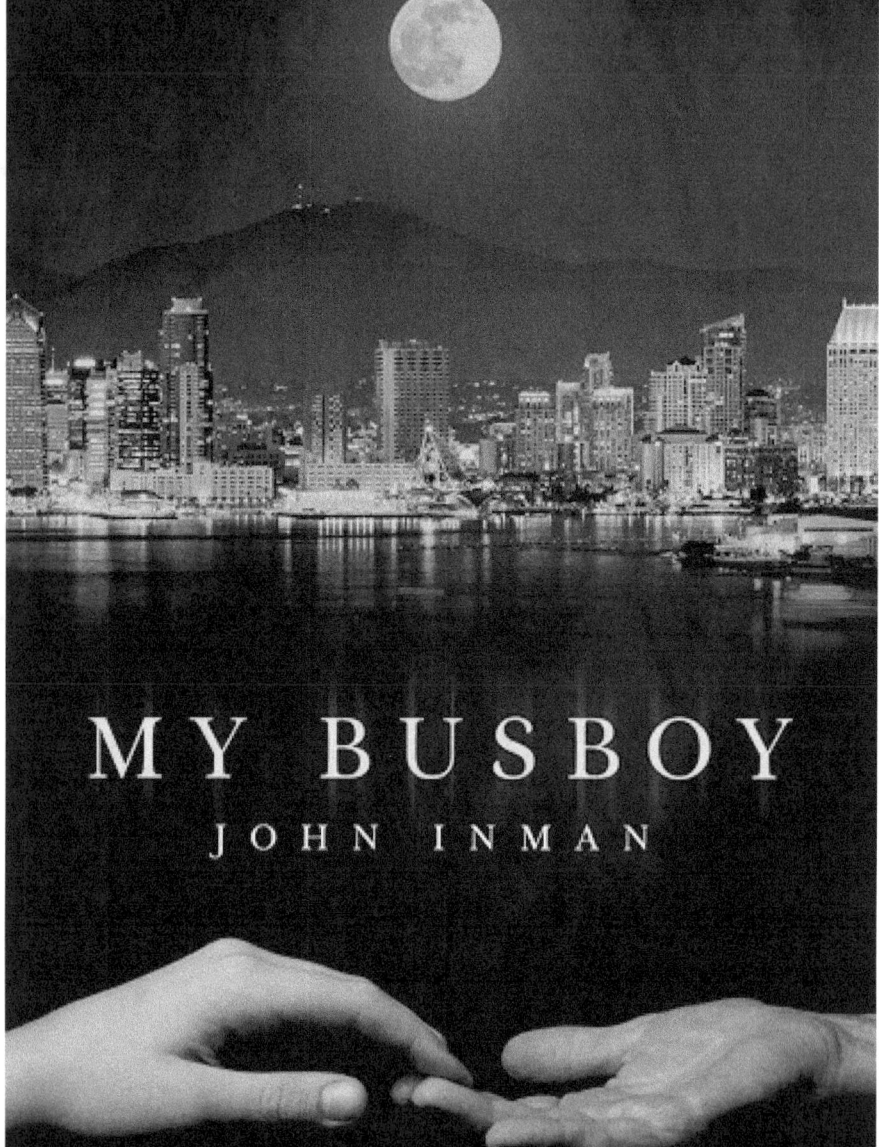

MY BUSBOY

JOHN INMAN

Robert Johnny just turned thirty, and his life is pretty much in the toilet. His writing career is on the skids. His love life is nonexistent. A stalker is driving him crazy. And his cat is a pain in the ass.

Then Robert orders a chimichanga platter at a neighborhood restaurant, and his life changes—just like that.

Dario Martinez isn't having such a great existence either. He needs money for college. His shoes are falling apart. His boyfriend's a dick. And he has a crap job as a busboy.

Then a stranger orders a chimichanga platter, and suddenly life isn't quite as depressing.

But it's the book in the busboy's back pocket that really gets the ball rolling. For both our heroes. That and the black eye and the forgotten bowl of guacamole. Who knew true love could be so easily ignited or that the flames would spread so quickly?

But when Robert's stalker gets dangerous, our two heroes find a lot more to occupy their time than falling in love. Staying alive might become the new game plan.

www.dreamspinnerpress.com

TWO
PET
DICKS

Old friends and business partners, Maitland Carter and Lenny Fritz, may not be the two sharpest pickle forks in the picnic basket, but they have big hearts. And they are just now coming around to the fact that maybe their hearts are caught in a bit of turmoil.

Diving headfirst into a whirlwind of animal mayhem, these two self-proclaimed pet detectives strive to earn a living, reunite a few poor lost creatures with their lonely owners, and hopefully not make complete twits of themselves in the process.

When they stumble onto a confusing crime involving venomous reptiles, which is rather unnerving since they're more accustomed to dealing with misplaced puppy dogs and puddy tats, they take the plunge into becoming real-life crime stoppers.

While they're plunging into that, they're also plunging into love. They just haven't admitted it to each other yet.

www.dreamspinnerpress.com